ABOUT THE AUTHORS

Kasey Michaels is a *New York Times* bestselling author who is celebrating the publication of her fiftieth novel this year. In addition to writing for Silhouette Books, she has long been known as one of the premier authors in the field of Regency Romance and mainstream historical romance. Ms. Michaels recently was honored with the *Romantic Times* Career Achievement Award for Regency Historical novels, and is also a recipient of the Romance Writers of America RITA Award and various Waldenbooks awards. Her career has been the subject of a Lifetime Cable TV program, "A Better Way," and she has appeared on the "Today" show. Ms. Michaels enjoys hearing from her readers, and you may write to her in care of Silhouette Books.

Muriel Jensen is the award-winning author of almost fifty books that tug at readers' hearts. She has won a Reviewer's Choice Award and a Career Achievement Award for Love and Laughter from *Romantic Times* magazine, as well as a sales award from Waldenbooks. Muriel is best loved for her books about family, a subject she knows well, as she has three children and eight grandchildren. A native of Massachusetts, Muriel now lives with her husband in Oregon.

Rebecca York is the pseudonym of Ruth Glick and Eileen Buckholtz. Between the two of them, they have authored over sixty-five books, including the highly successful 43 Light Street series for Harlequin Intrigue. Called "Harlequin's first lady of suspense," Rebecca York has been honored with a Career Achievement Award in Romantic Mystery by *Romantic Times* magazine and with a RITA Award nomination from Romance Writers of America. The writers live in Maryland with their respective families.

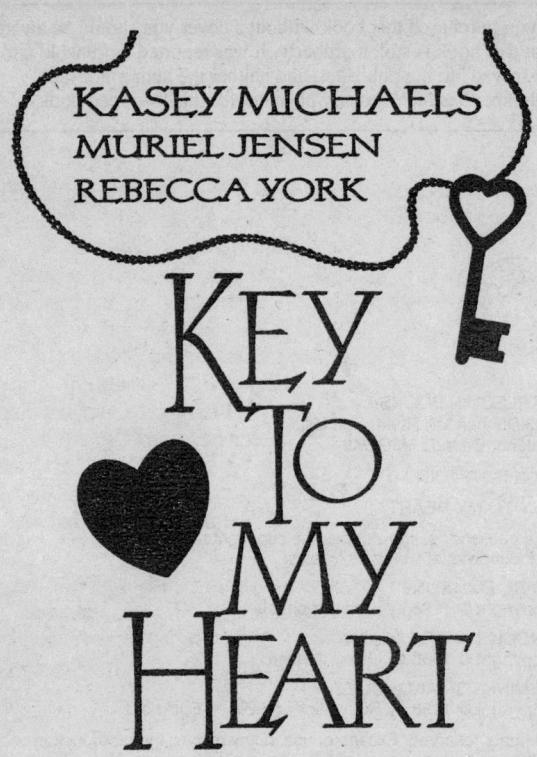

KASEY MICHAELS
MURIEL JENSEN
REBECCA YORK

KEY TO MY HEART

Harlequin Books

TORONTO • NEW YORK • LONDON
AMSTERDAM • PARIS • SYDNEY • HAMBURG
STOCKHOLM • ATHENS • TOKYO • MILAN
MADRID • WARSAW • BUDAPEST • AUCKLAND

If you purchased this book without a cover you should be aware that this book is stolen property. It was reported as "unsold and destroyed" to the publisher, and neither the author nor the publisher has received any payment for this "stripped book."

HARLEQUIN BOOKS
225 Duncan Mill Road, Don Mills,
Ontario, Canada M3B 3K9

ISBN 0-373-83349-0

KEY TO MY HEART

The publisher acknowledges the copyright holders of the individual works as follows:

LOVE, EMMALINE
Copyright © 1998 by Kasey Michaels

KNOCK THREE TIMES
Copyright © 1998 by Muriel Jensen

REMINGTON AND JULIET
Copyright © 1998 by Ruth Glick and Eileen Buckholtz

All rights reserved. Except for use in any review, the reproduction or utilization of this work in whole or in part in any form by any electronic, mechanical or other means, now known or hereafter invented, including xerography, photocopying and recording, or in any information storage or retrieval system, is forbidden without the written permission of the publisher, Harlequin Enterprises Limited, 225 Duncan Mill Road, Don Mills, Ontario, Canada M3B 3K9.

All characters in this book have no existence outside the imagination of the author and have no relation whatsoever to anyone bearing the same name or names. They are not even distantly inspired by any individual known or unknown to the author, and all incidents are pure invention.

This edition published by arrangement with Harlequin Books S.A.

® and TM are trademarks of the publisher. Trademarks indicated with ® are registered in the United States Patent and Trademark Office, the Canadian Trade Marks Office and in other countries.

Printed in U.S.A.

CONTENTS

LOVE, EMMALINE   9
by Kasey Michaels

KNOCK THREE TIMES   133
by Muriel Jensen

REMINGTON AND JULIET   255
by Rebecca York

To Hilda Charles, with love.

LOVE, EMMALINE

Kasey Michaels

Dear Reader,

Sometimes a wonderful character comes to you in a dream, or while watching a show on television, or while picking out groceries in a supermarket. A writer never knows when a wonderful character will tap her on the shoulder, introduce him or herself and tell you his or her story.

And then, sometimes, that "magic" happens an entirely different way, with the character coming to the writer, not unexpectedly, but when *asked* to call. Emmaline Whipple was one of those times.

My editor phoned me, you see, asking me to do a story about Valentine's Day. Needless to say, I was thrilled to agree, as Valentine's Day is such a wonderful, romantic holiday. My editor asked just one itty-bitty thing of me—could I possibly work a "key" into the story.

A key? Well, sure. But what kind of key? I'd said yes, but now I was stumped. Completely out of ideas. So I sat and I sat. And I thought and I thought. And then Emmaline Whipple, dear, sweet Emmaline Whipple, came tapping on my shoulder. I turned, looked at her, and she was holding a key. The key to Emmaline's inn. She sat down, poured me some tea, told me about her Albert, about Emmaline's, about her sentimental feelings for Valentine's Day.

And I fell in love!

I only hope, dear reader, that you will feel the same way about Emmaline as my Molly and Tim do, as I do. I know I'll be thinking about Emmaline Whipple this Valentine's Day, and wishing her love.

Aren't happy endings wonderful?

All the best,

Kasey Michaels

Prologue

13 February 1998

My dearest, dearest Albert,
Do you see the date, darling? I'm writing it a new way now. I believe the English do it that way. So elegant, don't you think? Or perhaps it's some new computer thingamajig, in which case it isn't half so elegant, I suppose.

But I digress, don't I? You always said that. "If there's a long way to get there, my Emmaline will find it!" Oh, how I miss hearing your voice, even when you were teasing me....

One more day, darling, and it will be fifty-four years since you got down on your knee in this very parlor, Mama's parlor, and proposed to me. Do you remember? I do. As if it happened only yesterday. You were so flustered, running your finger around the inside of your collar as if its starched fabric might choke you, your handsome face so white, I truly feared you might faint right there at my feet.

But I said yes, didn't I, dearest Albert? Yes, yes, a thousand times yes!

How I miss you, dearest Albert, even though I still feel your presence every day. Your sweet love surrounding me. How could fifty-two years pass so quickly? Why have the last two dragged on for decades?

No, no, I'm not complaining. Truly, dearest, I'm not! It's just that winter has been so long this year, and Emmaline's so empty of company.

That all changes this weekend, my darling! I've told you their names, haven't I? Molly Bryant and Timothy Fitzgerald. Such lovely names! Would I consider opening Emmaline's for them, just for the weekend? Silly children! How could I possibly say no? It's just as we've always said in our brochures—Valentine's Day is always very special at Emmaline's.

What does it matter if we've never had a paying guest for that weekend, not in all these years? You, dearest, were always the only company I needed. You, Albert, my very own valentine.

Just think, dearest. Emmaline's will be open for Valentine's Day for the first time in its history. Oh, Albert, the plans I've made for our young couple...!

Yes, yes, I know. Bryant and Fitzgerald.

They're not married. But they are engaged, and certainly that must count for something. When Tim phoned me—such a nice boy, telling me to call him Tim—he explained all of that. They're engaged, and will be married in June, but they felt they needed some time alone, some time together, some time away from the wedding preparations.

I simply couldn't say no, couldn't face another Valentine's Day alone.

And never call me a fuddy-duddy! This is the nineties, after all. I'm "hep"...or "with it"...or whatever they're calling a wink and a smile these days. Besides, Albert, I seem to remember a certain summer evening you and I spent doing a little winking and smiling of our own a few weeks before our own wedding. Remember? Oh, we were so naughty!

I've prepared the bridal suite for Tim and Molly—I'm sure she'll let me call her Molly. Just as I've told Tim to call me Auntie Emmaline. After all, it will be just the three of us for the weekend.

My, this is long, isn't it? Quite the most I've written in weeks. I really must go now, dearest, to check on the bits and pieces that still must be done before our lovers arrive for their romantic tryst. Don't you adore that word, Albert—*tryst?* Goodness, I believe I'm feeling giddy!

I love you, dearest, even though we're apart now. I will always love you. I'll put this with your pipes, as always, where you can find it....

Love, Emmaline

Chapter One

THERE WERE PROBABLY places more unappealing than a New Jersey seaside vacation town in the midst of a cold February rain. Grayer. More drab. Quieter. More deserted.

Alcatraz came most readily to mind....

Timothy Fitzgerald tooled his brand-new Mercedes across the Ninth Street Bridge and onto the main drag in Ocean City. Was there ever a "Ninth Street Bridge" song? Simon and Garfunkel, maybe?

Nah. Who'd write a song about a bridge? Okay, maybe the Bridge of Sighs, or whatever that one in Italy was called. That could inspire a song. But not the Ninth Street Bridge.

Unless...

"My love, she upped and left me," he sang out over the sweep of the windshield wiper, beating his fingertips on the steering wheel, giving himself a slow, country-music background beat. "She left me standin' on the ridge. My love, she upped and left me—" Words failed him for a moment. "Yadda-yadda-yadda, she left me standin', standin' all alone on that there ridge."

He peered through the windshield as he drove

and sang, looking for the turn onto Wesley Avenue, pulling to a halt when the traffic light up ahead flashed Caution. "I'm so lonely now, so lonely...so I'm jumpin' off the Ninth Street Brrrrr-*idge*."

As sad songs went, this one had gone fairly badly, so Tim discarded it, looking around the deserted intersection, waiting for the traffic light to change.

No cars coming to his left. No cars approaching to his right. He could have a picnic in the middle of the intersection, including dessert, and never be in danger of being run down.

So why was he sitting here?

Good question. He was sitting here, the last living cell in a dying organism, because the damn light was red. Can't go through a red light, Molly always said. It didn't matter if it was two in the morning and nobody else was awake, let alone out on the road. A law is a law is a law. Period.

Tim drew his mind away from memories of Molly, concentrating on the only other thing he could think of and not think of Molly. "'Bridge Over Troubled Water'? Okay, that's one. But it's not the one. There's another. Simon and Garfunkel. Simon and Garfunkel singing 'The Ninth Street Bridge Song.' Nope, that's not it. It doesn't sound right. There have to be a couple more syllables in the title. Yeah, well, I'll get it, sooner or later."

A man approached the Mercedes from the right. Dressed in a bright yellow rubber slicker, he stepped off the curb, then stopped directly beside Tim's car and looked to the sky, as if he might be expecting a plane to land in the wide street.

"Keep moving, keep moving," Tim urged, knowing the large, single windshield wiper was going to swoop to the right at any second, sending a powerful shower of rainwater smack in the man's face, like a wave crashing on the shore. The car might only be a week old, but he already knew its power—and its little idiosyncrasies.

He reached for the control knob to turn off the wiper.

"C'mon, buddy, keep—*whoops!* Too late. Sorry about that," he said, waving at the man now wiping water out of his eyes as the light turned green and he drove on, still on the lookout for Wesley Avenue.

"Molly would have slid under the seat," he told himself as he drove down the next block, smiling as he could picture his former fiancée's reaction. She'd be embarrassed, of course. Mortified. And then, as she'd be sliding her spine down the seat, she'd start to giggle. That sweet, delicious, faintly naughty giggle.

God, how he missed her!

But he wasn't going to think about Molly. About how he missed her. Or at least he wouldn't, not after this weekend. Unless he phoned her next week. He wasn't quite at grovel level yet. But he was close. Too damn close...

He saw the sign for Wesley Avenue and hung a left, then squinted through the rain until he saw the street sign for Delancey Place, and turned right, slowing down as he began to run out of street numbers—and out of street. Because, only a short block in front of him, there was little more than gray skies, a strip of boardwalk, some sand and a very large ocean.

And then he saw it. Grandma's gingerbread house.

Four stories high, its clapboard siding and ornate, carved woodwork painted at least six different, appealing—and peeling—shades of green, the Victorian bed-and-breakfast sat on the corner of Delancey Place and Corinthian Avenue. Right where the brochure said it would be.

Only, the photograph in the brochure didn't do the place justice. The building was magnificent! Comfortably old, welcoming in its very shabbiness—which, in his mind, Tim quickly amended to *hominess*—it stood amidst great, hulking, anonymous modern monstrosities, each built higher than its neighbor in order to get a better view of the ocean a person could walk to in less than a minute.

It was like being able to see the secret portal to a time warp. Climb the wide wooden stairs that rose above the brick ground floor, walk across the slats of the wraparound front porch—and step through the door, into the previous century.

That's all it would take. Just a few steps, and all the clocks would turn back. To a simpler time, a quieter time, a time where women wore long, rustling skirts and men were in charge. Where a man's opinion was never second-guessed, his decisions were taken as the final word and he controlled the checkbook.

Tim rolled his eyes, knowing he was thinking about Molly again. Thinking something that would send Molly Bryant into a pithy lecture on the equality of women, or the stupidity of thick, insensitive men, or something like that.

And, just for good measure, she'd then work her argument around to money—who should spend it, how it should be spent and how most of it should be put in a sock and tucked under the mattress.

One way or another, in any argument, Molly always found her way around to the subject of money. And how he, one Timothy Fitzgerald, hadn't a clue on how much it was worth.

You throw money around like it was water was one of her favorite sayings and, even after long months of hearing it, Tim would still be damned if he knew what in hell that meant. Who threw water around? Why would anyone throw water around? What would you have to put it in first, in order to throw it around?

"Stop it!" he ordered himself, giving the steering wheel a solid slap with his palm before pulling to the curb and turning off the ignition. "Just *stop* it. And, while you're stopping it, ask yourself again why you made a reservation in a dry town. You can't even drown your sorrows at a local tavern, Fitzgerald, you know that? Dumb. This whole idea was dumb, dumb, *dumb*. But it's still the only thing that's going to keep you from going over to Molly's and begging her forgiveness because *she* was wrong!"

Pulling his weekend case out of the back seat, he dashed across the sandy pavement and up the nearly dozen steps, nearly coming to grief before he realized that, at least where it fell on wood, the icy rain was beginning to freeze.

As it was only three o'clock or so, and it could only grow colder as the day went on, Tim resigned himself to staying at the bed-and-breakfast at least until morning. The roads leading out of Ocean City would be slick as an ice-skating rink in another hour.

He looked around for a doorbell and, finding none, lifted the brass knocker in the shape of a dolphin and banged it three times. As he waited for someone to answer his knock, he looked around the porch, shivered and realized that February, icy rain and the wind coming off the ocean all combined to make for one damn cold day.

It was a nice porch, though. Classic Victorian. Wide, long, it wrapped around the front and one whole side of the large old house built for an age now long gone. The wooden balustrades were originals, from what he could tell, and they were beautifully carved, if in need of paint. In fact, the whole place could use a good painting. Keeping clapboard and wood in A-one shape so close to the ocean and salty air had to be a challenge.

The owner had to feel like he was painting a bridge. Start at one end, or on one floor, and by the time you got to the other end, it was time to start the whole business all over again.

A bridge. He kept coming back to that. "Ninth Street Bridge," he said, trying to sing the words. "No, more syllables. *Twenty*-ninth Street Bridge? Damn it! Molly would know. She knows all the Simon and Garfunkel songs. And all the Beatles songs," he added, remembering how he had boxed up her full set of CD's and sent them back to her by special messenger the same day the package holding the engagement ring—the *insured* package, which was *so* like her—had arrived at his office.

"Come on, come on, come on," he chanted, watching the still solidly shut door. Then he looked at a small hand-painted plaque that hung beside the double doors. "Welcome to Emmaline's. Please don't just stand there—come on in!"

"Cute. Nothing like inviting burglars," Tim said shortly, and then turned the brass handle, pushing the right-hand door open onto a square, smallish room—or a fairly large foyer. He wasn't sure.

He was sure of a couple of things, however, as he ran an assessing gaze around the crowded, heavily decorated room. The place looked just as he'd supposed—as if he'd stepped through some sort of time portal, back to a quieter, gentler age. An age when burgundy velvet, curly-legged furniture, flocked wallpaper, and bric-a-brac were king.

He was also sure he heard a vacuum cleaner being run somewhere in the house—a nice, homey sound.

And he smelled apple pie. Hot, homemade apple pie. He smiled, and stepped up to the small counter that must serve as the reception desk, ringing the small silver bell he saw sitting on the doily-covered surface. He cocked an eyebrow at the plaster cupid hanging over the desk, the yards of red, construction paper hearts strung around nearly every piece of furniture, every lamp shade, ever corner cornice, then dismissed it all as the owner's campy idea of how Valentine's Day must have been celebrated back in the old days.

He shrugged out of his jacket as he took another deep breath, the aroma of cinnamon and apples soothing him even while making his stomach growl in anticipation, in protest at being denied this treat for even a moment.

He listened as the vacuum was cut off. A few seconds later a blue-jean clad teenage girl entered the foyer, earphones clapped to her head as she sang along with whoever was belting out disjointed lyrics that couldn't have had anything to do with the English language as Tim knew it.

The feeling of going back in time left him, although the aroma of baking pie didn't.

"All right, Fitzgerald, so it's not the Ritz," he said as the girl, still singing, handed him the key to his room, pointed toward the stairs and left the room. The vacuum roared to life again a few seconds later. "But, then again," he took another deep breath, "how bad can it be?"

MOLLY'S LATE-MODEL CHEVY crawled across the Ninth Street Bridge as she gripped the steering wheel with both hands and chanted desultorily, "Bridge freezes before other road surfaces. Bridge freezes before—*whoops!* Almost lost it there."

She'd reached the point of no return just as she'd turned onto the Atlantic City Expressway, halfway to her destination, just as far from her Allentown home. And, since she'd come that far, she'd decided to press on. She had been sure the temperature would rise as she got farther into New Jersey and closer to the shore. But the weather had played one of its nasty tricks on her, turning the storm into a Northeaster, its main force hitting the New Jersey shoreline much harder than it was doing farther inland.

Had she made any decision in the past weeks that hadn't come back to bite her?

Drizzle had turned to rain, the rain to rain and wind—and now the temperature had plummeted into the teens. By the time she'd turned off the expressway, the roads were little better than an ice-skating rink, and Molly Bryant couldn't skate.

She was cold, her spine and shoulders ached from holding the wheel so tightly, her eyes stung from concentrating on the icy streets beyond the water-washed windshield. And she was hungry, but not enough to chance pulling into the parking lot when a pair of golden arches appeared to her right.

All she wanted to do was find Emmaline's and park the car.

It wasn't as if she disliked driving. She rather liked cruising highways like the Atlantic City Expressway—long, well-kept stretches of macadam that took her to new and exciting places.

But she hated ice. Hated it, hated it, hated it. With a purple passion.

Damn you, Timothy Fitzgerald, she swore silently as she looked to her left and saw the Wesley Avenue street sign five seconds too late to safely brake and make the turn. She was so angry, she missed the next turn, as well, and only turned left when she reached Atlantic Avenue and sensed rather than saw that it presented her last chance to turn before she ended up in the ocean. *Damn you, Timothy Fitzgerald, for not being with me.*

She inched the car along for another dozen short blocks, sure she was lost, then sighed in real relief when she saw the sign marking Delancey Place.

Emmaline's was easy to spot, for Molly had been staring at the brochure for days, telling herself that anything was better than staying at home, waiting for her mother's almost hourly phone calls begging her to "give the poor boy another chance, sweetie."

And why shouldn't she take advantage of the reservation she and Tim had made in such happy anticipation three months earlier? They'd already paid for the weekend, hadn't they? A phone call late last night to Emmaline's had confirmed Molly's suspicion that Tim had forgotten to cancel the reservation, thereby probably forfeiting their money.

Which was just like him. He'd had three weeks to cancel the reservation, but he hadn't. He'd written the check, and that was the end of it, as far as he was concerned.

Honestly. The man threw money around like water.

Molly scowled into the rearview mirror as she remembered for, oh, only the ten millionth time or so, their last, huge argument three weeks ago. The one that had ended with Tim slamming out of her apartment—and getting in the last word, as usual—saying, "You want to save money, Molly? Well, just remember. It would be cheaper all around if we just didn't get married at all!"

He had to have thought she'd phone him in the morning. He had to have thought she'd come to her senses—as he always termed her endless capitulations—and apologize for having the audacity to point out that their wedding bills were soon going to rival the national debt. She'd tell him, he must have supposed, that a champagne toast at the reception was much better than using a good, and much cheaper, table wine. She'd tell him that doves being released as they left the church was simply a smashing idea. She'd tell him two weeks in Cancún was definitely a more reasonable honeymoon than a week in the closer, less expensive Pocono Mountains.

In a pig's eye, she would!

And she didn't.

Not this time.

All right, so maybe she'd come from a less

financially secure background than Timothy Fitzgerald, boy tycoon—or at least he acted as if he was. Maybe she did hold on to her pennies a little hard—made them squeal for mercy, according to her spendthrift fiancé. So what?

Because it wasn't the money. Not really. It was the whole way the two of them looked at life, that's what it was, even if Tim refused to see it that way. But if they had argued almost daily over catering estimates and prices for the honeymoon, imagine what would happen when it came to buying a house, choosing a college for their children.

Oh, yes. A broken engagement was much better than a broken marriage.

Which is why Molly, after crying for most of the night, had slipped her cherished engagement ring from her finger the next morning and sent it—insured, of course—to Tim's office.

And she wasn't sorry!

Except when her mother phoned to harangue her.

Except when the bridal shop employee had phoned to tell her that her headpiece had arrived.

Except for the day the wedding invitations had been waiting for her when she got home from work.

Except for every moment she was awake, and for every long hour she tossed and turned at night in her empty bed, and for all the times she wanted to hear Tim's voice, see his smile—even when she longed to beat him into a jelly for not breaking down her door and begging her forgiveness.

Three weeks. It seemed like a lifetime. Because she missed him so much. Because she loved him so much.

How many times had she picked up the phone to call him? How much longer would she last before she did make that call? She hadn't run to the Jersey shore to make use of reservations already paid for—she'd run to escape the temptation to call Tim.

And now, here she was, sitting in her car, watching the black Mercedes parked in front of her turn into one huge icicle. Nice car. She'd always loved Mercedes. So classy. So elegant. Such a very good buy, if one only had the money for such luxury and dependability.

Now she hated the Mercedes she was glaring at as if it had been put there just to mock her. She'd finally agreed with Tim that they should have such a car, but she'd wanted to lease it. Leasing made sense. All her research told her that. Tim, of course, had wanted to buy the car outright. Which was economically idiotic.

What had that been? Fight number 192? She'd stopped keeping count.

Molly looked into the rearview mirror one last time, pushing at her chin-length burnished curls and pursing her lips, seeing that she'd eaten all of the lipstick off her bottom lip, probably after that limousine had slid into her lane near Exit 9.

But, all in all, she didn't look that bad. A little worse for wear, that's all. Five pounds lighter than she had been three weeks ago. With slightly dark bruises under her eyes, the legacy of too many sleepless nights, too many tears. She started to reach into her purse, meaning to rummage around for her lipstick and compact, then realized what she was doing.

She was in Ocean City, New Jersey. In February. Alone. She needed lipstick about as much as the streets around her needed another inch of ice.

She was here for a rest. And an exorcism. She was going to walk the boardwalk—even if there were gale warnings posted, damn it! She was going to sleep late, eat too much and cry until Timothy Fitzgerald was cried straight out of her system.

And all without interruptions from her well-meaning mother or phone calls from her friend Alice Ann, who was to have been her maid of honor. Alice Ann had never met Tim's older brother, Matthew, but she'd seen a photograph Molly had sent to her in Chicago, and she now seemed to hold Molly personally responsible for ruining what Alice Ann had seen as a definite upswing in her social life.

After all, hadn't Alice Ann met her last boyfriend at her uncle Jonathan's funeral? Only Alice Ann would see a funeral, or her best friend's wedding, as a prime dating opportunity!

Reaching into the back seat, Molly pulled her garment bag over the headrest and onto the seat beside her, then reached back once more to grab the smaller overnight bag. Two nights, two bags. It was her greatest failing, this tendency to overpack. She hated packing for a trip, deciding what she'd need, what would be too much.

So she just took everything.

Tim had grumbled good-naturedly last November, when they'd sneaked away for a weekend in New York, and he'd ended up lugging three suitcases filled with both autumn and winter clothes as she'd explained that November was a fickle month, and she had to be prepared.

But at least then he'd carried the bags for her. This time she was on her own, and as she stood outside the car and surveyed the long flight of ice-slick stairs, she cursed Timothy Fitzgerald yet again—even as she wished they could have come here together, as they'd planned.

Because Tim would have loved the place.

Emmaline's was lovely, even in the midst of an ice storm. Perhaps *especially* in the midst of an ice storm. There wasn't much light on this dark, damp afternoon, but every bit of it seemed to be centered on the sparkling ice that turned each romantic bit of gingerbread, each wooden curlicue, each carved balustrade marching along the curving porch, into fantasy iced confections.

Tim loved old houses. In that, he was a bit of a rebel, as architects went, preferring personality over anonymous glass and sleek functionality. His latest project, a small neighborhood of Victorian-looking craft shops that also served as homes for the owners, had been written up in more than one architectural magazine, and it was one of Molly's favorite projects, as well. Oh, he'd designed his share of shopping centers, Tim had, but it was projects like Jordan Village that held his heart.

Yes, he would have adored Emmaline's.

Molly shook her head, shivering as she realized she was still standing on the pavement, her garment bag slung over one shoulder, her bulging overnight case pulling at her left arm. With one last look at the icy steps, she took a deep breath and slid her feet, one after another, toward the stair railing to her right.

And fell flat on her garment bag.

The pain in her right ankle was sharp and immediate. "Damn you, Timothy Fitzgerald!" she snarled out from between pain-clenched teeth, knowing she was being ridiculous, and more than a little redundant. Tim had nothing to do with her fall. But she'd been cursing him for three weeks, and it was fast becoming a habit. A habit she'd break this weekend, along with other habits, such as putting an extra potato in the oven, or setting two places at the table before realizing what she was doing. Or waking in the middle of the night and turning on her side to cuddle, just to discover that she was alone in her bed.

"Oh, for crying out loud, Molly, just get up!" she told herself as she grabbed on to the railing and slowly pulled herself onto her knees. Slowly, and still favoring her now-throbbing ankle, she inched her way up the dozen steps on her shredded panty hose, then hopped to the door.

"Welcome to Emmaline's," she recited, smiling wanly as she read the hand-painted wooden plaque beside the door. "Please don't just stand there—come on in!"

"Sure. Come on in. Just come on in! The one time you'd overtip shamelessly for a bellman," she groused, biting back a whimper as she pushed open the door, then limped inside, walking on only the toes of her right foot.

"Oh, my!"

Molly let the garment bag slide off her shoulder as she looked at the woman who had come out from behind the small registration desk and was now rushing toward her. She looked like the Good Witch from *The Wizard of Oz*—only, in miniature.

Dressed all in a light blue gauzy dress that fell in flounces to just above her ankles, the petite woman was a spectacular vision in lace collar and cuffs, a large cameo brooch at her throat. She was also eighty if she was a day, but her hair was a blond mist around her head, a fuzzy haze of curls that would have done justice to a fairy's glittering tiara. Her lips were red as cherries, and matched the two circles of color on her papery-thin cheeks. Blue eye shadow that matched her eyes made her appear more whimsical than comical.

Molly fell in love with her on sight.

"Oh, you poor dear thing!" the old woman chirped, taking Molly by the elbow and easing her into a red velvet armchair beside the door. Molly caught the sweet scent of lavender and made a silent bet with herself that the dear old lady whipped up batches of it from scratch in her kitchen. "You're Molly, aren't you? Well, of course you are. Who else could you be? I'm Emmaline. Emmaline Whipple. But you must call me Auntie Emmaline. Everyone does. Do you think it's broken? Your ankle, that is?"

Molly flexed her foot, then shook her head. "No, I don't think so. But I'm not going back out there until the spring melt, I can tell you that," she added, smiling as Mrs. Whipple—Auntie Emmaline—cluck-cluck-clucked her tongue, a sound Molly had read about in books, but never actually heard.

"Oh, that's all right, then, isn't it?" Auntie

Emmaline said, beaming at Molly. "There's nothing more cozy than Emmaline's bridal suite in a winter storm. You can just snuggle up in the bed, listening to the waves break on the shore, a cheery fire in the fireplace. You go on up now, dear, and turn on the fire if it isn't already on. It's gas—Albert talked me into converting both the fireplaces, in the parlor and in the bridal suite—and quite easy to work. Leave the bathroom door open as you take your bath, and you'll soon be warm as toast. You *can* make the stairs now, can't you?" she added, looking as if she might burst into sympathetic tears if Molly said she couldn't.

Pressing her hands against the arms of the chair, to help boost her to her feet, Molly tentatively put weight on her right foot, then stood up. "Almost as good as normal!" she lied, trying not to wince. Even if her anklebone was sticking through her skin, Molly wouldn't complain. It would be like spanking a puppy for wagging its tail. She looked to her left. "My luggage—"

"Will be upstairs as soon as I can find Tabitha and pry those horrid things off her ears long enough to tell her to carry them up to you. The luggage, of course, not her ears," Auntie Emmaline ended, giggling. "You just go along now, dear, and don't worry about a thing. Little upsets like this never last. Besides, Auntie Emmaline has a *wonderful* Valentine's weekend planned for the two of you!"

Molly hesitated as she mounted the first two steps that made up the landing before the stairway turned to the left, rising along the wall. "Two? Oh, but, you see, there's only—"

The good witch who was Emmaline Whipple fluttered her beringed hands, making shooing motions, indicating that Molly shouldn't be standing around on her injured ankle. "We'll talk later, dear. You just go now, and soak in a hot tub. You look rather like a drowned kitten, if I must say so, love, and you'll catch your death of cold if you don't do something about it right away. Tabitha will bring your luggage up directly."

Molly bit down her protest and headed up the stairs, responding to the older woman's wisdom just as she had done when her mother had said those same motherly words: *You'll catch your death of cold.* Such phrases were like a mother's curse, and nearly always came true. *Wear a hat or you'll get an earache. Stop running, young lady, or you're going to fall. Shave your legs before you're fifteen and the hair will grow back dark, and twice as thick.*

And there was one more "motherism" Molly couldn't get out of her brain. *Let Tim walk out of your life without talking to him one more time, little lady, without trying to work out your problems, and you'll regret it for the rest of that life.*

"Yes, Mother," Molly grumbled under her breath as she half pulled herself up the wide, shallow staircase, stopping only as Emmaline Whipple called to her, then floated to the stairway Good-Witch-like and handed up the key to the bridal suite.

Molly took it, then let it lay in the palm of her hand as she looked at the large, old-fashioned key. It was shiny, almost like brass, with a small gap-toothed bottom straight out of another century. But it was the design on the other end of the key that brought a sad smile to Molly's lips.

The key was topped by a lovely golden heart. It was beautiful. Perfect for a bridal suite.

Molly blinked back self-pitying tears and continued climbing the stairs.

Chapter Two

AND THERE IT WAS. Emmaline's bridal suite. Oh, yeah. Molly couldn't miss it, even at the end of a long, twisting hallway. It was, after all, rather difficult to overlook a doorway decorated in doily-edged red paper hearts. The hand-painted sign over the door, spelling out Bridal Suite in gilt-edged, curlicue letters was equally difficult to overlook. Or forget.

She could have asked for another room. She *should* have asked for another room. But it was too late now.

Molly slid the key into the lock, turned it and pushed into the room.

Tears stung at her eyes as her gaze was captured and held by the bed settled into an alcove at the other side of the large chamber. Constructed of what had to be solid cherry, the top of its mattress stood a good three or more feet above the floor, a small set of cherry steps sitting beside it on a needle-point floral rug.

Its four tall posts supported a canopy that dripped white eyelet, a material that also made up the bedspread that trailed nearly to the floor, ending in a deep, double row of ruffles.

There had to be a dozen or more colorful, floral pillows piled against the carved headboard and, hanging on the wall just above the headboard, a huge gilt, near-naked gilt cupid complete with bow and quiver smiled at her.

Leered at her.

Tim would have taken one look, named the silly-looking figure and they both would have laughed until their sides hurt...then made love on the bed.

The scent of real, homemade rose potpourri drifted to Molly's nostrils as she tore her watery gaze from the enormous bed and did a small investigation of the remainder of the room.

Red cabbage roses—as huge as melons—scattered on an ivory background papered the walls. A massive, burled-front, marble-topped bureau stood against the far wall.

A dozen perfume bottles of varied and whimsical shapes sat on a mirrored tray atop the bureau, their contents most probably colored water, as Molly couldn't remember ever seeing green or blue perfume. There was also a pair of crystal table lamps complete with dripping crystal pendants positioned at either end of the bureau top, their reflections clear in the massive, cherry-framed mirror.

There was another mirror in the far corner, one of those freestanding contraptions, a six-foot-long oval that could be positioned every which way. Tim would know the name of it. A dressing mirror? Maybe. Maybe not. Whatever it was called, Molly had always wanted one.

At least she knew what the tall chest set to one side on the window wall was called. A highboy. Queen Anne, she believed. She particularly admired the short, fat, deep green tassel Mrs. Whipple must have hung from the top center drawer.

She wasn't as sure she liked the piece of pottery sitting on the top of the highboy—a foot-high antique jug in the shape, she was sure, of Bacchus, the Greek god of wine. Or was that fertility? Well, one often led to the other, in any event.

Molly giggled. For shame, Mrs. Whipple!

In front of the white organdy-covered double windows sat an old wicker carriage; in it, a life-size baby doll with a china face and wearing the most beautiful christening gown Molly had ever seen. She limped across the largest of four or more needlepoint rugs scattered around the room, barely noticing that, yes, the gas fire had already been turned on in the ornately carved marble fireplace, and stroked a finger down the doll's pink cheek.

Why, Auntie Emmaline, you're just one great big sentimental sweetheart, aren't you?

Wiping at her eyes—her lamentably easy-to-moisten eyes, at least for the past three weeks—Molly turned and looked at the bureau once again, noticing that there were doors at either side of it. One must lead to a closet, the other to the bathroom.

Did the bathroom door open into two rooms? Was she going to have to share the bathroom with another guest? For she could hear the shower running, and whoever was in it at the moment was singing. Singing badly. Off-key. Almost as off-key as Tim could be when caught up in murdering one of his silly, self-composed country music songs.

Molly sighed and slipped out of her shoes, kicking them to one side as she began opening her blouse. She was so tired, exhausted actually, and as soon as her luggage was brought to her, she was going to unearth the rose bath salts she'd brought with her and sink into a nice hot tub. At least the bathroom would be warm after the singing cowboy got done with his shower.

She'd gotten to the third button before the water cut off in the bathroom. Her blouse was lying over the back of the overstuffed armchair and she was unzipping her jeans when the bathroom door opened.

On *her* side.

"...she left me standin', standin' all alone on that there ridge."

Molly heard the words, recognized the voice and quickly rezipped her jeans.

She watched, while simultaneously trying to

find the sleeve opening of her blouse and not having much success, as Timothy Fitzgerald walked into the room, rubbing at his wet head with one towel, another, larger one loosely slung around his waist. "I'm so lonely now, so lonely...so I'm jumpin' off the Ninth Street Brrrrr-*idge*."

"Timothy Fitzgerald," she growled, realizing she'd put the wrong arm in the wrong sleeve and tearing the blouse off again, so that she was standing in front of her former fiancé in bare feet, jeans and a flimsy lace bra, her blouse wadded against her breasts. "How *could* you!"

He stopped rubbing at his wet hair and let the towel drop from his right hand to his left as he goggled across the room at her. "Molly?"

"Yes, Tim—*Molly!*" She all but ripped her blouse, trying to find the correct sleeves, then jammed her arms into them, one after the other. "But don't worry. I was just leaving."

He grinned then, damn him. Grinned as wide as the Cheshire cat, and with twice the innuendo. "Doesn't look that way, Moll. You've got the buttons hooked all wrong. And you're not wearing shoes, mean as I am to point out these small lapses."

Molly looked down at the buttons on her blouse and muttered to herself as she slid them out of the incorrect holes and started over. "This is just like him. Straight down to the ground.

Happy as a lark, smiling and singing one of his awful songs. I can't get out of here fast enough!"

Tim walked past her, his chest still glistening with water droplets from his shower, and pushed back the ruffled organdy curtains, peering outside. "You like driving in ice storms now, Molly? My, how a person can change in only three weeks. Why, I remember a time you couldn't even *walk* across a slightly icy pavement without landing on your—"

"Shut up, Tim. Just shut up, okay!" Molly commanded, picking up her shoes and sitting down on the overstuffed chair to put them on. The left shoe went on fine. The right one? Well, that was another story. Her foot might not be broken, but it had already swollen up enough that it hurt too much to try to shoehorn herself into her loafers. She'd have to unearth a pair of sneakers from her luggage.

Her luggage! Somebody named Tabitha was going to be bringing up her luggage any minute now. Oh, no. Her luggage and Tim's luggage were not going to inhabit the same room. No way. No how.

Except, now that she needed it, her luggage was still downstairs, and she was here. Upstairs. With Timothy Fitzgerald. In the bridal suite with Timothy Fitzgerald. She'd look at the cupid, but knew it probably wasn't just leering now. It had to be bent over, holding its little gilt sides, laughing its little gilt head off!

She hefted the loafer in her hand, contemplating throwing it at Tim's head, then gently, oh, so gently put it down and sat back in the chair, her shoulders slumped against the cushions.

"I hate you, Timothy Fitzgerald," she proclaimed from between clenched teeth as Tim let the curtain fall and walked across the room once more, to stand in front of her. She refused to look up into his face, but she could see the water droplets clinging to the hairs on his straight, bare legs. She could, peering up through her lashes, watch the steady rise and fall of his nicely muscled chest as he breathed. She could imagine what was hidden under that scandalously small scrap of terry cloth. "I hate you *so much*."

"I'm glad to see you, too, Molly," he answered with maddening calm, turning to go to the closet. He opened it and pulled out a suitcase, tossing it onto the bed and zipping it open.

"Don't put that suitcase on there!" she exclaimed, not wanting to talk to him, but worried for the eyelet bedspread that had to be one of Auntie Emmaline's treasures. "You'll ruin the spread, you idiot."

Tim looked at the bedspread, then picked up the suitcase and laid it on the floor. "When you're right you're right, darling. Besides, if we ruin the thing, we'll probably have to pay for it," he added, his brown eyes narrowed and glinting, probably because he'd just remembered that he was angry with her, and why. He put a hand to the towel at his waist. "Now, Ms. Bryant, do you want to turn your back, or should I ask if you want to buy a ticket to the great unveiling?"

Molly sniffed. She snorted, actually. It looked like their last fight was about to take up where it had left off three weeks ago. Well, she was ready for him! "You don't have anything I haven't seen before, Tim. Unless you've *bought* something new?" she ended sarcastically, then quickly turned her head as the towel dropped to the floor. She was angry, yes, but she wasn't nuts. One look at Tim in the nude, a single glimpse of the body she knew so intimately and had missed so much, and she would be telling him *three* weeks in Cancún couldn't be all that expensive, after all. Maybe a month would be too short.

She heard the rustle of legs being shoved into jeans and the slide of a zipper before she turned to look at him once more. His upper body was still bare, his broad shoulders exposed for her admiration, and his longish, light brown hair was adorably tousled against his forehead. He grinned at her, his brown eyes dancing with mischief, and she longed to belt him.

"You're enjoying this, aren't you?" she said accusingly.

"You betchum," he answered brightly, pulling a long-sleeved denim shirt out of the suitcase and putting it on. "I guess I should have known you'd rather come here alone than think we'd paid for the weekend and then not used it, right? It's vintage Molly Bryant."

Molly looked to the window and heard the slap of icy rain against the panes. "Which doesn't explain why *you're* here," she pointed out, silently praying Mrs. Whipple had just a small vacant room left for the weekend. Something in the attic, under the eaves. Or in the basement. Anywhere. Anywhere that wasn't here, in this room, with this man and her rapidly crumbling defenses.

"You want honesty, Moll? Because I'm not proud, I'll give you honesty. It was the phone," Tim said, walking past her and back into the bathroom, just to appear again, comb in hand, pulling it through the tangles of his damp hair. "I came here to get away from the telephone. Every time it rang, I hoped it was you. And every time it rang, it was my mother. Or my brother. Or my father. It didn't matter who it was, as they all were saying the same thing."

Molly rolled her eyes in commiseration, because she *didn't* hate Timothy Fitzgerald. She loved him. She just couldn't marry a man whose basic ideas so badly mismatched with hers. "Don't let that nice boy get away?"

"Substitute *sweet little girl* and, yes, you've

got the idea." Tim gifted her with one of his most endearing grins. "So, how *is* your mother?"

"I don't wanna talk about it," Molly mumbled quickly, gingerly lifting her right foot onto her left knee and beginning to massage her sore ankle. "The invitations arrived last Tuesday."

She looked up at him through her lashes as he laid the comb on the bureau and then knelt on the floor at her feet. "Bet that really bites you, huh? I mean, with the printing already done, they can't be returnable. Don't worry, Molly, the bill also arrived last Tuesday. I already paid for them."

"This has nothing to do with who *pays* for them!" she exclaimed, wishing he'd understand that the invitations weren't about money, they were about a wedding that was supposed to take place and now wouldn't. Besides, they'd already had their argument over the cost of the simple, elegant invitations, which had been top of the line. He'd won that argument, as she recalled, and she'd won the less expensive napkins for the reception argument.

Not that any of that mattered now. Nothing mattered now, except that Tim was kneeling in front of her, so close that all she had to do was reach out her hand and...no! She wasn't going to do it! It was over. The engagement was over!

He reached up and placed a hand on her instep

and Molly sucked in her breath, trying not to moan—not in pain, but in relief, for at last they were physically touching. She ached so badly to touch him, to have him touch her, hold her, tell her he still loved her.

"What did you do to your ankle, Moll? Did you slip on the ice?"

She nodded, then kept her head down, her hair falling forward to help hide her stinging eyes as Tim moved her hand away and began inspecting her ankle, measuring the severity of her injury.

"You need ice on that, if you don't want it to swell too much. I'll phone down for some."

Molly bit her lip, nodding once more, then looked around the room. "I don't see a phone, Tim. I think you'll have to go downstairs and ask Auntie Emm—I mean, Mrs. Whipple."

"Will do," he said, getting to his feet, her foot feeling strangely cold now that his hand had been removed from her flesh. "And I'll get your luggage while I'm at it, okay?"

"No, Tim. That's *not* okay. I'm going to ask Mrs. Whipple for another room. I can't stay here. Good Lord, Tim, how could you even think such a thing?"

He grinned, wickedly. "I'm a cockeyed optimist? I figured you'd be a big fan of that old saying, 'Two can live much more cheaply than one'? I thought I could talk you into bed so that we could make up? As I recall the thing, Moll, and I recall it too damn often, we do *make up* really, really well," he offered, then sobered. "All right, all right. I'll talk to—what did you say her name was?"

"Mrs. Whipple. But she'll tell you to call her Auntie Emmaline. She's a sweetheart, Tim. Didn't you meet her when you signed in?"

"Signed in?" Tim laughed. "I could have stolen everything in the reception area, Molly. I could have ransacked the kitchen for the apple pie I could smell baking. I could have run off with the family silver. The only thing I couldn't do was to sign the register. Not unless I wanted to surgically remove a pair of headphones from some teenage girl who probably would have given keys to Jack the Ripper, along with directions to the nearest victim."

"Oh," Molly said, remembering how happy Mrs. Whipple—oh, the heck with it, *Auntie Emmaline*—had appeared when she saw her. She understood now. The dear old woman had no idea that she and Tim had come here separately, not knowing the other one had the same plan. She had no idea her bridal suite was being occupied for the weekend by two people who believed they had waved their final goodbyes to each other.

What had the woman said to her? *Auntie Emmaline has a wonderful Valentine's weekend planned for the two of you!* Yes, that was it.

"Tim?" Molly ventured hesitantly as he

slipped his bare feet into a pair of unlaced sneakers. "What are you going to say to her? I mean, I think she has the whole Valentine's weekend planned out for couples. We'd be a real wet blanket on the group for the whole weekend. You know, everyone else holding hands and sighing—us throwing sarcastic remarks and salad plates at each other across the dinner table? Maybe we *both* should leave?"

He looked at her for a long time, his eyes dark and unreadable, until she shifted uncomfortably in the chair. "Right," he said at last, and headed for the door. "If that's what you want, Molly. I'll go tell her." With a quick motion of his head, he indicated the cupid over the bed. "You stay here and let Jasper over there keep you company, okay. I'll be right back."

The door closed behind him and Molly dropped her head into her hands. "Jasper," she said quietly, looking up at the grinning cupid. "Of course. It's the perfect name. And no, Tim," she added, her voice breaking. "That's *not* what I want. It's just the way it has to be."

TIM RAN MRS. WHIPPLE to ground in the kitchen, and soon found himself sitting at the table, a large glass of cold milk and a thick slice of warm apple pie in front of him.

He doubted he'd ever be sure exactly *how* he'd ended up there, his mouth full of pie as Auntie

Emmaline bustled around the kitchen, a frilly, starched white apron looped over her head and tied around her infinitesimal waist. But there he was. And there she was, chattering at him as she lifted lids and watched and stirred, not bothering to check to see if he was still listening to her—which he was, avidly—as she told him all about Emmaline's Valentine's weekend.

He listened, and he smiled, and he had a second helping of pie. Then he gave Auntie Emmaline a kiss on her rouged, papery cheek, accepted the small tray she handed him; it was a silver tray holding a fork and napkin, another slice of pie, another glass of milk and a blue plastic ice bag. He walked back into the Reception area, looked around with new eyes at all the Valentine's Day decorations, hefted Molly's garment bag onto one shoulder, stuck her overnight case under his arm—the woman packed like she was in charge of troop movements on Napoleon's retreat from Moscow!—and headed back upstairs.

He employed his free—well, nearly free—left hand to open the door to the bridal suite, walked inside and laid the silver tray on top of the bureau. He shrugged the garment bag off his shoulder and let the overnight bag drop onto the carpet.

Then he turned to look at Molly. To tell Molly want he had to tell her. And then duck...

He took a deep breath, then announced bluntly,

"We can't do it, Moll. We can't leave. Neither one of us. It would break her heart."

Molly was still sitting where he'd left her, looking so sweet, so vulnerable, so madder than hell. Before she could say a word, he snatched five silly knickknacks—was that one a real Dresden figurine, sitting right alongside a chipped, dime store figure of a pink poodle?—and a lace doily from the small table beside the chair.

He just as quickly moved the table in front of Molly. He slid the tray onto the table, unfolded the embroidered linen napkin—two red hearts entwined on a cream background—and placed it in her lap. He shoved the heavy, antique silver fork into her right hand. "Trust me, Moll, it's delicious. You eat. I'll talk. Okay?"

"You met Auntie Emmaline, didn't you?" Molly asked, looking at him, then sadly shaking her head. "What happened?"

Tim distractedly ran a hand through his hair and began to pace. "She's a widow," he began, beginning where Auntie Emmaline had begun. "Fifty-two years of marriage to her Albert, and two long years without him." He pointed to the carriage and doll. "No children—that's the christening gown she sewed and embroidered by hand before they were married and moved into this room, by the way."

"Oh, God," Molly said, sighing. She still held

the fork in her right hand, not moving a muscle. "Go on."

"Yeah, right," Tim said, taking another deep breath. "This was her parents' house, but she and Albert were young, and the house was large, and... Anyway, they lived here for all of their married lives. After her parents passed away, Albert had the happy idea of turning the place into a bed-and-breakfast, and they ran it, together, for the last half century or so. Albert named it Emmaline's because her parents had willed the property to her."

Molly had begun to eat the pie. "That's sweet," she said, putting down the glass and sliding her tongue over her upper lip, to rid it of a small milk mustache.

Tim closed his eyes on the sight of her pink tongue gliding along her lip, finding that he was in real, physical pain.

"It gets sweeter," he warned, abusing his already mussed hair once more. "Albert proposed on Valentine's Day—right here, downstairs, in the parlor, as Auntie Emmaline calls it. Anyway, Valentine's Day became their favorite holiday. They even advertised it in their brochure, remember?"

"I remember," Molly said around another forkful of pie. He'd known she'd like it. Molly had a real sweet tooth. And she was looking less edgy already, more mellow. Well, that'd change soon enough.

He walked over to the bed and sat down on the low cherry blanket chest that sat at the foot of it. "The thing is, nobody ever showed up. *Ever.* Think about it, Molly. February. New Jersey. Cold, windy, rainy, *icy.* Who wants to come to the seashore in the middle of winter, right?"

"Right," Molly said, dragging out the word as she looked at him. He couldn't quite meet her eyes, so he looked at the ceiling instead, and noticed that it was one of those old-fashioned ceilings with a domed top and finely done stuccoed decoration above the wide, intricate molding. Vines, and leaves, and—those were bluebirds mixed in there, weren't they? Nice architectural interest. "Tim?" Molly prompted as he considered the logistics of a domed ceiling over the more trendy tray ceilings he'd chosen for the house he wanted to build for Molly and himself. At least in the bedroom suite.

"Hmm?" he asked, then shook his head, trying to clear it. There was no sense thinking about his and Molly's dream house, not when there wasn't going to be a marriage. "Oh. Oh, yeah. Back to Auntie Emmaline's romantic Valentine's weekends. Nobody came. Never. But Auntie Emmaline remained hopeful, and she and Albert decorated the house every year—you've seen some of it, Molly, in the reception area. She's even got cupids and hearts hanging from the ceiling in the kitchen, for crying out loud."

He couldn't sit still any longer, and stood up, beginning to pace once more. "This year was going to be the same, or so Auntie Emmaline figured, with nobody showing up for the special weekend. In fact, hardly anyone stays at Emmaline's anymore even in the summer months, not with all the newer, air-conditioned hotels on the beach. And Auntie Emmaline isn't getting any younger, she told me, although you couldn't prove that by me, watching her bustle around that old-fashioned kitchen so fast, she made my head spin. She says one of her greatest loves is cooking, baking. Anyway, she closed Emmaline's at the end of November, for the very last time, actually—" he stopped and turned to face Molly "—and then she threw out the mattresses in all the guest rooms."

The heavy silver fork hit the plate with a *clang*. "She did *what?* Emmaline's is *closed?*" Molly looked at the bed. "But—but the brochure? And the *reservation*. She took our reservation, Tim. How can the place be closed?"

"The For Sale sign is on the side of the house, on Corinthian Avenue. I parked out front, and didn't see it. And she took our reservation for two reasons, Moll. One, your mother never throws anything out, and that brochure she gave you is about five years old. And two, because we asked to come here on Valentine's weekend—Auntie Emmaline's and Albert's favorite holiday. She couldn't resist, she told me. Putting up the decorations one last time. Having young lovers—and, hey, I'm just telling you what she said—*trysting* in the bedroom she and Albert had shared on their honeymoon fifty-four years ago."

He dropped his chin to his chest. "She enters some kind of combination retirement and nursing home as soon as the house is sold. She gets one whole room to herself, she says. No kitchen."

"Oh, God," Molly said, her hand going to her mouth as her tear-bright eyes touched something deep in Tim's heart. "That's the saddest thing I've ever heard. Tim, what are we going to do?"

Yeah. Right. What were they going to do? Emmaline Whipple's was the only other furnished room in the bed-and-breakfast, something he was sure Molly had already figured out. She probably had also already figured out that she couldn't drive with her right ankle injured—not while he was around to stop her. Besides, the ice storm of the century was going on right outside their window.

They couldn't leave. Period.

And they couldn't hurt Auntie Emmaline, which demanding separate rooms would most certainly do.

"It's obvious, isn't it?" he said when Molly didn't try to answer her own question. "We stay here for the weekend. We play happily engaged couple. We eat the individual heart-shaped meat loaves Auntie Emmaline was sticking in the oven when I left the kitchen. We smile, we hold hands, we admire all the decorations—and we promise not to kill each other. Unless you have a better idea? You know, like telling that dear old lady the truth, and breaking her heart? I mean, she already wrote to Albert, telling him we were coming."

"She—she *wrote* to him?"

Had to be a dry town, didn't it? Tim, who was not a drinking man, longed for a long, cold beer, or a short, warm shot of Scotch. "That's what I said, Moll. She writes to him. Tells him everything that's going on. Then she leaves the letters on the table—the one holding Albert's collection of pipes in the parlor. And he takes them."

"The pipes?"

Tim grinned at Molly's incredulous question. "You know what I mean, Moll. Albert takes the letters. Auntie Emmaline swears it. That's her biggest concern, you know. That she has to leave Albert here alone when she goes into the home. But, at the same time, she says she's glad he'll still be here, to take care of their memories."

"Well, that tears it. I think I'm going to cry," Molly said, pushing the table away from her and getting to her feet.

"Yeah, I know," Tim admitted, rubbing at his

chin. "So, Moll, what do you say? Do you think we can make it to Sunday without coming to blows over the fact that I forget to turn out lights and let the hot water run while I'm shaving—thus throwing money around like water? Hey, wait a minute! Is *that* what it means?"

"I'm not sleeping with you," Molly declared flatly, obviously willing to overlook his reference to her pinch-penny economies and his own spendthrift ways.

"Fair enough," he agreed, pleased by her quick capitulation. He knew Molly, and she would rather swallow broken glass than hurt a nice old lady like Auntie Emmaline. "I promise to be good."

"Oh, that'll be easy enough, Tim," she told him, pointing to the chair. "Because *that's* where you'll be sleeping!"

Tim eyed the chair owlishly. "You're kidding, right? I'm six-foot-two, Moll. I can't sleep in that chair."

"And I have to keep my ankle elevated," she answered reasonably. "So *I* can't sleep in that chair. Unless you have a better suggestion?"

Tim hadn't been named Most Innovative of his graduating class for nothing—although, granted, the award had been for his design of an office building that had all the modern conveniences but carried the interesting architectural design of a more gracious, bygone era. Still, innovation was innovation, and a little expert "stealing" of old ideas, reworking them for his own use, could still be called innovative. Or, at the least, damned inventive.

"If I remember my history correctly, Moll, the early American settlers used to have something they called bundling. Because it was often cold in the cabin when young couples were courting, they were tucked up into a bed—bundled—with a rolled blanket or something stuck in between them, just to keep Colonial Tom, Dick, or Harry honest, I suppose. There's about a half-dozen extra blankets on the shelf in the closet, Moll. And that bed is large enough to hold four people."

"Bundling," Molly said after staring at him so long, he wanted to wipe at his chin, sure there was a piece of pie crust hanging from it. "Now *you've* got to be kidding. We wouldn't last five minutes, and you damn well know it."

"No, I don't know that!" Tim exclaimed, while his brain whispered *Damn straight I know that, Moll.*

"It won't work," she persisted, hands on hips.

"Are you doubting me, Molly? Do you think I'm that rotten, that weak—that *desperate?*" he asked, doing his best to look pitiful when, in truth, he was already planning his first moves after the lights went out and they were alone in bed. "Or are you doubting yourself?"

"Oh, that's low, Fitzgerald," she spat out.

"Really *low!* All right, I'll do it. But first, I'm going to search these drawers for a hat pin I can keep under my pillow. Auntie Emmaline must have one around here someplace. *That* ought to keep you honest."

Tim let out a sigh of relief, then went to the closet to pull out the folding luggage rack he'd seen in there earlier, so that Molly could unpack.

"I suppose that also means I don't have to ask you if that brand-new black Mercedes I saw out front is yours, do I? You know. The big one, with the teardrop headlights?" she asked silkily, so that he felt a shiver race down his spine, for once again she'd zeroed in on one of his impulse expenditures. "I mean, as long as we're being so *honest.*"

He hefted the overnight case onto the luggage rack and grinned at her. "Yeah, Moll. I wanted it, and I got it. Last week. But I leased it, Moll. That has to count for something, doesn't it?"

"Tell it to Jasper, Fitzgerald. I'm no longer interested," Molly bit out, then turned her back on him, sat down on the chair once more, laid the blue ice bag on her ankle and proceeded to finish her pie.

Chapter Three

MOLLY'S HOPED-FOR long soak in a hot tub turned into a quick lather and rinse under a tepid shower—Auntie Emmaline's hot water heater obviously had known better days. But that was all right, because Molly had done a slow burn of her own while showering, thinking about the fine mess she'd gotten herself into this time.

Only, this time, she hadn't stumbled into the sticker bushes on her own. This time, she'd had help. Plenty of it! In the form of one Emmaline Whipple. With more than a little assistance from one Timothy Fitzgerald. And the fickle winter weather. She could even lay some of the blame at her mother's door, and even at Alice Ann's.

Actually, when she got right down to it, nearly everyone and everything—perhaps the whole world—had conspired against her.

And she couldn't see any way out of her dilemma. She was here. Tim was here. The ice storm was here. Dear, sweet, soon-to-be dispossessed Emmaline Whipple was here. Why, the way things were going, Molly was about ready to believe Albert was here.

And a heart-shaped meat loaf was waiting for her downstairs.

Molly pulled on a pair of tan-and-white houndstooth check wool slacks—she adored lined wool slacks, as the silky material felt so good sliding against her panty-hose-clad legs when she walked. Tim, when she'd admitted as much to him, had said that was because she was a "sensual woman."

She'd told him he was right, as she recalled now, and then went on to prove his theory, falling onto his bed with him. They'd missed the early showing of the movie they'd planned to attend that night. And the second show, as well. And dinner. But that's all they'd missed....

"Oh, that's good, Bryant," she told herself, roughly wiping the steam from the mirror with a hand towel. "You just keep reminiscing like that, and you'll land yourself straight in another fine mess. Now, just get yourself dressed, get yourself downstairs and get this evening *over with!*"

With her own warning ringing in her ears, she quickly topped the slacks with a soft white angora sweater sporting a huge cowl collar, then looped a tan, mauve and white silk flowered scarf under the collar and let the ends hang free nearly to her waist.

She'd washed her hair that morning, and it still looked full and squeaky-clean, sleekly falling from its center part to end in a knife-sharp edge just below her chin on the sides, slightly shorter in the back, cupping her nape. A dash of mauve lipstick, a little mascara, a quick spray of Chanel, and she was done.

She was ready to walk the plank, or to go down to dinner, which was, Molly knew, pretty much the same thing.

Taking a deep, steadying breath, she opened the bathroom door and stepped back into the room.

Tim was lying stretched out on the bedspread, his arms folded behind his back, looking very much at his ease. "I've always liked that sweater," he said, grinning at her. "All soft, and fuzzy, and *touchable*."

"I'll go change," Molly bit out quickly, then found her sneakers and sat down in the chair, hoping the right one would fit. The swelling had gone down in her foot, but her ankle was still puffy, and hurt like hell if she tried to put her full weight on it, not that she'd tell Tim that. "And we don't have an audience yet, so you can stop complimenting me, okay?"

He jackknifed into a sitting position, his long legs dangling over the edge of the bed. "Yeah, but the curtain goes up in five minutes, Moll, and I need to get into character. I think I'm a method actor."

Molly had been bending over from the waist, attempting to tie her sneakers. She looked up at him through the veil of her hair and said, "Oh, you've got a method all right, Fitzgerald," she agreed tightly. "And so do I." She sat up once more, pushing her hair back into place by simply running a hand through it, so that it naturally fell back into the lines of its very good cut. "Did you happen to see the straw hat hanging on the bathroom wall, Tim? The one with the silk flowers on it?"

Tim frowned. "Can't say as I did. Why?"

She grinned. "Oh, that's too bad. You should have noticed. Everybody's hanging big straw hats on walls these days. It's a very nice, homey decoration. Complete with hat pin," she ended, reaching under the cowl collar and pulling out the long, thin, pearl-topped pin, holding it up in front of her, turning it this way and that, admiring its sharp point.

Tim slid off the bed and onto his feet. "That's sadistic," he said, slipping into his loafers. "But very good, Moll. Very good."

"Even excellent, Fitzgerald," she said, feeling fairly smug. "I've even been rehearsing my lines. Make my day. I'm your worst nightmare. And this one—you feel lucky, punk?"

"You may have overestimated your charms, Moll," Tim said, walking past her to open the door to the hallway. "Did you ever think of that?"

"Maybe," she said, walking through the doorway ahead of him. "But I've never underestimated *you*, Timothy Fitzgerald. Well, now, I'm starving! Shall we?"

She all but skipped down the long hallway ahead of him, knowing that, for just this once, she'd gotten in the last word in one of their arguments. And, man, did it feel *good!*

That good feeling lasted about fifteen more seconds, until Molly walked through the reception room, pushed back the floor-length ropes of beads that hung inside the archway and walked into the "parlor." She stopped dead just on the other side of the archway, so that Tim almost stepped on her heel behind her.

"Can you believe this?" she asked, letting the lengths of beads slide through her fingers as she slowly entered the room, looking to her left, looking to her right, looking up to the ceiling—and finding Valentine's Day decorations wherever she looked.

There were, as Molly now termed them, the prerequisite red construction paper hearts, garlands of them swooping from corner to corner, even hanging in an X running diagonally across the ceiling.

Lace, handmade doilies covered every table surface, draped over the backs and arms of every chair, both love seats—the Victorian, heart-backed burgundy velvet love seats.

Old Valentine's Day cards, some of them ancient and touchingly sentimental, some of them obviously homemade, a few of the more modern ones sporting color drawings of Mickey Mouse, even Daffy Duck, marched along the mantel, spilled across the broad windowsills behind the frilly white Priscilla curtains.

It was as if Valentine's Day had up and exploded in the room.

That was all bad enough.

But there was more.

Auntie Emmaline must have been collecting cupids for half a century. Elegant crystal cupids. Pricey porcelain cupids, painted by a master hand. Plaster of Paris cupids, the sort of cheap ornament a person won at the county fair if the guy couldn't guess your correct weight.

Cupids with glitter on their fat bellies. Cupids holding bows and arrows. Nearly naked Cupids lying on their sides, with flowerpots growing out of their backs—complete with tacky plastic flowers. A cupid holding a ukelele and wearing a hula skirt, "Hawaii 1956" painted on its bare chest in bright, neon pink.

A cupid with a clock in its belly. A cupid with plastic, stuck-on googley-eyes that jiggled if you picked up the statue and gave it a shake.

Here a cupid, there a cupid, everywhere a cupid, cupid.

Molly walked up to the hula cupid and gave it a gentle nudge. It had been constructed in two pieces, and the top half, the half with the green plastic grass skirt attached to it, began to dance.

"It's just enough, isn't it?" Tim joked from behind her. "I mean, one more would be too many, but this is just right, just enough. Wouldn't want to be tacky, right? How many do you think there are, Moll—fifty?"

"At least," Molly answered, grinning up at him. "And I'll bet Auntie Emmaline and her Albert gave them all to each other over the course of their marriage, and that there's a lovely story behind each gift, each card. She probably keeps them stored in the attic, and brings them out every Valentine's Day."

She frowned then, as another, more sobering thought struck her. "Auntie Emmaline will never be able to take them all to the retirement home with her, Tim. Will she?"

"No," he agreed, looking around the large, cluttered room. "I suppose she won't. She told me she's hoping to sell most of the furniture to whoever buys the place—but this stuff? She has some valuable pieces mixed in with the rest, Moll, but most of this stuff is purely sentimental. Look, Moll—there's Albert's pipe rack over there on that table. And Aunt Emmaline's letter."

Molly bit her lip and turned to see a rack holding about a half-dozen pipes. Lovely old pipes, their ends well bitten. There was also a cherry tobacco holder on the small end table. And a letter—folded, but not in an envelope. "Albert must be coming by later, since it's still here," she said, wishing she didn't want to believe that Albert really would be stopping by to pick up his mail, his love letter from his wife. "Tim! What are you doing? You can't touch that."

But Tim was already holding the letter in his hands, unfolding the two sheets of thick stationery and beginning to read.

"Tim!" Molly protested again, thrusting her hand, fingers spread, in front of the paper. "There are laws against this sort of thing."

"I'm not stealing, Molly."

"No," she said as he brushed her hand away, "you're just tampering with the U.S. Mail. I think that's a felony, Fitzgerald. And its definitely an invasion of Auntie Emmaline's privacy."

Tim grinned at her. "Are you going to quote me chapter and verse of the U.S. Postal Code now, Moll?" He held out the letter to her and she took it, hating herself, but taking it. "See? No envelope. No stamp. We're back to invasion of privacy, Moll. Surely only a misdemeanor."

"I don't care," she said, shoving the letter back at him, then reaching for it again, before he could read what Emmaline Whipple had written. "That's personal correspondence, and we shouldn't read it. Just put it back, Tim. *Now*."

"Personal correspondence? Written to a dead man, Moll?" He held the letter above his head, so that she couldn't reach it. "Besides, don't you want to know what Auntie Emmaline said about us? She told me she'd written Albert all about us. Come on, Molly. Just a peek?"

"You're incorrigible!" she told him. But she was weakening. Besides, what harm could it do? Surely Albert wasn't going to complain.

"Yes, I am. And despicable. And nosy as all hell. So are you, except I'm more honest, Moll. I admit it," Tim said, sitting in the huge, worn wingback chair Albert Whipple must have sat in every night, packing his pipe and gazing into the fireplace, his Emmaline sitting on the smaller, matching chair—cutting out red construction paper hearts and pasting them on paper doilies. "Ah—here we are. Listen, Molly. 'I've told you their names, haven't I? Molly Bryant and Timothy Fitzgerald. Such lovely names! Would I consider opening Emmaline's for them, just for the weekend? Silly children! How could I possibly say no? It's just as we've always said in our brochures—Valentine's Day is always very special at Emmaline's.'"

Molly dropped into Auntie Emmaline's chair, bonelessly, as if all the stuffing had gone out of her, the way most of the stuffing had disappeared from the worn, pink satin cupid pillow she'd moved out of her way so that she could sit down in the first place. "Oh, yeah. I'll agree with that. Valentine's Day at Emmaline's is special, all right. Unique, even."

"*Shh!* There's more, Molly. I'll just give you the highlights, okay? Here's one— 'Oh, Albert, the *plans* I've made for our young couple!' What plans, do you think? I'll bet that sentence has you trembling in your shoes, Moll. I know I am."

"I really couldn't say, Tim," Molly told him sweetly. "But if she wants us to bob for apples in a big metal tub, the way we used to do at Halloween when I was a kid, I'll be more than happy to hold your head under the water for, oh, five or ten minutes."

He lifted his head for a moment, to glare at her.

"No, no. Don't thank me," she said, holding up her hands. "It's the least I can do, *darling*."

"You're still crazy about me, aren't you? I have a sixth sense about these things, and I can tell," Tim all but purred, smiling, then read on a little more, chuckling deep in his throat. "Oh, Molly, you're really going to love this one— 'And never call me a fuddy-duddy! This is the nineties, after all. I'm "hep"...or "with it"...or whatever they're calling a wink and a smile these days. Besides, Albert, I seem to remember a certain summer evening you and I spent doing a little winking and smiling of our own a few weeks before our own wedding. Remember? Oh, we were so naughty!'"

"Put it away, Tim," Molly pleaded, caught between being embarrassed and wanting to weep for the young Emmaline and Albert, their good times all behind them and gone. Like hers and Tim's. "Please, Tim."

"Not until you read the last paragraph, Molly," he said, sighing. "Here—" He handed her the second page of the letter. "Read it."

Molly didn't want to read Auntie Emmaline's letter, but something in Tim's eyes, some sadness, some never-before-seen wistfulness, compelled her. "'I love you, dearest, even though we're apart now,'" she read, her voice low, faint. "'I will always love you. I'll put this with your pipes, as always, where you can find it.'"

She folded the letter and laid it in her lap, stroking the stiff stationery with her fingertips as she ended, "'Love, Emmaline.'" Her voice ended on a sigh, and her breath caught in her throat. "Oh, Tim..."

"Yeah. I know. Give it to me, Moll, and I'll put it back where we found it."

They sat in silence for a while, staring into the flames of the fireplace across the room, the only sound the ticking of the mantel clock. And then, out of the corner of her eye, Molly saw Tim hold out his hand to her, across the small space, the wide miles, dividing them.

She put her hand into his, closing her eyes as he squeezed her fingers.

Neither of them said a word....

THE DINING ROOM at Emmaline's was just behind and to the left of the parlor and, in its day, the large cherry table must have been scene to many a rollicking party as Aunt Emmaline's and Albert's guests slid their chairs beneath its immense surface.

But, for tonight, there were just the three of them, so that Emmaline had set their places fairly close together, taking the head of the table, and the hostess's chair, for herself.

The serving table as well as the dining room table boasted tall, branched silver candelabra, which Emmaline had fitted with red candles in honor of the holiday before switching off the crystal chandelier overhead. A lace tablecloth older than Tim and Molly put together covered the table.

She looked so sweet, Auntie Emmaline did, sitting there in her big, high-backed chair, her blond ringlets curling damply against her papery cheeks after she'd worked in the heat of the kitchen. So pixielike, so very happy to have guests at her table.

Why, she'd even asked Tim if he'd say grace for them, a request that had nearly reduced Molly to giggles. Until Tim, never missing a beat, had suggested the three of them join hands, then improvised the loveliest little speech that somehow included giving thanks for Auntie Emmaline, for Valentine's Day and even for the heart-shaped meat loaves that sat under a silver dome on the server table behind Molly, waiting for them when they were done with their fruit cup and homemade potato leek soup.

The meal had been delicious, if slightly agonizing for Molly, who had to remember to pepper her conversation with "darlings" and "sweethearts" because Tim, who really did seem to be getting into his part, kept asking her opinion on every subject they touched upon, ending all of his sentences with those same endearments.

Plus one. And if he called her his sugar sweetums just one more time, she was going to brain him with one of the candelabra!

"There now, another meal at Emmaline's has just about come to an end. How was it, children? It was good, wasn't it?" Emmaline beamed at Tim. "Well, it had to be, Tim, didn't it? You ate two of my meat loaves. I usually stick to a brown gravy with meat loaf, but seeing that it's Valentine's Day weekend, well, I couldn't resist a red sauce, now could I? Tabitha's mother gave me the recipe. She told me it would taste like a great big, juicy meatball. It's strange. I didn't think Rollins was an Italian name, did you?"

Tim hesitated as he was about to down a heart-shaped petit four in one bite, and looked to Molly, who was sitting across the table from him.

Feeling faintly sorry for him, she stepped right into the breech, carefully explaining to Aunt Emmaline that one didn't necessarily have to be Italian to know a good meat loaf or, for that matter, a good meatball recipe. "Tim's mother likes to say she's as Irish as Paddy's pig, but she makes the best pork-and-sauerkraut dinner I've ever tasted."

"Goodness, Molly, you're right!" Emmaline grinned down the table at the two of them. "And isn't it nice that you and Tim's mother get along so well? My Albert adored my parents. Why, he was forever teasing me that he and my mother were going to run off together to Atlantic City to watch the horse dive off the end of the Steel Pier. And Mama said she'd do it, too. Why, she said she'd even take her bathing suit along and see if she could ride the horse for its dive—there were these lovely young girls who dove with the horses, you know. Mama was such a stitch! Is your mother still alive, Molly?"

Tim grinned as Molly glared at him across the tabletop. Her mother adored Tim. "Oh, yes, Aunt Emmaline, my mother's still very much alive."

"And kicking. Isn't that right, darling?" Tim added facetiously, and Molly wished the table weren't so wide, so that she could kick *him* under the table. "In fact, Auntie Emmaline, Molly and

I are each fortunate enough to both have our parents still with us."

"So your father will be giving you away, Molly?" Emmaline pressed her hands together in front of her. "Oh, how lovely! You must tell me everything. Is it to be a very large wedding?"

"Yes."

"Not really."

Molly glared at Tim—who had denied theirs was to have been a large wedding—as he smiled at Emmaline, who was looking from one of them to the other, an adorably confused frown on her wrinkled, little pixie face.

"Not large, if you're thinking global, Auntie Emmaline," Tim explained, ignoring Molly's fairly inelegant snort—that she quickly changed into a cough. "Not small, if you're thinking a trip to the local justice of the peace. Right, Molly darling?"

Molly hadn't known until that moment that it was possible to smile and still grit one's teeth—and still speak at the same time.

"The guest list topped three hundred guests, *darling*," she said as sweetly as possible. "I'd hardly call that small." *And, at about thirty-two-fifty a head for the dinner and an open bar, I'd hardly call it cheap, either! But you won that battle, didn't you, Fitzgerald? And the others, as well. Invitations for over three hundred people.*

Wedding favors for over three hundred people. And the costs going up, and up, and up.

"Poor darling. She worries about our budget," Tim explained to Emmaline, somehow making all of Molly's perfectly rational objections to spending tons of money on one single day sound trivial. "But you only get married once, if you do it right, so why not go all out, I say. Isn't that so, Auntie Emmaline?"

It was a pity Tim had finished off the last of the petit fours Emmaline had so proudly served to them on a doily-lined silver tray, because Molly was now longing to leap across the table and rub a half-dozen of the pink-and-white-iced confections in his grinning face.

"Well," Emmaline answered slowly. "I don't know, Tim. Albert and I married during the war, you know, and the ceremony and reception were right here, in the parlor of Emmaline's. I believe we ate cucumber sandwiches and root beer, if memory serves—and it usually does—and with only about a dozen people in attendance. Still, I wouldn't change a single moment of our wedding day."

Ha! Take that, Fitzgerald, and stuff it into the hole in your wallet! Molly thought triumphantly, beaming down the table at dear, sweet, sensible Auntie Emmaline.

"Of course," Emmaline added after a moment, "if we could have, I'd have *adored* a large wedding. It's so romantic, you know. A big church wedding, and a reception people would talk about for years! Wearing a long white gown that cost the earth—covered with lace and encrusted with pearls, with its train sweeping along behind you as if you were a princess. Attendants dressed in lovely gowns of their own, perhaps with live flowers in their hair. Flowers *everywhere*. The groom and his gentlemen dressed in tuxedos and looking so handsome. And dancing, of course. Dancing to a real, live orchestra. Oh, and doves. I know I would have wanted doves released into the skies as Albert and I walked out of the church. Flying up to a cloudless blue sky, flying free, off to whisper to the heavens that they'd seen a love born, a love grow."

As Emmaline sat back in her chair, a beatific smile on her face, Molly looked across the table at Tim.

He wasn't smiling smugly. He wasn't waggling his eyebrows at her as if to say, "See? Told you so!" No, he wasn't doing either of those things.

He was simply looking at her. And his eyes were sad.

She picked up her cup, lowered her eyes and took another sip of tea.

"NO WONDER YOUR EYES are brown, Fitzgerald!" Molly boomed as he closed the door to the bridal suite behind them two hours later. "Because you're nothing, Fitzgerald, if you're not full of—"

"*Ah-ah,* Molly, remember—you're a lady," Tim cut in just as Molly was going to stop speaking anyway, he was sure, because Molly Bryant never said anything the least bit risqué. Except, maybe, for "Damn you, Timothy Fitzgerald!" She'd been saying that a lot lately. But he'd begun to think of that as just a slightly different sort of endearment.

"How *could* you?" Molly went on, pacing the carpet as she flapped her arms, a furry angora 727, flapping her wings as she headed down the runway. "How could you have invited Auntie Emmaline to our wedding? There isn't going to *be* a wedding, Fitzgerald, in case you've forgotten that one small fact."

"What can I say, Moll? I lost my head? I got carried away in the excitement of the moment?" Tim offered, pulling his crew neck sweater off over his still-attached head, then running a hand through his mussed hair. Man, was Molly mad!

"The excitement of the moment?" Molly shook her head. "What are you talking about? We were looking at Auntie Emmaline's photo albums, that's all. Photographs of her wedding to Albert."

"I know, I know," Tim said, raking a hand through his hair again. He'd done a dumb thing.

Dumb, dumb, *dumb*. "Be happy it wasn't home movies of the wedding, Moll, or I probably would have asked her to be our flower girl."

"We're not having a flower girl, Timothy," Molly informed him as she sat herself down and unlaced her sneakers. He watched as she eased the sneaker off her right foot, trying not to wince. When was she going to admit that her ankle still hurt like hell? When was she going to admit that *she* hurt like hell? Just like he did. "And do you know *why* we're not having a flower girl, Timothy? Because we're not having a wedding—*that's why!*"

"We could," he offered quietly.

He watched as Molly blinked several times, probably to keep from crying. He hoped it was to keep from crying. It might be mean, but he was suffering. He'd like to think she might be suffering a little bit, too. "No, Tim," she said sadly. "We couldn't. We've tried, we're really tried. But we can't. We might love—*have loved*—each other, but we have completely different ways of looking at life."

"We both like Bruce Willis movies. We both hate broccoli," Tim offered, trying to lighten the suddenly dark, heavy mood in the bridal suite.

She looked up at him with huge guppy eyes. He adored guppy eyes, and Molly's were the most beautiful shade of green. "There are differences even there, Tim. I'd rent Willis movies.

You'd buy them. Buy them, watch them once or twice and then stack them on the shelf of the expensive piece of furniture you bought to hold all your purchased, barely watched videos.''

"Yeah. But we've still got our hatred of broccoli," he said, aiming for some humor one more time, and missing—badly. "I like owning my own videos, Moll. Where's the harm?"

Molly got up, grabbed the pair of navy blue flannel pajamas from the bed, where she'd laid them earlier and made for the bathroom. "The videos are just one small example, Tim, and you know it." She half walked, half limped into the bathroom, leaving the door partially open behind her. He listened as she brushed her teeth, waiting for her to speak to him again. Because she would, sure as God made little green apples. "Our fights over the wedding expenses is just another one," she said over the sound of running water. "Symptoms of a larger problem. I save money, you spend it. It's as simple, and as complex, as that."

"I spend it, yes," he called to her through the half-open door. "I also *earn* it. Lots of it. I work hard, I play hard. It's called the American Dream, Moll. Maybe you've heard of it?"

"And you own your own company," Molly said, coming back out of the bathroom, dressed in the flannel pajamas now—*his* old flannel pajamas, he noticed. The legs dragged on the floor and she'd rolled up the sleeves three times. Her face was shiny and clean and she smelled of honey and lemon. She went to the closet and hung up her slacks and sweater. "Which means you have to make your own preparations for retirement. And have you, Tim? Have you put one red cent away in an IRA, a savings account—*anywhere?*"

"I've got some stocks," he said, unzipping his jeans. He'd be damned if he'd go hide in the bathroom, as Molly had done—just as if they hadn't been undressing in front of each other, or undressing each other, for almost a year now. "Some bonds. A couple of things."

"Yeah. Right," Molly said, turning toward the bed, her arms full of blankets she then dropped onto the floor. "You're a grasshopper, Tim. Oh, you might work more than a grasshopper. You work very hard, actually. But you don't put anything away for winter."

"Wait—I think I know this story. *Aesop's Fables,* right? I'm the grasshopper, so you have to be the ant. The ant who works hard all year and puts most of what he gets away for winter."

"We live in Pennsylvania, Tim. Cold winters," Molly said succinctly, turning back the eyelet bedspread and folding it neatly at the bottom of the bed. The quilted coverlet and top sheet followed. "Very cold winters."

"But Molly Bryant will have her savings and

her grocery coupons and her big ball of string, or sealing wax, or whatever the hell old maids collect to keep her warm. Is that it, Molly? How do you sleep nights, Moll—with all those pinched pennies screaming at you as they writhe in pain?"

She hesitated a moment as she bent down to pick up the blankets, but didn't say anything. Or hit him, which he had to consider a good thing, because he was laying it on pretty thick, and she had to be madder than hell at him.

"I love you, Moll," he said as she unfolded the first blanket, then rolled it up, placing it lengthwise, square in the center of the bed. "Can't we work this out?"

"You want to go to bed with me, and you'd say anything, promise anything, to get what you want," she said, still with her back turned to him. "And, much as I want to go to bed with you, I'm not going to do it. Going to bed with you has never solved anything."

"Maybe not for you," Tim quipped, and was immediately sorry, for now she did turn to him, and he saw the tears coursing down her face. "Aw, Moll—" he began, reaching for her.

She held up her hands in front of her, warning him not to come any closer. "No, Tim. Not again. Just go brush your teeth and come to bed. We'll talk again in the morning if you want, not that it'll do a bit of good."

"That's what I like best about you, Molly," he rasped, angry now. "You're such a cockeyed optimist. Go to bed, would you? Just go to bed."

By the time he'd finished in the bathroom, the bedroom was dark, and Molly was under the covers on her side of the wide bed with her back turned—a thick roll of blankets and a chasm as wide as the Grand Canyon between them. He crawled under the covers and lay on his back, looking up at the white eyelet canopy that was partially visible in the light coming through the window from the streetlight on the corner.

"Just tell me one thing, Molly," he said at last.

The sheets rustled as she turned onto her back. "What? I thought we weren't going to talk about this anymore tonight."

"We're not. But I've got one other question. Is there a Ninth Street Bridge song, Moll? You know—one of those Simon and Garfunkel things you like?"

She was silent for a few moments, then softly began to sing the chorus.

"You're kidding. That's it? Isn't that 'Feeling Groovy'?"

"No, Tim, it's 'The Fifty-ninth Street Bridge Song.' You always got that one wrong. Now, good night, Tim. I want to go to sleep now."

"Yeah. Right. I'll go to sleep now, while I'm

so happy, feeling so damn *groovy*." Tim slid an arm behind his head and stared up at the canopy.

He was in bed with the woman he loved.

Alone in bed with the woman he loved.

The operative word being *alone*.

And he remembered another vintage Simon and Garfunkel song, one he'd always liked, but never quite understood. "At the Zoo." How did it go? Something about everything taking place at the zoo?

"Welcome to the zoo, Fitzgerald," he grumbled. "Just don't feed the animals."

"Did you say something, Tim?" Molly asked from her side of the Grand Canyon.

"Nope," he answered, turning onto his stomach, giving his pillow a solid punch. "Just wondering out loud what Auntie Emmaline is making us for breakfast."

"Stacks of heart-shaped buttermilk pancakes with a strawberry topping would be my guess," Molly said, sounding more cheerful.

Tim smiled into his pillow. "Yeah. I suppose so. Good night, Moll."

"Good night, Tim. Oh, and Tim?"

He turned to her at once, instantly hopeful.

"I love you, too," she said softly, wistfully, so that he knew there was a big "but" coming next. And there was. "But it just won't work out."

He settled back against the pillow once more, knowing he was in for a long night.

But, then again, the ice was still outside, Auntie Emmaline was being just as romantic as she could be and there was always tomorrow....

Chapter Four

MOLLY AWOKE SLOWLY, smiling as she felt the warmth of Tim's body as she snuggled against him, wrapped spoonlike around his back.

Content, she floated back down toward sleep once more, and into her favorite dream.

How she loved the mornings. Waking with Tim beside her. Feeling the warmth, the solid strength of his body. She burrowed deeper under the small mountain of covers, pressing her cheek against his shoulder, sliding her arm more fully around his back, gently trailing her fingertips along the flat of his stomach.

He turned in her arms, reaching out for her, just as he always did. Still asleep, but yet aware. Seeking. Finding.

He kissed her hair, the column of her throat as she stretched up her neck, allowing him to do as he willed. His hand found her breast and she sighed her eager submission. His leg slid over her lower body, wakening it even as her mind still floated inside a dream, arousing her, giving her life.

His hand moved at the buttons of her pajama top, sliding them free of their moorings, slipping inside. Once more seeking. Once more finding.

Finding more.

His mouth followed where his hand had been. He pressed his mouth against her warm, willing flesh, blazing a trail of soft kisses that ended as he opened his lips around her nipple, laving at it with his tongue, teasing it with his teeth.

She rose against him, then slid oh-so-slightly to her left, wordlessly telling him to come even closer, to let her feel the full weight of his body on hers, pressing her into the mattress, allowing her to slide her leg up and down the length of his, feeling his hair scratch against her skin, deepening her sensations, this prelude to their physical joining.

He was nothing if not responsive, for his body knew just what to do, just what she wanted. Even though he, too, was still caught between waking and sleeping, the both of them remaining locked in a sensual dream that straddled the realm of fantasy and their small, private kingdom of reality.

Her eyes still closed, Molly smiled as Tim rose up slightly, preparing to do as she'd silently asked. He kicked at the mound of covers, pushing them down and away from them, revealing both their bodies to the air.

The cold air.

The very frigid air.

And the dream shattered. Molly came fully awake, her eyes opening and her brain awakening in an instant. She knew where she was. She knew who was there with her. Her body stiffened, even as her pajama top slid off her shoulder, exposing more heated skin to the chilly air of the room.

The bridal suite.

She put her palms against Tim's shoulders and gave a mighty push. "Get off me, Timothy Fitzgerald. How dare you try to take advantage of me like this?"

Clad only in running shorts, his upper body bare, Tim raised himself up on his elbows and peered down at her, his grin maddening, so that she longed to punch him. Or kiss him.

No! She longed to punch him. He hadn't been asleep at all, the bum. His eyes were too bright, too alert, too brimming with mischief. He'd been awake for at least an hour. Awake enough to have surreptitiously removed the rolled blankets that had been jammed between them. Awake enough to know that she always reached out for him in the morning—and he was damn well going to make sure she found him!

Because Molly knew Tim well enough to know that he was a slow riser, a lazy riser. The sort of person who woke slowly, stretched languidly and lay in bed for long minutes before facing the day. It was one of the things she loved about him most, the way he gave himself up to lazy minutes of cuddling and talking in the mornings, the way he never hopped out of bed and straight into a shower, as if eager to leave her.

So he'd been awake. Awake, and waiting for

her. And she'd come to him as surely as Lassie arriving home at the end of every episode. Damn him!

"Damn you, Timothy Fitzgerald!" she thundered, pushing him over onto his back and quickly pulling the front of her pajamas together as she sat up in bed, reaching for the covers. "Of all the rotten, sneaky—"

He remained lying on his back, his arms crossed behind his head. "Was it almost as good for you as it almost was for me?" he asked, still grinning. And then he gave a small, involuntary shiver. "Is it just the shock of being rejected by the love of my life—again—or is it cold in here?"

"It's both!" Molly told him, grabbing one of the rolled-up blankets from the bottom of the bed, unfolding it and then draping it around her shoulders as she sat cross-legged on the mattress. "And it's not just cold in here, Tim. It's *freezing*."

She watched as he sat up and grabbed another of the rolled-up blankets for himself, then got out of bed, walking over to the large, fat silver radiator that ran beneath the length of the double windows. "Cold," he said—unnecessarily Molly thought. "Emmaline's has gas heat, I believe, but it won't work without electricity. The ice storm must have knocked down the power lines."

"The fire's still on," Molly pointed out, then physically pointed to the small fireplace.

"It would be," Tim told her, trying the light switch as he looked up at the ceiling light, which remained off. "The kitchen stove will work, too. But not the lights. Not the heat, or the hot water, for that matter, if the water heater has an electric igniter. I wonder how Auntie Emmaline is. We've got the fireplace, so it's warmer in here than in the rest of the house. She's got to be freezing. Get dressed, Moll. We'd better check on her."

"Right," Molly said, agreeing with him, for she was also worried about the little old lady, who barely had enough meat on her bones to keep her warm in the summertime. "And then we're going to talk about where we're sleeping tonight, Timothy Fitzgerald. Because you don't play fair."

"You've got that in one, Moll," he agreed, winking at her even as he headed for his suitcase and something to cover his bare legs. "But, then again, everything's fair in love and war, or something along those lines. I'm an architect, not a poet. And a lover, not a fighter, come to think of it."

"A lover?" Molly was dragging her own suitcase out of the closet now, glaring at him as he pulled on heavy wool socks, for the wooden parquet floor was like a block of ice in between the needlepoint rugs. "That's not what I'd call it, Fitzgerald. Our engagement is off, remember?

O-F-OFF! Just because I was still half-asleep, you had no right to—to—"

"Take what you offered? Respond in kind? Hope that maybe you'd changed your mind?"

"I did *not* offer!" Molly shouted, throwing the pajama top onto the bed and pulling on a warm sweatshirt of Tim's she'd borrowed, then inadvertently shrunk in the wash and then gratefully inherited. "You *tricked* me."

"Yeah," he answered, looking at her bare breasts, which she hastily covered, pulling down the sweatshirt. "And it almost worked. And I didn't do it because I'm some sex-crazed idiot. I did it because you do still love me, Molly. You said so."

"I love panda bears, too, Tim. That doesn't mean I'd let one balance my checkbook."

Tim took a moment to look up at the ceiling. "Here we go again, boys! Molly, do you have any idea of how much money I make? How much I made just last year?"

He angrily rummaged through his suitcase, coming up with a sweatshirt that exactly matched Molly's, a soft gray sweatshirt with Wanda's Bait And Party Shoppe emblazoned across the front in bright green lettering. He'd seen the sweatshirt somewhere, and ordered it as a joke.

And now he'd bought a new one, of course, to replace the one she'd shrunk. Hell, he'd probably bought two. Maybe a gross of the damn things!

She watched as he pulled the sweatshirt over

his head, jamming his arms into the sleeves all in the same motion, then emerging from the material and scrubbing at his mussed hair with both hands. "You've got it on backward," she pointed out, trying not to grin.

Tim looked down at his chest, swore under his breath, and pulled his arms back out of the sweatshirt, swiveling the whole thing around on his neck and finding the correct armholes. He then went on as if he hadn't been interrupted, answering his own question. "No, you don't. And do you know why you don't? Because you don't *want* to know, that's why. Every time I try to tell you, you start quoting chapter and verse on how much I *spend*, never on how much I *earn*. Why is that, Moll? Huh?"

She had a second pair of thicker, woolly socks on now, and a pair of jeans. It wasn't until she was lacing her sneakers that she realized that her ankle didn't hurt anymore, or at least not much. And her feet fit inside the sneakers, both of them. "Because," she said reasonably, although she couldn't help glaring at him as she spoke, "it doesn't matter how much you earn. You still spend too much. Indiscriminately. Without waiting for sales, or comparing prices, or considering a purchase before making it. Like the wedding invitations."

Tim rolled his eyes. "Yeah. Right. We could have gone cheaper. We could have shopped around. We could have tried to find a real *deal*.

Molly, you *loved* those invitations the moment you saw them. Nothing else was going to be the right thing, because you'd already found the right thing. So what was the point?"

Molly blinked back tears. Not angry tears. Just tears. "I'm just not used to that, all right?" she blurted out, heading into the bathroom to grab some deodorant, to brush her teeth and to splash some cold water on her stinging eyes.

He followed her. "Just not used to it, Molly?" he asked, reaching past her to the clutter of bottles on the counter top. "Or not thinking you *deserve* it—because you weren't the one to earn it?"

"Oh, that's low, Fitzgerald. *Low*," she told him around the toothbrush in her mouth, ducking under his arm and heading back into the bedroom. Once again, he followed her. He was like gum stuck on the bottom of her shoe—she couldn't get rid of him!

"Is it, Moll?" he persisted, taking her by the shoulders and maneuvering her back into the bathroom—which was a good thing, because she needed to rinse and spit. "Is this whole thing, this whole argument—this whole breaking of the engagement—because *you* believe you should be paying for the wedding on a nursery school teacher's salary? I know your parents can't, and I don't expect them to, not when the wedding's so large."

Molly rinsed her mouth, splashed cold water

on her face and then blindly reached for a towel, which Tim handed her. "The bride and the bride's family are *supposed* to pay for the wedding, Fitzgerald. It's traditional."

"It's a bunch of *bunk*, that's what it is," Tim responded tightly.

"It's also only a small part of the problem," Molly informed him, opening the door to the hallway, then hugging herself, rubbing her hands over her upper arms, for it was even colder out in the hall. And much darker. "I've got three-year-olds in my class who know more about the value of money than you do, Fitzgerald."

"Oh, yeah? Do they know it can't buy love?" Tim groused, pushing ahead of her down the stairs and heading for the kitchen.

"Maybe not buy love, Fitzgerald, but it appears it can fairly easily *heal*—by leasing a Mercedes!" Molly called after him, wanting to do nothing more than head back to the bridal suite and throw herself on the bed, to cry until her tears were all gone.

But she couldn't. Auntie Emmaline was somewhere in this cold, dark house. Alone. Without heat. And believing she had two Valentine lovebirds under her roof.

Molly took a deep, steadying breath, pinned a smile on her face and set off down the stairs, thinking it might be a good idea to turn on the fireplace in the parlor.

As she walked into the room, she glanced toward the table holding Albert Whipple's pipe. Auntie Emmaline's letter.

Except that the letter was gone.

But that wasn't all.

Molly shivered as she inhaled the faint, lingering aroma of a good pipe tobacco that floated in the air.

"Tim? *Timothy*," she called out, her voice barely raised above a whisper. She forgot to turn on the fire as she slowly backed from the room, then trotted toward the kitchen.

It was 7:00 a.m. And the day, Valentine's Day, was just beginning.

TIM TRIED THE DOORKNOB once more, smiled and slipped the screwdriver into his back pocket. "When you're good, Fitzgerald, you're good," he congratulated himself, knowing he'd only replaced a doorknob, not built another Taj Mahal. But, hey. A job done well was a job done well, right?

So far, he'd changed three doorknobs on the smaller guest rooms on the third floor, replaced the guts of the commode on the same floor, unstuck an attic window Auntie Emmaline wanted unstuck—he didn't know why—and sanded the bottom of the door leading to the attic so that it wouldn't rub against the floor when it was pulled open.

That last one had been a bonus Auntie Emmaline hadn't even put on the list he'd had her write as he'd scarfed down a thick stack of—just as Molly had guessed—heart-shaped buttermilk pancakes. With strawberry syrup on top.

He looked at his watch, seeing that it was almost noon, time for lunch, then glanced outside to see that, unbelievably, the sun had come out after a day and night of storms. He walked to the window and pushed back the organdy draperies, to see water dripping off the icicles hanging down from the eaves of the multilevel roof. There had been a lot of ice out there, but it was melting now. Melting fast. Auntie Emmaline had said that ice storms never hung around the seashore too long.

He'd already found rock salt in the storage area on the ground floor, right where Auntie Emmaline had told him it would be. He'd bundled up and gone outside to sprinkle it on the sidewalk that angled around the property, and now the bright winter sun was probably doing its own melting job on the wooden front steps leading up to the porch.

Maybe, after lunch, he and Molly could take a walk down to the beach. The sand couldn't be frozen, after all, and there was hardly any breeze. With the noonday sun to warm them, hell, it was probably warmer outside than it was inside the old inn.

Tim picked up the small toolbox he'd unearthed in the storage area and headed back down two flights of stairs, frowning as the second step from the bottom of the flight leading to the reception area squeaked as he put weight on it. He'd noticed that last night, and again this morning. He could fix it. With the right tools, in fact, he could fix almost anything, and had, ever since his father had given him his first toolbox when he was six.

"Tinkering" his mother had called what Tim and his father had done nearly every weekend, when the Fitzgerald family had had more than enough money to hire workmen, plumbers, painters, all sorts of handymen. But that wasn't his dad's way, or Tim's. They both liked working on the family home, putting bits of themselves into it, learning its idiosyncrasies, adding personal touches that sprang from their own creativity, their own inventiveness.

There was nothing like hands-on experience, Tim believed. In drawing all his own plans for his latest project, to joining the workmen on site from time to time, just to keep his hand in, to feel the satisfaction of driving nails, to breathe in the smell of freshly sawed wood.

He could do wonders with Emmaline's, he knew, starting with an overhaul of the ancient plumbing, then an updating of the electrical system. He'd put in a new, oversize water heater. Update the circuit breaker box. Fix that length of rain gutter he'd seen hanging by a single bracket as he'd walked around the house earlier, sprinkling rock salt.

How many weekends would he have to spend hand-sanding the old, flaking paint from the balustrades on the porch before he could repaint them? Three? Six? Oh, sure, they could be replaced with new ones. But throwing out the old ones would be criminal. A waste.

A man could really enjoy this place. With Molly puttering in the overgrown gardens at the back and on one side of the house, or sitting in a rocker on the porch, talking to him as he worked, their summer weekends could be so full—just as they'd fill the bedrooms with their children. Kids loved the shore, playing in the sand, jumping waves, body-boarding.

And this was Ocean City, after all, advertised on billboards as America's Greatest Family Resort. The dozens of blocks of beachfront boardwalk were lined with miniature golf courses, water slides, amusement rides, movie theaters, T-shirt stores and pizza shops. What better place could there be for a family vacation house?

"Stop it, Fitzgerald," he warned himself as he cut through the parlor on his way to the kitchen, following his nose, which told him somebody had been baking chocolate-chip cookies. "One, first you've got to convince Molly that she didn't mean it when she called off the wedding. And, two, you're never going to convince her of that if you tell her you're thinking of buying this white elephant. *Impulsively* buying this white elephant. She'd just see it as another case of throwing money around like water.''

He was almost into the dining room, and on his way to the kitchen, when he stopped, turned and stared at the table beside Albert Whipple's chair. Son of a gun. The letter was gone. The teenager who helped out around the bed-and-breakfast—Tabitha?—hadn't been here, so she couldn't have taken it. Because that's the conclusion Tim had come to—that Tabitha took the letters, letting Auntie Emmaline believe Albert had come for them.

That left Auntie Emmaline herself. She wrote the letters. She put them out for Albert. And then she gathered them up again, telling herself Albert had shown up during the night and read them. She probably had dozens of her letters to Albert, all tucked up in a box somewhere.

Yeah. That made sense. Sad sense, but sense nonetheless.

Because there simply was no other explanation. Was there? He noticed that the lid of the tin that once held Albert Whipple's loose tobacco wasn't quite on straight, and decided to fix it. Funny. There was fresh tobacco in the tin. Half a can. Now, why would Emmaline keep pipe tobacco around? Why, now that he'd taken time to notice, it almost smelled if someone had recently smoked a pipe in the room.

Which was beyond silly. Downright spooky. ''Maybe Auntie Emmaline has a secret vice,'' he told himself, mostly to hear a human voice in the quiet room. But he didn't believe what he'd said. And he didn't want to believe what he was thinking....

Entering the kitchen, he was immediately struck by how cozy it was, how warm, even though the heat and electricity were still off. Molly had her back to him, bending over the open oven door of the large white porcelain gas stove, slipping a tray of cookie dough onto the wire shelf.

She was wearing a huge, white, ruffled bib apron and, as she turned to say something to Auntie Emmaline, her cheeks were flushed with simple pleasure and heat—and dusted with white flour. "That's the last one, Auntie Emmaline. Tim loves chocolate-chip cookies, as I said, and man cannot live on angel food cake and heart-shaped cut-out cookies alone, right?"

Auntie Emmaline was perched on a white wooden stool, her small feet resting on the crosspiece, as the stool was tall and Aunt Emmaline was not. "Albert adored sand tarts," she said, smiling, her wrinkled pixie face nearly beatific. "I could never make enough for him. But, as my mother always said, the way to a man's heart leads straight through his stomach. Tim will be so pleased that you made these just for him."

"Only if he can have one of them before lunch," Tim said, letting the swinging door shut behind him, keeping the heat in the kitchen. Sunlight was streaming through the windows that faced the water, but the kitchen would soon cool off once the oven wasn't in use anymore. "And, speaking of lunch—what are we having? This handyman is starving."

Molly looked at him for a moment, pushed her hair back behind her ears and walked over to the refrigerator. "There's some lunch meat in here we should eat before it goes bad. Auntie Emmaline's putting a huge turkey in the oven when the cookies are done, and that ought to keep the kitchen warm at least until suppertime. After that—"

"Oh, the electricity will be back on by then, dear," Auntie Emmaline said. "It always is. That's why I told Albert not to bother fixing the generator the last time it broke."

"You have a *generator*?"

The question came from both Molly and Tim, both of whom had turned as one to look at Auntie Emmaline.

"My goodness! Anyone would think I'd just said I've got a tail hidden under my skirts and cloven feet under these shoes. Of course I have a generator. We ran a bed-and-breakfast, my dears. We couldn't allow our guests to freeze, now could we?"

"That's rational, I suppose," Tim said as quickly Molly slapped mustard on two pieces of bread, threw a few slices of bologna on top of one slice, slapped the two slices together and handed the sandwich to him—all in the space of ten seconds.

"Go. Do," she said, shaking her head as he dutifully turned toward the basement stairs. "Oh, and wait a moment."

He turned back to her questioningly, the toolbox in one hand, the sandwich in the other. Then he smiled, opened his mouth and clamped his teeth around the still-warm chocolate-chip cookie she held out to him.

Yeah, he could buy this place. He could see a lifetime of summer weekends in this place.

But only if Molly would agree to share them with him.

MOLLY LOVED THE FEEL of wind in her face, even a cold February wind. She loved the way it blew her hair away from her face, the way she had to lean into it, move with it, dance with it, become a part of it.

The wind smelled of sand, of sea. Of life. Vitality. Promise.

She didn't remember when she had allowed Tim to take her hand, but she also knew she didn't want him to let her go. She just wanted to keep walking, walking. Walking the length of this hard-packed, sun-kissed winter beach.

They had walked for blocks, each one marked by the long, rusted drainage pipes that ran into the ocean at each street corner. They'd walked from Delancey Place all the way to the Eighth

Street Music Pier, the long yellow building that was the only one on the ocean side of the boardwalk, jutting out almost to the shoreline. At times, they'd had to climb the wooden stairs to the boardwalk, at places where the beach had eroded in the winter storms, but always went back onto the beach at their first opportunity.

They didn't speak, not much, except to read the signs above the closed stores to each other, or to wonder aloud what it must be like to sit inside the Music Pier on a warm summer's night, the sound of the waves blending with the orchestra as they played the music of Lloyd Webber, of Gershwin, of Mozart. Maybe even a Beatles tune or two.

But now they were back at the Delancey Place beach once more, and Tim let go of her hand in order to slide an arm across her shoulders, steering her toward the boardwalk once more, and the steps that led back to the street.

Molly looked up at him, at the way the breeze ruffled his long hair, dusting it across his forehead, whipping it away again. He'd turned up the collar on his winter coat after wrapping his wool scarf around her throat and he had his other hand stuffed into his pocket, but he'd never said he might be cold.

And neither had she. Because she wasn't cold. Not really. At least, not cold enough to cut their walk short, to lose a single precious moment of this strange, quiet interlude devoid of joking, or everyday conversation. Or argument.

"It's getting dark," Tim said as they walked the short block back to Emmaline's.

"Everywhere except at Emmaline's," Molly said, rather proudly. "Aunt Emmaline told me that generator hasn't worked in ten years. However did you fix it?"

He grinned down at her, wickedly, the Timothy Fitzgerald she had grown to know, grown to love. "I'm good with my hands," he quipped, adding, "or so they tell me."

One of those hands was now sliding down her arm, his hand brushing against the side of her breast. She could feel his touch, even through the thickness of her parka. "Very funny, Fitzgerald," she said, slipping out from beneath his arm and clambering up the stairs leading to the porch. "Want to bet it smells delicious in there?"

"I always try to bet on a sure thing," Tim answered, holding open the door for her, then putting out a hand to stop her as she moved to go inside. "We're having a good day, aren't we, Moll?" he asked, his brown eyes suddenly serious.

"Yeah, Fitzgerald," she agreed, reaching up one mittened hand to cup his cheek. "We're having a good day. A real good day."

"Oh, goodness me—*kiss* her, Tim," Auntie Emmaline said, and Molly turned her head to see the old lady sitting behind the reception desk, busily cutting out red construction paper hearts.

"Auntie Emmaline!" Molly exclaimed, shocked to see the woman dressed all in ancient red velvet, a wide band of ivory lace tucked around her neckline, a brooch nestled just in the center. "Shame on you."

"No, shame on Tim, for just standing there when he should be kissing his sweetheart. It is Valentine's Day, you know. Now go on, Tim— kiss her. Emmaline's hasn't seen a pair of young lovers in much too long."

"Yes, ma'am," Tim said dutifully, and pulled Molly close against him. "Don't fight me, Moll. Remember what we decided. We're only doing this for Auntie Emmaline."

"Liar," she whispered, her palms against his chest. "You're doing this for you."

"Ah, sugar sweetums," he whispered right back at her as he moved his mouth to within a fraction of hers. "You know me so well."

His lips were cold and salty from the winter wind, yet still warm, heated by a rapidly growing desire. His tongue was even warmer, and she opened her mouth to let him inside. She felt a furnace fan into flames deep within her, a fire so hot, their two bodies melded together in the open doorway, the February chill no threat against the warmth of Emmaline's reception area, and the quick, hot heat generated by this unexpected, soul-searing kiss.

Tim moved away first, drawing back slightly although he didn't release her from his embrace. "Method acting," he said quietly, bending forward once more to lightly kiss the tip of her nose. "I think you're getting a handle on it, Moll."

How could he be so calm, so controlled, when she felt as if she could melt into a puddle on the floor? "Damn you, Timothy Fitzgerald," she said, remembering not to move away from him too quickly, to appear the least bit angry.

Flustered, however, she decided, was all right. Auntie Emmaline probably expected her to look flustered.

"Ah, Tim, that was sweet," the old woman said, sighing. "I'll bet you were a real ladies' man before Molly captured your heart. Come here, won't you, and keep me company while I finish this. You can tell me how you and Molly met."

The mantel clock chimed out the hour of four, and Molly smiled at Auntie Emmaline, mumbled something about soaking in a hot tub and raced up the stairs, leaving Tim behind to fend for himself.

Four o'clock. Only four o'clock, with dinner and an entire Auntie Emmaline planned romantic evening still to be gotten through. Without arguing. Without giving in, as she'd always given in, because Tim would never change—he didn't even know he *should* change.

That didn't frighten her. Not really. What

frightened her was that she was beginning to think she didn't want him to change. That she liked him, loved him, had fallen in love with him, just the way he was. Because of what and who he was.

"We're going to have to talk," she told herself as she poured bath salts under the force of the water running into the old-fashioned clawfoot tub. "We're going to have to really, *really* talk about this. Unless he calls me his sugar sweetums again, of course," she amended, struggling out of her sweatshirt, getting it caught behind one ear and having to tug on it so that her head popped free abruptly, her hair falling into her face. She blew it away with a swift exhalation of breath. "Because then, love him or not, I'm going to have to kill him."

Chapter Five

THE POWER CAME BACK ON just as they sat down to supper, kicking off the generator and turning on the chandelier over the dining room table.

"Oh, pooh," Auntie Emmaline said, pouting as she looked up at the bright lights. "That isn't the least romantic, now is it?"

"No, Auntie Emmaline, it's not," Tim said, tossing his napkin onto the table and walking over to the light switch, returning the room to the more "romantic" darkness of candlelight.

Molly looked beautiful in candlelight. Of course, Molly looked beautiful in any light. That's how he'd first seen her, as he'd told Auntie Emmaline that afternoon. In candlelight. Across a crowded room. The whole bit. And he'd known, right there and then. He'd just *known*.

Of course, it had taken Molly a little longer to figure out what he'd already known, but he was a persistent sort, and he'd finally convinced her she couldn't live without him.

Not that she wasn't trying...

"I thought we'd play Hearts after dinner, if you'd like," Auntie Emmaline said, breaking into Tim's thoughts as he absently chewed on juicy, delicious turkey. "It's a card game," she ended hopefully.

"That sounds very nice, Auntie Emmaline," Molly said, smiling across the table at Tim. "Tim is very good at games, aren't you, darling?"

Oh, boy. She was still ticked off about the kiss. That had to be it. "Love them," he said cheerfully, refusing to look away from her. "I'm especially good at Monopoly, although some people don't believe me."

"Monopoly!" Aunt Emmaline clapped her hands, clearly excited. "We have that in the closet in the parlor. Albert and I played all the time. Do you know that each of the addresses is a street in Atlantic City? Ventnor, Pacific—Boardwalk, Park Place, you know, the *blue* ones? I'd end up with the purple ones—Mediterranean, Baltic and such. The low-rent district, I suppose you'd call it. But Albert *always* ended up owning both Boardwalk and Park Place. He built hotels there, every time. And I'd land on them, every time. Oh, Albert was ruthless when it came to Monopoly. He used to tease that Donald Trump had nothing on him. I do so miss playing Monopoly."

"Then we'll just have to play Monopoly, Auntie Emmaline," Molly said. "I think I even remember the metal player pieces from the set I had as a child. Let's see. I'll be the car, you can be the thimble, Auntie Emmaline—and Tim can be the old boot."

"Boot, huh, darling? As in 'giving him the?'" Tim asked, frowning comically. "I guess that'll teach me to brag about my Monopoly skills, huh?"

"Let's just say we'll see who gets bragging rights *after* the game, all right?" Molly answered, reaching for the gravy bowl. "Auntie Emmaline, I'm so glad you taught me how to make this gravy. It's delicious. In fact, everything's delicious. I think that walk on the beach really gave me an appetite."

"Me, too," Tim answered, knowing only Molly understand *exactly* what he meant. And, damn, he knew her legs were long, but not *that* long. How'd she managed to kick him in the shins from way over there?

"Sorry, Tim," Auntie Emmaline said, smiling at him. "My foot was falling asleep and I kicked it out, to *wake it up*. Did I hurt you?"

Tim looked at Aunt Emmaline closely, seeing the hint of mischief in her eyes. She knew! She knew he and Molly were in the middle of an argument. How did she know? Or was there some woman-only sixth sense that told her? Some sort of built-in radar? Probably. It would be just like them. Always finding a way to be one up on the poor, unsuspecting men on the planet. And, like with any woman, she'd automatically put all the blame on him.

"That's all right, Auntie Emmaline," he said, still trying to believe the old woman didn't know what he thought she knew. That he was being a jerk, a stupid, desperate jerk.

Auntie Emmaline smiled at him, then winked, a knowing, mischievous batting of one wise old eye. "Yes, it will be all right, if you realize what's happening and wake up in time, or so Albert always said. Otherwise, everything just goes all numb and unfeeling. As good as dead, actually. And that's *not* good, is it?"

Tim looked at Molly, who was staring at her plate as if the turkey leg on it had suddenly come to life and she expected to see it go dancing across the table. "Um, yes. That's right, Auntie Emmaline," he stammered uneasily, then quickly changed the subject, talking about the rain gutter that needed repair. Talking about feelings wasn't safe. Rain gutters were safe.

THEY'D ALREADY PLAYED Monopoly—Auntie Emmaline had won handily—and they were all content to sit in the parlor and leaf through the old woman's photograph album.

The album was thick and quite old, its pages black construction paper, the photographs held in place at each corner with small white triangles glued to the page. The cover was faintly battered, white leather long since turned ivory, and a pink satin ribbon poked through the metal-edged holes in the binding, holding the pages in place because the original lacing had long since cracked and broken.

Glenn Miller tunes played on the ancient phonograph in the corner across the room, the tunes dating from the Second World War.

"And that's Albert in his army uniform, just as he finished his basic training. He was in the big one, you understand, WW Two."

Auntie Emmaline sighed, obviously remembering a frightening time, now far in the past. "That was the longest year of my life, the year my Albert was gone. He finally took a bullet in the hip at Messina, and was sent home. He limped ever since, especially in damp weather, not that either he or I minded. At least he came home. So many didn't."

She pointed to the picture once more. "Young Georgie Someone or other took this particular photograph, as I recall. I remember Albert telling me Georgie had never left Pennsylvania, or even his Scranton farm, until he was drafted. Georgie was married—they had a child, a son, I believe. That's him, that's Georgie," she said, pointing to another picture, one in which the young Albert Whipple had his arm around the shoulder of another soldier. Both of the men had their uniform hats tipped back on their foreheads as they mugged at the camera. She sighed again. "Poor Georgie. He never got to go home to Scranton."

Tim and Molly exchanged uneasy glances over Auntie Emmaline's head as they sat on either side of her on one of the love seats, flames dancing in the fireplace across the room, the photograph album open across the old woman's knees.

War had separated Emmaline and her Albert. What was separating them? Stubbornness? An unwillingness to compromise? Pride? It all seemed so silly, so petty. So very sad.

"Well, that's enough of that, isn't it," Auntie Emmaline said bracingly, turning another page. "Oh, my. Now how did that happen? This one came out of its holders, and isn't in the right place. Look, Molly, dear. This is a photograph of both Albert and me standing alongside the Steel Pier, just before he received his draft notice for the service. My goodness, would you look at my dress? How *short* it is, blowing like that in the wind. Of course, it did show off my ankles quite nicely, and those silly, strappy white shoes I adored, even if they did pinch. And that hair! I don't remember having quite so much hair."

"You were a real looker, Aunt Emmaline," Tim told her. He leaned over and gave her a kiss on the cheek. "You still are."

Molly took the photograph from Aunt Emmaline before she could slide it back in between the pages, tracing her fingertip down the smiling images of Emmaline and Albert Whipple. They were standing with their backs to the railing of the Atlantic City boardwalk, the photograph in black-and-white, although Molly could imagine the red of the roses in Auntie Emmaline's dress, the blue of the sky behind them.

They looked so young in the picture, Emmaline and her Albert. So very happy. As if life held nothing but good things for both of them. Fifty-two years together. Fifty-two years of loving, and laughing, of tears and disappointments. And a lifetime of memories, the good obviously far outweighing the bad.

She carefully laid the photograph back and allowed Aunt Emmaline to turn the page.

"Oh, you don't need to see that one," Aunt Emmaline said, quickly trying to turn yet another page.

"No, you don't, Auntie Emmaline," Tim protested teasingly, stilling her hand. "What is it? A picture of you and Albert cavorting in the surf?"

He pressed the page back down, to see a large, full-color photograph of Emmaline's, of how Emmaline's looked during its heyday. The large building was painted green, just as it was now, but all the woodwork, all the gingerbread trim, was a pale, butter yellow, the front doors a brilliant, welcoming red.

He could see the faint outline of organdy tieback curtains at every window, butter yellow window boxes filled with geraniums and some sort of fragile, trailing vine beneath every window. The porch and front steps were stained, not painted, the wood a warm brown. The shrubs in the short front yard were well trimmed; petunias lined the walkway.

And, posed stiffly on the small spit of grass, their smiles bright even as they squinted into the camera, were Albert and Auntie Emmaline, both proudly pointing to a large, oval, pale green, freestanding sign with the word Emmaline's painted on it, Established 1948 beneath it.

It was the most beautiful photograph of the most beautiful, wonderful house love had ever built.

"Why didn't you want us to see this, Auntie Emmaline?" Molly asked. "Isn't this a picture of a happy memory?"

"Yes, dear, of course," Auntie Emmaline said, nodding, then pulling a white lace-edged handkerchief from her apron pocket and wiping at her eyes. "Oh, I'm being silly, I know. It's just that this photograph makes me sad. We loved Emmaline's as if this house was our child, and it doesn't look like this anymore. Albert and I got older, and families grew and didn't come back to us anymore with their children and their sand buckets and their laughter. We took down the window boxes in 1978—Albert couldn't keep them up anymore, you understand. Well, to be truthful, neither of us could keep up with it all. Emmaline's is just old now, I suppose, and fairly useless. As I am."

She trailed her fingers over the photograph, pausing as she reached the sign that no longer stood outside the house. "But I do miss the way it was. Oh, yes, I surely do." She closed the cover on the photograph. "Now," she said, smiling brightly—too brightly, "who else wants a cup of hot chocolate? I've got marshmallows, you know. Those little ones that melt so nicely."

Tim and Molly watched as Auntie Emmaline slid the photograph album back into its spot in the bookcase and all but ran out of the room, heading for the kitchen. Molly gave a small cry and made to follow after her.

Tim grabbed her hand, pulling her back down on the love seat. "Let her go, Moll," he said gently. "She needs to be alone for a while."

"But it's so sad, Tim," Molly said, turning to look at him, her own green eyes sad, and bright with unshed tears. "All the years, all the memories. And she has to leave here for some stupid, antiseptic retirement home. What will Albert do without her?"

Tim looked at her owlishly. "Albert, Molly? Isn't that, well, a little overly romantic?"

"So what if it is?" she countered, bristling. "It's Valentine's Day. I'm *supposed* to be romantic! You know, Tim, you could stand being a little bit more like Albert Whipple. I mean, it couldn't hurt!"

He watched as she flounced out of the room, then sat gazing into the fire for a long time, looking at the vast collection of Valentine's Day cards, the even more vast collection of cupids.

And then he smiled, got up and headed for the reception area. He rummaged behind the desk, found everything he needed and took the stairs two at a time, heading for one of the vacant guest rooms where he'd seen a small writing desk—a man with a mission.

MOLLY AND AUNT EMMALINE shared a mutually pleasant hour together over hot chocolate and sand tart cookies before the older woman's exaggerated yawns convinced Molly that she should excuse herself and go upstairs—to kill Timothy Fitzgerald, who seemed to have disappeared without a trace or a word of explanation.

"I think I'll sleep in tomorrow, dear, if you don't mind," Aunt Emmaline said as Molly put the cups and dishes in the sink, running water in the cups so that they wouldn't stain. "Then we can have a lovely brunch before you and Tim have to head back to Pennsylvania. Not that I'm in any rush to see you leave, but my Realtor phoned earlier today, while you two were out on the beach. He's bringing someone by tomorrow at two." She frowned. "He said something about the man having plans to tear Emmaline's down and replace it with one of those huge modern monsters. So many of the old houses have been replaced. But perhaps he won't, if he finds Emmaline's as charming as you and Tim tell me do."

"Oh, Aunt Emmaline, no!" Molly dropped the cookie plate into the sink, nearly breaking it, and raced back to the table. "You can't let them do that." She bit her lip then, subsiding into her chair. "That's why you didn't want to look at the photograph of Emmaline's tonight, isn't it? Because somebody might tear it down? Because it breaks your heart to think about such a thing?"

Aunt Emmaline wouldn't meet her eyes. "Well..." she said slowly, tracing the bright floral pattern of the oilcloth tablecloth with one beringed finger. Then she lifted her head and smiled at Molly. "But don't you worry your pretty little head, dear. Time passes, and life goes on. I'm leaving anyway, aren't I? Now, why don't you take a glass of milk and some chocolate-chip cookies up to Tim as you go? He's probably hungry after all the chores he did for me today."

Molly did as she was told, bending down to kiss the top of Auntie Emmaline's vibrantly blond curls before leaving the room, Tim's milk and cookies balanced on a small silver tray.

Emmaline Whipple watched her go, then smiled in the warm, homey kitchen. She looked suddenly younger, almost girlish. "We've got 'em, Albert, just as I thought we might," she whispered at last, brushing crumbs off the tabletop and into her hand as she prepared to wash the few dishes and go to bed. "Such sweet children they are, just like our own grandchildren would be. And now you don't have to worry, my darling. Because you're not going anywhere."

"WE HAVE TO TALK," Molly said abruptly, closing the door to the bridal suite behind her and leaning against it. "I mean, we really, *really* have to talk."

"All right," Tim said, sitting up on the bed. He was already dressed in a dark gray T-shirt and matching shorts, his long legs bare, his hair still slightly damp from the shower. He patted the mattress beside him, waggling his eyebrows at her invitingly. "Let's *talk*."

"In your dreams, buster," Molly said, sniffing. "Over here, on the floor, in front of the fireplace. You can have your bedtime snack, courtesy of Auntie Emmaline, and I can watch where you're putting your hands. Too many of our talks— okay, our *arguments*—end with us making love, and nothing gets accomplished."

He waggled his eyebrows again, and grinned. "Works for me."

"Okay, so we got a few things accomplished," she admitted, fighting a smile of her own at his silliness. "But you know what I mean."

"Yeah, Moll, I do." He sobered, jackknifing off the bed and taking the tray from her, then sitting cross-legged on the carpet in front of the fireplace. "I've assumed the position, ma'am," he said, inviting her to join him by waving a hand at the spot across from him. "Now, what are we going to talk about?"

"Me, mostly, I guess," she said, sitting down

across from him, admiring the way the light of the fire brought out a faint golden glow in his hair, his skin. "And about what a jerk I am."

"A jerk? *You?* No, you're going to have to repeat that, Moll, because I think you've got your pronouns mixed up. *I'm* the jerk."

Molly rolled her eyes. "Oh, this is great. Now we're going to argue about which one of us is the bigger jerk? That ought to get us far." She leaned forward slightly, picking up a cookie and prying out one of the chocolate chips, placing it in her mouth. "Let's split the difference, okay? We've both been jerks."

"Fair enough," Tim agreed, taking her chocolate-smeared index finger and putting it in his mouth, gently sucking off the chocolate. "Um, good. Oh, sorry—am I breaking a rule? Go on."

"You're really trying to drive me crazy, aren't you, Fitzgerald?" Molly asked, already feeling her insides untensing. It was going to be all right. Everything was going to be all right. Because they loved each other. And everything else was secondary.

"Trying to drive you crazy? Hmm, let me work on it for an hour or two, over there, on the bed, and we'll see how it goes," he suggested, then quickly held up his hands as if to erase what he'd just said. "All right, all right, I'll be serious. You want to talk? Let me start, okay? I spend too much money. There, I said it. I don't put much of anything away, plowing money back into the business, spending the rest. Pretty much living the good life, huh? And I'm wrong to do that. But, at the same time, since I'm being honest here, I don't think I'm a clipping grocery coupons sort of guy. So, I've decided to let you handle the family finances. Fair enough?''

She looked at him for long moments, then shook her head. ''No, Tim,'' she said at last. ''That's not enough. I don't want to be in charge of the family budget. Not all by myself. I don't want to always play the heavy, running around after you saying not to buy this, to save that. But I do want to *share* in planning that budget you're talking about, in the decisions *we* make regarding spending and saving and whatever. Money's important to me. Security's important to me. You've always had both, so you don't know what it's like not to have them.''

He looked at her measuringly, then nodded. ''You know, Moll, I'll never have to worry that you might have married me for my money. Hell, you've never even asked how much I earn in a year. You just keep telling me to shut off the hot water when I'm shaving.''

''I know, I know,'' Molly said, shaking her head. ''And that's my fault. I yell about hot water bills and wedding costs and car leases because I don't know how to say what I really mean. And what I really mean, Tim, what I really don't want—what I'm really *afraid* of—is ending up like poor Auntie Emmaline downstairs. She and

Albert worked hard—I'm sure they did—and yet look at her, Tim. She's losing her house, being forced into some awful retirement home. Money has never been something for me to enjoy. It's always been something you save. Something you might not have enough of if you spend it today with the idea that you'll still have more tomorrow."

She took a deep breath. "But what I want most today, what I want tomorrow, and for as long as I live, is your love, Tim. And I almost threw it away for what I thought would be security. I couldn't have been more wrong. I just think we need to find a balance between the two."

"I love you, Molly Bryant," Tim said then, and she thought he was going to kiss her, lift her into his arms and carry her to bed.

But he didn't.

He stood up, walked over to the marble-topped bureau, opened the top drawer and pulled out the saddest, most obviously homemade, ridiculous, *wonderful* Valentine's card she'd ever seen and laid it in her lap. Her four-year-old nursery school children were more proficient with glue and paper.

"I bought you a diamond tennis bracelet for Valentine's Day, Moll, and I still want you to have it," he said, sitting down beside her as tears fell onto the crushed red construction paper and ragged heart-shaped doily surrounding the words *I love you, Molly; Be my Valentine for Now and*

Forever. "But I think Albert had the right idea. The best, the most precious presents, come from the heart, not from a jewelry store. They might cost a lot less, but they're worth a lot more. Am I learning anything, do you think, Moll? Is there hope for me? Hope for us?"

She laid her head against his shoulder. "Damn you, Timothy Fitzgerald," she said, wiping at her wet cheeks. "If you get any more perfect, I'm going to develop an inferiority complex, you know that? How did I ever get so lucky?"

"It's your legs, Moll. You've got great legs. I never could resist them," he teased, lifting her chin so that he could look into her face. "And those big green eyes. And the way your hair kind of slides and moves when you walk, as if you're always walking toward a gentle breeze. And your nose—I'm particularly nuts about your nose. And your mouth…oh, yeah, Moll, your mouth…"

He pressed her back onto the carpet and Molly heard the glass of milk tip over onto its side. But that didn't matter. A little bit of spilled milk could wait. She could always clean it up later.

What really mattered was the *now,* this precious moment. She'd always be practical about some things. A lifetime of being practical and sensible and, yes, sometimes a little frightened, didn't become altered in the space of a single kiss.

But, she thought as Tim's hand found her

breast and she sighed into his mouth, living for the moment wasn't all that bad....

"You make *how* much?"

Tim grinned in the near darkness, the only light in the room coming from the moon outside and the gas fire that burned in the fireplace. "That was last year, Molly. I should make half again that much this year, thanks to the project I bid on last month. You've just been sleeping with the architect for the new shopping center in Bethlehem Township. I found out last week. Don't you feel honored?"

"I feel speechless, actually," she told him, threading her fingers through the soft mat of hair on his bare chest. "Why didn't you ever tell me this before?"

"You didn't want to know, remember?" he reminded her, and she turned her face into his shoulder, because he was right. "You just kept saying it didn't matter what I made—just what I spent. Or something like that."

"Oh, it was exactly like that, Tim," she said, sighing. "Don't try to be kind. It's way out of character, for one thing. And it's true. But I'm still paying for half of this wedding, okay? After that? Be warned, all right, because, oh, buddy, do I ever think I'm going to learn to love charge accounts!"

"But you'll still shop around and wait until everything's on sale?"

"You know I will," she answered, nipping at the tender flesh on the side of his throat. "I've got to ease myself into this spending stuff. Which," she added, sighing, "brings me back to the wedding. I still don't want a big one, but I do want to spend a lot of money. See? I'm beginning to compromise."

"I don't understand," Tim said, levering himself up on one elbow and looking at her as she gently rolled onto her back on the mound of pillows. "How can we have a smaller wedding and still spend a lot of money?"

She reached up a hand and slid her fingers into his hair. "Well," she said, smiling a secret smile, "I don't want the church, but I'm keeping the gown. I don't want the large reception, but I still want the doves you mentioned. Oh, and one more thing. Just a little thing, you understand. I want you to buy Emmaline's so that we can have the wedding in Albert's parlor."

She kept a determined smile on her face, even as her stomach did a small flip. And she waited. She watched Tim's face, hoping to see some sort of reaction. Praying for the reaction she wanted.

"You want to buy Emmaline's?" he said at last. She couldn't decide if he was shocked, or angry, or just too incredulous to believe he'd heard her correctly.

"Yes, Tim, I do." She rushed into speech, her words all but tumbling over themselves. "I know it will be expensive. The place needs all sorts of work. But you could do most of it, couldn't you? I mean, you're so handy, and you like puttering, right? I'd help you, and bring you lemonade when you got thirsty, and bandage your thumbs when you hit them with the hammer. We could replace the window boxes, or unearth them from the storage area under the house, or whatever. Why, I'll even bet that old sign is still around somewhere. We could find it and fix it, and put it back in the lawn. Not that we'd actually run a bed-and-breakfast, because that's not practical, or even anything I'd want to do. And then there's Auntie Emmaline. She could stay, couldn't she? Because I really love her. Because she'd make a great Auntie Emmaline to our kids when we have them, baking them sand tarts and serving up heart-shaped buttermilk pancakes. And because otherwise Albert—"

She broke off, biting her lips together, averting her eyes from Tim's.

He reached out and stroked her cheek. "Because otherwise Albert couldn't get his letters," he finished for her. "Moll, you don't really think—"

"I don't know *what* I think, darling," she said, feeling tears pricking behind her eyes once more. Happy tears. Joyful tears. "Auntie Emmaline might write the letters and then pack them away in a box somewhere. She might even smoke the pipe. Or Albert might stop by and sit in his chair at night and read the letters while he enjoys his pipe. And I don't really care. I don't care if Albert's spirit is still here, if he and Auntie Emmaline will always, one way or another, be here with us. In fact, I'd like to believe they will be."

"It's not a practical purchase, Moll," Tim said, gathering her close. "Not moneywise. The place is a white elephant. The siding will drink paint, the heat bills will be enormous—unless, of course, I have a heat pump installed. That will help. And the foundation's solid. I checked it out this morning, when I was finished kicking the generator back to life. And—"

Molly sat up straight, knocking his supporting elbow out from under him. "Whoa, buddy. Back up a minute, okay. You *kicked* the generator back to life? I thought you said you fixed it."

"I did," he said with a wicked smile. "I worked on it for a half hour, then decided to drop-kick the damn thing into next week. My foot's sore, but it worked. A good kick, Moll, it's the handyman's ace in the hole. I'll bet there's a lot of good dropkicks waiting for me in this place."

She shook her head as she looked into his wickedly dancing eyes. "You love this house as much as I do, don't you, Tim? Can we really do it? Can we buy Emmaline's?"

He reached up a hand, tracing his fingers down her cheek, along the length of her throat, onto the curve of her breast. "You throw money around like water, don't you, darling?" he quipped, grinning.

"Damn you, Timothy Fitzgerald. You want this house as much as I do. But I'll pay you for it, somehow. We can call it a shameless bribe, if you want. And I'm *utterly* shameless," she promised, lowering her body onto his. "Wanna see how much?"

"Oh, yeah," Tim breathed against her mouth. "Oh, yeah, I sure do, Moll. I'm by and large an honest man, but I find myself suddenly very open to bribes...."

Epilogue

6 June 1998

My dearest, dearest Albert,
Well, my darling, we couldn't have asked for a more perfect day, from start to finish.

Molly was beautiful, of course, and Emmaline's staircase never looked lovelier than when she floated down it, her long gown trailing behind her, her father all misty-eyed and proud, his chest puffed out as he waited for her at the bottom of the stairs. She wore the small key I had copied from the key to the bridal suite, and it looked lovely around her neck, hanging from the thin gold chain I picked out, matching quite well with her gown, if I do say so myself. She says she'll treasure it always, and I believe she will. Molly's wonderfully sentimental, Albert. I do adore her so much.

Tim stood at the entrance to the parlor, very handsome, a little nervous, looking at Molly with such love shining from his eyes. Oh, Albert, I started to cry, he loves her so much. Then the second step from the bottom squeaked as she put her foot on it, and Molly and Tim looked at each other and laughed. Poor Tim. He vows that step won't defeat him, but it defeated you for all those years, didn't it, darling?

The ceremony was very sweet, and so are Molly's and Tim's parents, whom I've already told you about when I met them all at Easter time. Black Jack Fitzgerald, as Tim calls his father when he's joking—so much love in that family, dearest, in both those families—vows Emmaline's is like a putterer's dream come true, and he wants to come back here next weekend with his wife, to see what he can do about that door to the third guest room. You remember, darling—the one that refuses to stay open by itself?

So, even though Molly and Tim will be in Cancún for their honeymoon, Emmaline's will be brimming with life again next weekend. Black Jack took me aside and whispered that he was fairly sure his wife would like heart-shaped pancakes for breakfast on Sunday morning. And then he winked at me! Tim certainly came by his mischievous ways honestly, didn't he, dearest?

We had a lovely luncheon after the ceremony, and then we all went outside to watch as the doves were released into the bluest blue sky I've seen in many a year. The sun shone down on Molly and Tim as the photographer snapped photographs of them in front of the sign, and then we posed on the porch. All of us, the whole family.

Emmaline's has never looked better, darling, except, of course, when you had charge of everything. The window boxes are full, the shrubs are trimmed—and I always did like that butter yellow color best.

I'm so lucky, Albert. I'd hoped, I'd wished, and I kept Emmaline's for you. But I never thought to keep it for me. I never thought I'd have a family again after you, my dearest family, my only home, had gone away.

I know you won't mind that I've also given Molly and Tim the christening gown as a wedding present. Molly took me aside after I gave her the present, to ask me how I knew, as she hadn't even told Tim until last night. I told her, Albert. I could see the new softness in her eyes when she and Tim were here last weekend, a new glow. If I'm counting correctly, and I believe I am, we'll have a baby in the house just in time for Valentine's Day next year. Isn't that wonderful?

Well, I'm off to bed, dearest, for it has been a long, happy day. I thought of you so many times during this day, Albert, and all

my memories were happy ones. They always were. They always will be.
                              Love, Emmaline

P.S. Hey, Albert! Just thought we'd say thank you for everything before we head out. We figure there has to be at least one cupid somewhere in Cancún, and we're on our way to find it. We left a small gift for you—some of your favorite tobacco. And Albert? Don't worry, we'll take good care of your Emmaline. We love her, too, you know.
                        Love, Tim and Molly

KNOCK THREE TIMES

♥

Muriel Jensen

Dear Reader,

The date of the spring equinox is about March 20, but I celebrate it when the first Valentine's Day card appears on the rack at Paramount Drug Co.

The Oregon coast is one of the most beautiful places in the world, but winter here can best be described as "character building." Snow is a rarity and slows down life and business in our hilly community, so we try to relax and enjoy the novelty of it when it comes.

The rain, however, is eternal. It begins early in the fall and is with us through spring. Everything is gray—sky, river, outlook. Rain runs in sheets down windows, puddles in the streets and on your lawn, seeps down your collar, into your basement and eventually your brain.

It's like *Waterworld* without Kevin Costner.

Then Valentine's Day cards appear with their messages of love. They're often covered with roses and make it possible for us to endure the wait for the real ones that are still sleeping. And everything is red! Wonderful, bright, passionate red. In a world of gray there is nothing more beautiful.

Love is like that—a spot of color where you sometimes think there's nothing, where it seems nothing will ever change, where winter is so pervasive it becomes a mood.

Let's combat winter by sowing love—on the cheeks of little children, on the heads of dogs and cats, in the lives of senior citizens and on the lips of our lovers.

Plant it everywhere until it feeds the world!

Muriel Jensen

P.O. Box 1168
Astoria, Oregon 97103

Chapter One

"THE GIFT HUNTER. This is Lindy, how can I help you?"

Jade Barclay looked up from a red box frothing with white tissue as her young assistant answered the phone. It wasn't just that she felt she had to monitor Lindy's job performance. It was that she *knew* disaster would result if she didn't.

There'd been the woolly white goat The Gift Hunter had delivered to a startled little white-haired woman in a second-floor apartment. A telephone call made on the spot revealed that the woman's husband had asked that the shopping service buy her a woolly white *coat*.

Lindy had apologized for her error in taking the message, then several days later transposed the last two numbers of an address and delivered a basket with erotic massage gel and edible panties to the minister at Angels Episcopal Church, rather than to the young newlywed wife whose husband had planned an amorous evening.

After a scathing phone call from the minister's wife who suggested that Jade's immortal soul was in danger—Jade issued a new office rule.

Lindy was to let the answering service get the phone when Jade wasn't there.

"I think we can do that, Mr. O'Brian," Lindy said. "Let me check. Hold on, please." Lindy covered the receiver with her hand and looked across the room at Jade. "This man needs four gifts by tomorrow," she said, her blue eyes wide with concern. They matched her blue hair, which stood up in spikes like a crown of spears all around her head. "He wants to know if that's even possible with Valentine's Day just four days away."

Of course it wasn't. Jade looked around the living room of her waterfront condo. It also served as The Gift Hunter's office and was littered from end to end with flowers, candy, negligees, sexy undies for men and women and a myriad other gifts that clients had ordered and asked her to wrap and deliver.

She had enough work to keep three people busy until Valentine's Day. And then someone would have to redo everything Lindy did.

But if that was *Jack* O'Brian, none of that mattered.

Jade replaced the lid on the gift box and walked across the room toward the phone.

O'Brian had used her service only once before, several months ago. He was leaving for a working weekend at a client's vacation retreat the following day, he'd said, and needed casual clothes for the trip. His voice had been deep, resonant and sort of liquid. She'd felt it move thickly over her like warm honey or molten gold.

Then she heard someone else claim his attention, and he told her quickly that he'd like the clothes delivered to his office before six. It hadn't occurred to her until he'd hung up that he hadn't been very specific about what he'd wanted.

So she'd put her instincts to work and gone with the image his voice created in her mind. Tall. Elegant. Even his casual clothes would be dressy.

She'd bought everything in black with a Calvin Klein label—slacks, T-shirt, sports coat.

His voice had lived in her memory since then, and sometimes, in the dark of night, she imagined it whispering her name.

Jade took the phone from Lindy. "Mr. O'Brian." She used her competent, professional voice. "Can you tell me what you had in mind?"

"Miss Barclay?" he asked.

It *was* him. And he remembered her! That velvet-shadows voice made a warm little puddle of her heart.

"Yes, Mr. O'Brian." Her competent voice again, but slightly cracked.

"I apologize for being so last-minute," he said. She heard papers shuffling. "But I've just wrapped up a case that had all my attention."

She knew he was an attorney. She'd delivered

the clothes to a law office on High Street and left them with an attractive, middle-aged secretary.

"That's all right," she assured him. "It's the pressures of last-minute shopping that keep me in business. But successfully rounding up what you want that quickly will depend on what it is."

"A chenille robe for my mother," he said, launching efficiently into a list. "A weekend stay at Seafoam Lodge for my sister Diane, and dinner reservations at Brighton's for my sister Donna."

"Reservations for two?" Jade leaned over the desk, the phone cradled between chin and shoulder as she took notes.

"Yes," he replied. "I'm providing a friend of mine as her escort. I've been trying to get them together for a long time."

A matchmaker. She liked that. "All right. Reservations for two. And the fourth gift?"

He cleared his throat. "Something in black lace."

Her heart gave an erratic little lurch then settled down into quiet disappointment. He had someone.

"A negligee?" she asked.

"Well...no." He cleared his throat again. "One of those one-piece things that's sort of like...bra and panties together."

"A teddy."

"I guess." His voice grew firmer. "I'll have

my secretary give you the addresses. Can you take care of all that and deliver everything tomorrow? Except the teddy. I'd like that brought to my office."

Jade couldn't help but wonder if he had a liaison with a co-worker, or if he was going straight from the office to a dinner date. Or if they would even bother with dinner.

"I'll take care of it," she promised firmly.

"Thank you, Miss Barclay. I appreciate it."

"My pleasure, Mr. O'Brian."

Actually, Jade thought, pressing the off button on the phone and replacing it on its base, Jack O'Brian was probably in for a lot more pleasure than she was.

"He sounded like a babe," Lindy said, looping thin gold cord into the holes punched in the white gift tags Jade had cut out of French drawing paper. She sighed as she made a slip knot in the cord. "I wish Brad Pitt would call and ask us to shop for Gwyneth. She'd take him back— I know it."

Jade studied the notes she'd taken. She'd go to Yvette's for the teddy, to Nightwear, Inc. for the robe. "There probably isn't anything he'd want," she said absently, "that he can't get on Rodeo Drive."

Lindy raised an eyebrow. It was pierced with a tiny silver ring. "I don't think he's the horsey type."

Jade bit back a groan. "Rodeo Drive is an upscale shopping area in Beverly Hills," she said, feeling old. There was a certain innocence lost in the realization that many things in life were unattainable—such as a credit card for a shop on Rodeo Drive. Or a man like Jack O'Brian. "It doesn't have anything to do with horses."

"Oops." Lindy hunched her shoulders in embarrassment.

"You can't know that if you've never been there." Jade tucked Jack O'Brian's list in the front pocket of her purse where all the orders for the next morning's shopping were filed. Then she grinned at Lindy. "And didn't you see *Legends of the Fall?* He rides like a champ."

Lindy rested her chin in her hand and her eyes looked dreamy. "I wonder if I'll ever find anybody like him."

"Sure, you will." Jade offered the reassurance as though she believed it. It could very well be true for Lindy. It just wasn't true for Jade. Not that she wanted Brad Pitt, anyway. "You might not find a movie star, but I'm sure you'll meet someone wonderful."

Lindy turned moodily toward Jade. "How come you never found anybody?" she asked with brutal honesty. "You're kind of pretty."

Jade smiled at her young associate, inured to her remarkable ability to put her foot in her mouth and bite down on it without even noticing it was there. It was all part of the Lindy mystique. It was Jade's theory that the girl was from another planet, but Betsy, Lindy's mother and Jade's neighbor across the hall, insisted that Lindy's father had played football for Oregon State. He'd just never scored. Or graduated.

"It's an old story, Lin," Jade said, digging through a stack of plastic drawers in which she kept bows. She withdrew a pearlescent white one. "I just move too fast to get to know anyone. I shop all morning, wrap and take orders all afternoon, go to class a couple of nights a week."

Lindy threaded gold cord through another card. "What do you want a degree in business for anyway? If The Gift Hunter keeps you too busy to meet men, why would you want the business to get bigger?"

"It's what you do in life," Jade replied patiently. "You keep trying to improve yourself. Learn more. Do more."

"But...don't you want to love more, too?"

Before Jade was forced to admit that was a very profound question, there was a quick rap on her front door followed by the entry into the room of a small, plump brunette in a gray wool suit. She'd apparently left her shoes in her condo across the hall.

"Hi, girls," Betsy Bowers said, going around the desk to kiss her daughter's cheek. She looked around at the flowers and lingerie. "This place looks like a bordello. Where are the men?"

Jade stuck the bow on a corner of the red box, then looked up at her friend with a rueful smile. "As your daughter just pointed out to me, I don't have any."

Betsy shook her head at Lindy. "That wasn't nice." Then she turned a grin on Jade. "Seems I've pointed that out to you a few times, too. When are you going to do something about it?"

Jade attached a tag to the bow. "When The Gift Hunter makes it to the New York Stock Exchange."

Lindy stood, pulled her short leather jacket off the back of her chair and shrugged into it. "What does that mean?" she asked Betsy.

"It means never," Betsy replied. She went to the sofa to finger a red silk nightshirt and heaved a gusty sigh. "I'd love to have one of these. But when you have to sew two together so they'll fit, it sort of loses its sex appeal."

Jade swatted Betsy's shoulder and held the nightshirt up to her. "Just buy a Large and you'll look ravishing."

Betsy shook her head. "I don't even think an Extralarge would fit. I'm getting fat and ugly."

"You're not ugly," Lindy denied staunchly, completely surprised when Jade put a hand over her eyes. "What?"

"Go on home." Betsy turned her daughter

gently toward the door she'd left open. "I brought home kung pao chicken and put it in the oven to keep it warm. Help yourself. I'll be right there."

As Lindy waved at Jade and disappeared across the hall, Betsy took the nightshirt from Jade and replaced it on the sofa. "We may as well just face it," she said gloomily. "I'll never be thin again, and you'll never make time for a man."

"It's not that I don't want one...." Jade denied.

Betsy nodded. "I know. Wonderful men are few and far between. And if you're going to rearrange your life for him, he should be special. At least I date once a year and try to find one."

"How're you doing?" Jade teased, though she knew the answer.

"About as well as you."

"That's pathetic."

"I noticed that. So I'm going to drown my sorrows in Szechuan. Want to come? There's lots."

"Thanks." Jade waved a hand around the room. "But I have to wrap all this tonight."

Betsy put an arm around Jade's shoulders and squeezed. "Lindy isn't being much help, is she? You can tell me the truth."

"She tries hard." Jade did her best to put a positive spin on Lindy's contribution to the business. "She's only sixteen, so of course there's a lot she isn't going to know."

Betsy studied her worriedly. "But it's been four months and she's really not catching on, is she?"

"She will," Jade fibbed. "One day it'll all come together for her and she'll be great. Meanwhile, she's fun to have around." Another fib. "Stop worrying. I'm not." Colossal lie.

But Betsy's relieved smile was worth it. She hugged Jade. "Thanks. After she was fired three times, her self-esteem was demolished, but I thought if someone had the time and patience to lead her through, she'd be a good employee. She's a good kid at heart."

"I know that."

"And she thinks you're wonderful."

Jade rolled her eyes, pushing Betsy toward the door. "She does not. She thinks I'm a shrunken old maid."

Betsy laughed. "You're not shrunken," she said.

Jade closed the door on her friend and turned to face her room filled with dozens of other people's tokens of love. For a moment she felt a physical pain.

It hurt to know that there was no one in Heaven's Harbor, Oregon—or even in the whole wide world—whom she could claim as family. Her parents, who'd died in the crash of a light plane when she'd had been seventeen, had been only children of parents who'd been gone for years. And Jade had been their only child.

She'd vowed then to find the perfect man as soon as possible and have six children so that when *they* had children, her life would be filled with family.

But that was taking longer than she'd planned.

She had scores of friends, many dear acquaintances and hosts of clients who thought kindly of her. But that wasn't the same as knowing that someone out there was planning a Valentine's surprise for her because she was family—or because she was the light in his heart.

She'd long ago accepted that she was alone in the world, but had found that the only way to function with that knowledge was to refuse to think about it, to become a sort of liaison between her clients and those *they* loved by finding them the right gift.

But every once in a while—like at Christmas and Valentine's Day—it became a kind of in-your-face reality. And she was forced to stare it down.

Well, she wasn't going to be the one to blink.

"Oh, quit sniveling," she told herself firmly, "and figure out how you're going to wrap that quilting frame."

Chapter Two

JACK HEARD HIS CHILDREN arrive even before they opened his office door and shoved each other through. They wore the blue-and-white uniforms of the Columbia Academy. And they seemed to be in the middle of a quarrel that had begun the moment Ashley, now eight, could talk, and it was still in progress.

Ashley was small and spindly with a serious Napoleonic complex. She turned and swung her backpack at her brother's midsection.

Andy, ten, fell to the pearl gray carpet with a cry of pain a stranger might have thought meant death. But Jack knew his son had been born with the De Niro-Pacino gene.

Ashley tossed her backpack at the client's chair and came around the desk to fall into Jack's lap. "You don't have sex with Natalie, do you, Daddy?" she asked, looping her arms around his neck.

It always amazed him that a fragile-looking little girl could cut to the heart of a matter with the surgical ruthlessness of a district attorney.

"Do you even know what sex is?" he asked, stalling for time as he pulled grass out of her hair.

"I do!" Andy leapt to his feet, apparently reborn, and came to sit on the edge of Jack's desk, facing him. "It's when men and women sleep together."

He was several inches taller than Ashley but just as wiry. In the depths of his eyes, though, was a charm and intelligence that already crackled with power.

Ashley would fight her way to the top in whatever she did, but Andy would have a strategy.

"But you can't do things when you're sleeping," Ashley argued.

"Well, that's the thing." Andy propped his feet on Jack's knees. "You don't really sleep. They just call it sleeping."

Ashley looked into Jack's eyes. Hers were dark blue and serious. "Do you sleep with Natalie?"

"No," he replied honestly. But he didn't add that he was hoping to change all that tomorrow night.

"Are you ever gonna?" Ashley chewed on the end of her long blond braid and waited for an answer.

Andy leaned forward. His hair was a shade darker than Ashley's and he liked it buzz cut so he didn't have to deal with it.

"'Cause if you are," he said, "Ashley thinks you should know that you can't marry her."

Jack had been seeing Natalie since that weekend at her father's place in the Cascades, but marriage hadn't crossed his mind. "I wasn't considering it," he said. "But why not? I thought you both got along with Natalie."

"She's nice," Ashley said, swinging her leg and bumping her oxford rhythmically against the side of his knee. "But she's not the kind of mom I want."

Andy rolled his eyes at Jack. "I tried to tell her that you have to like her for a wife not just for a mother for us."

"I'd never marry someone you guys didn't like." Jack took Ashley's braid out of her mouth and tossed it over her shoulder. "But what's wrong with Natalie?"

Ashley sighed, thinking. "It's the way she holds my hand. I don't remember Mom's face very well, but I remember her holding my hand. When we got to the street, she used to hold it so tight, I couldn't get away from her." She sighed and rested her head on his shoulder. "I used to like that. But Natalie doesn't do that. I can get away from her anytime I want to."

Andy grinned at Jack as though his little sister's thoughts were cause for their mutual male tolerance. "So I think we have to find a mom who pumps iron. Or do you think you could get a date with Sandra Bullock? She played a lawyer once so you'd have things to talk about."

"And she can drive a bus, so I wouldn't have

to worry about getting you to school on time." Jack laughed with Andy, then kissed Ashley's cheek and tuned in to her serious observation. "It could be that Natalie doesn't feel she has the right to hold you too tightly yet," he said. "You've only seen each other a couple of times."

"She hugs you a lot." Ashley played with his tie. "But she doesn't hug us."

"She might think it's too early for that, too."

Ashley dropped the argument, but Jack knew that didn't mean he'd won it.

Natalie Livingston was the very beautiful daughter of a long-standing client. She was CEO of her own cosmetics firm and not at all the kind of woman he'd ever expected to attract—or to be attracted to.

His wife had been small and dark-haired, an inveterate homebody who ran a successful desktop publishing company from their den, and who stopped everything the moment the children came home.

If he indulged himself, he could still feel her in his arms. And he could still feel his rage over her death two years ago. She'd been only thirty and on her way to deliver a job when a log truck jackknifed on a narrow road.

But he'd learned that anger was futile and exhausting, and that he had to function at top performance to stay ahead of his children.

So he'd learned to cope. And when Natalie had come on to him that weekend he'd spent at her father's place, he'd known it was time to think about getting on with his personal life.

He guessed he could thank Miss Barclay of The Gift Hunter for that. Though he'd hated the black outfit she'd bought for him, he'd been forced to take it with him because he had nothing between an Armani suit and a pair of sweats.

But Natalie had sought him out on the deck one quiet evening, brushed deliberately against him as she went to perch on the railing, and told him she'd always had a Black Knight in her dreams and now he was finally here.

Since then, they'd been to the opera, a Sonics game, met for lunch a few times and taken the children to a production of *The Nutcracker* during the Christmas holidays.

She'd made it more than obvious that she was ready to take their relationship to a new level. And he was ready, too. Sort of.

Well...he *felt* ready, as long as he didn't think about it too deeply. Then he knew clearly that something was holding him back. The trouble was that he couldn't identify what it was. He suspected it was the fear of being unfaithful to Rita's memory, something he knew he had to get over. Or it was the fear of facing his own future, something he'd never been afraid of before.

So he'd held back, unsure whether it was the

relationship or him lacking the passion that banished doubts.

He was growing impatient with his own indecision. He'd determined to resolve the issue the following night. He and Natalie were celebrating Valentine's Day several days early because she was hosting the gala opening of one of her exclusive cosmetics boutiques in San Francisco on the fourteenth.

"Can we have a cat?" Ashley asked into the silence.

Jack groaned. She'd asked the same question three times a day since she'd been given the video of *The Three Lives of Thomasina* as a birthday gift.

"Honey, we're not home enough," he replied, as he'd also done three times a day since that fateful birthday party. "It wouldn't be fair."

"But Isabel says cats fend for themselves. That it wouldn't be any trouble. And she wouldn't mind feeding it."

Isabel was their housekeeper.

"Then it would be Isabel's cat and not yours," he said reasonably.

Ashley sat up in his lap, folded her arms and frowned at him with great displeasure. "So we can't get the right kind of mom and I can't have a cat?"

He knew better than to try to placate her.

"That seems to be the way it stands at the moment."

She pushed against his windpipe and his knee and leapt to the floor. "I'll be in the front office when you're ready to go home." She grabbed her backpack and left his office with royal disdain.

Andy shook his head sympathetically. "At least she doesn't hit *you*. Can we have a dog?"

The Gift Hunter's phone rang off the hook the following afternoon. Jade put Heaven's Harbor Chocolates on hold while she dispatched Lindy with Jack O'Brian's deliveries.

"I thought you wanted to make the deliveries yourself," Lindy said as Jade handed her a large shopping bag that contained all the gifts.

"I did," Jade replied, "but I can't leave the phones, so I'm depending on you, Lindy."

Lindy looked worried. "What if I screw up?"

"Each package is labeled," Jade told her calmly, "so you shouldn't have any trouble. You're perfectly capable of doing this, Lindy. Just take each gift to the address on each box."

"Okay," Lindy said uncertainly.

"And pick up the flowers from Castlebaum's on your way back, okay?"

"Okay."

"Great."

"I'M SUPPOSED TO MEET HER at the restaurant?" Ross Mitchell sat in Jack's client's chair, looking concerned. "Why didn't you arrange for me to pick Diane up at home?"

"It's *Donna*," Jack corrected, leaning over his desk toward his good friend and stockbroker. "Not Diane, *Donna*. Believe me, you don't want to have dinner with Diane because she has three-year-old twin boys and a jealous husband who works construction. *Donna* is an artist and lives in Cannon Beach."

"And what is it you're thinking a stockbroker and an artist will have in common?"

Jack smiled at him. "You're both very strange. You may as well be strange together."

"Don't look now," Ross said, "but you've just bought into mining shares in Colorado."

Jack laughed. "Actually, I like her and I like you and I thought you might like each other. She's always stuck away in her studio, trying to make ends meet, and you're a workaholic, always trying to make ends meet for everybody else. You seem like a natural combination to me."

Ross nodded, then stood and reached across the desk to shake Jack's hand as he stood, too. "All right. Thanks. I'll let you know tomorrow how it went."

Jack walked Ross to the elevator. As the doors parted for Ross to get on, a tall, slender teenager with blue hair got off.

Jack and Ross exchanged an amused look, then Ross waved as the doors closed on him.

Jack returned to his office to find the girl with the blue hair standing before his secretary's desk, apparently waiting for her to finish a telephone conversation.

"Can I help you?" he asked.

As she turned to him, pretty blue eyes wide with surprise, he noted the ring pierced into the arch of her eyebrow and was proud that he withheld a wince. He would never understand why pretty girls did that to themselves.

"Mr. O'Brian?" she asked.

"Yes."

She smiled nervously and handed him a package wrapped in red-and-white paper. A sprig of white flowers was attached to a big red bow. "This is for you," she said. "Well, I mean, it's not *for* you, it's *from* you to somebody else."

"You're from The Gift Hunter."

"Yeah." She smiled, fidgeted, frowned a little worriedly, then offered him a clipboard and a pen. "Would you sign this, please?"

He put the box on the corner of Elizabeth's desk, signed the sheet and handed the clipboard back.

She gave the box one last look, smiled, then frowned again and left.

Jack carried the box into his office. It contained Natalie's teddy—and quite probably the next bend in the road of his life.

Chapter Three

"I've missed you *so* much." Natalie's face was less than an inch from Jack's.

They sat at a small table in the Siren Song Restaurant on the top floor of a beachfront hotel. She leaned seductively toward him, flowing red hair streaming over the shoulder of his suit coat and her own bare arm.

Her eyes wandered lustfully over his face. "Did you miss me, Jack?"

He knew stopping to think would be the wrong response, so he filled the silence quickly with, "I thought about you, Nat—"

"All the time?" She interrupted him, looking pleased, every movement of her body a signal that she was his tonight if he would just make the move.

He'd intended to. He'd planned to.

She leaned even closer, the low round neckline of her red silk dress revealing the tops of full alabaster breasts.

He reached for the box he'd placed at the foot of his chair and handed it to her.

"Oh!" She flexed her fingers greedily, moved the wineglasses and water glasses aside—all that was left of their meal—and put the box on the now-bare expanse of tablecloth.

She removed the sprig of flowers and tucked them in her hair, ripped off the paper and opened the box.

Watching her expression over the sheets of tissue, Jack was surprised when her wide smile of anticipation turned to a frown of confusion.

Then she reached into the box and pulled up a length of thick, fuzzy, bright red fabric. It was alternately patterned with large white hearts, and little white houses with chimneys puffing smoke. The windows were yellow, cozily representing lights within.

He stared at it, thinking it was the ugliest thing he'd ever seen, and wondering where in the hell it had come from.

She held it up, then dropped it back into the box and stood.

He stood with her, trying to catch her arm as she reached for her purse. "Nat, I..."

She shook him off, tears standing in her eyes. "I've tried hard with this relationship, Jack!" she whispered tightly as everyone else nearby turned to look at them. "But this is something you'd give your *mother* for Valentine's Day, not the woman with whom you intend to...to pursue a future! Good night!"

As Natalie stormed out of the restaurant, Jack sat down again and took a fistful of the ugly chenille robe. Of course, he thought, temper coming to life. The Gift Hunter was responsible for this.

JACK READ THE CARD in his hand and followed the third-floor corridor of the Coast Condominiums to suite 321. Then he rapped loudly on the door. It was after 10:00 p.m., but he didn't care.

He wasn't sure why he was so angry. Perhaps because it was the second time Miss Barclay had made a mistake with his order. But, then, his job was to defend people who made mistakes, so he should be more understanding.

He'd been telling himself that all the way over here, but he still wasn't convinced. All he was aware of was that he'd intended tonight to be something special and it had ended with Natalie storming out on him in tears.

He shifted the big white box to the other hand and knocked again.

The door was opened suddenly by a tall young woman wearing pearl gray silk. The gown was caftan-style and voluminous, but its silky fabric clung to perky, tip-tilted breasts.

For an instant, his anger fled—and so did every word in his vocabulary. He raised his eyes up an expanse of creamy throat to a softly rounded chin, pale pink lips and a straight, elegant nose.

Wary dark eyes fringed by thick lashes waited for him to explain his presence at that hour. Her face was framed by clouds of glossy dark brown hair that fell to her shoulders.

He thought absently that he'd imagined Miss Barclay as a silly blonde with a ponytail on the side of her head and lots of makeup. What other kind of woman would make her living shopping?

This must be her sister or her friend.

He pulled himself together by remembering that someone at this address had ruined his evening—and possibly his foray into the future with Natalie Livingston.

Just the thought of the red robe in the box under his arm reignited his temper. "I'd like to speak to Miss Barclay, please." His authoritative voice reflected his mood.

The woman opened her mouth to speak, caught sight of the box under his arm, the belt of the red robe hanging out of it, and said simply, "Uh-oh."

He recognized her voice. Miss Barclay. So his mental image of her had been wrong.

Her eyes held his for a moment as though she recognized him, which was impossible. Unless she recognized his voice as he'd recognized hers. She seemed about to smile, then changed her mind. Instead, she frowned apologetically.

"Mr. O'Brian," she said, stepping back to let him in and closing the door behind him. "I'm Jade Barclay. Your mother didn't like the robe?"

He thrust the box at her, working hard to ward

off the appeal of her soft brown eyes and the movement of the silk gown on her curves and around her ankles.

"My mother didn't get the robe, Miss Barclay," he explained stiffly. "My girlfriend did, and was very unhappy that I thought of her in terms of chenille at a time dedicated to lovers."

She opened her mouth, presumably to apologize, but he was working up a good head of steam. "And to compound the problem, I presume this means my mother is now staring at a tiny scrap of black lace and wondering what on earth has happened to the sanity of her only son."

She closed her eyes and shook her head, clutching the box to her. "Mr. O'Brian, I am so sorry." She spoke with sincerity but he was in no mood to be understanding.

"I'd say, Miss Barclay—" he reached behind him to yank the door open "—that The Gift Hunter has a serious problem with quality control. Good night." He left her apartment, pulling the door firmly closed behind him.

Jade dropped the box on the closest chair, pulled out the red chenille robe and held it up. How could anyone not love this robe, she wondered, with its cheerful little houses with the light in the windows and the hearts so perfect for Valentine's Day?

Of course, it had been intended for Jack

O'Brian's mother, but how could his girlfriend have missed its homey appeal?

Well. That wasn't her business. Her business was to get the right gift to the right person.

She sank onto the sofa with the robe and tried to reconstruct the time that afternoon when she'd put his order together. She'd wrapped the dinner reservations for one sister, and the faxed confirmation of the weekend stay for the other sister, in scarf boxes, then the teddy and the robe in garment boxes. She'd wrapped them all with red-and-white paper, attached red bows and sprigs of baby's breath, then attached the tags and addresses. What could have gone wrong?

Silly question. She'd had Lindy deliver them, that was what had gone wrong.

She fell back against the sofa cushions with a groan. And Jack O'Brian had been just as gorgeous as she'd imagined. Not very understanding, but definitely gorgeous.

"WELL..." Lindy sat in the middle of Jade's sofa in a long red-and-black overshirt, black tights and black high-tops. "I'm not sure what happened yesterday." She wound her fingers together and tears puddled in her eyes. "I was carrying the bag to the car and this kid on a skateboard bumped into me and everything went flying. There was nothing to get broken, but you'd put all the tags on the bows and all the bows came off and all those little notes you put on them with the addresses."

Jade wanted to scream. "*All* the tags came off?"

Lindy nodded. "I know it's weird, but the bag went flying...."

"Why didn't you call me?"

"Because you wanted me to do it right."

"But you ended up doing it wrong and the client is really angry with me."

A tear spilled onto Lindy's cheek. "I'm sorry. I guess I'm just not good at anything. I thought I remembered what went to who, but...I guess I was wrong."

Jade got to her feet and went for her coat. "Okay. Well, at least I know what happened. Can you wrap those scarves while I'm gone?"

Lindy took a tissue off the coffee table. "Okay. Do you want me to answer the phone?"

Jade nodded. She really didn't her want to, but kicking the kid when she was down didn't seem like a fair option. "Take good messages and be sure to get phone numbers."

"I'm really sorry."

"I know. And I can fix it, but it's always better to double-check when you're not sure rather than to risk doing it wrong." Jade pulled on her red wool coat and reached for her black drawstring bag. "Did you have lunch at school? In the freezer I have those burritos you like."

Lindy got boxes and tissue from the shelf. "Thanks, I'm fine."

"All right. I'm going to Jack O'Brian's office. I'm not sure how long I'll be, but I'll check in with you on my way back."

JADE HALF EXPECTED HIM to refuse to see her. But when his secretary buzzed him and announced her, there was an instant's silence, then he pulled his office door open himself.

He was in shirtsleeves, but no less gorgeous than he'd been the night before.

"Miss Barclay," he said politely, though not warmly. "Come in."

She preceded him into a book-lined office with mahogany furniture, an Oriental carpet and a white brocade sofa placed against a window that looked down onto the water.

She stopped in the middle of the office and turned to him, getting right to the point.

"The Gift Hunter would like to make amends for last night," she said, her hands in her pockets because she had his full attention and that made her fidgety. "I'll return everything, replace everything, whatever you'd like me to do. And I'll rewrap and redeliver free of charge." She drew a breath. "I'll even call the lady and explain that it was all my fault."

He went around his desk, gestured her to sit in the client's chair, then sat himself.

"Thank you," he said. "When she finally took my call this morning, I made it clear that it was all your fault, so that's already taken care of."

"Good. Were you able to get the teddy back from your mother?"

He shook his head. "I haven't been able to reach my mother. But in Natalie's case, I think jewelry might put her in a forgiving mind, so I would like to take advantage of your other offer."

Jade's eyes widened. "You mean you have to buy this Natalie jewelry so that she'll forgive you for *my* mistake?" She knew even as the words were coming out of her mouth how unprofessional they were, but it was too late.

His frown noted that also. "She's just come back from a business trip," he said. "Her sense of humor was a little strained."

"Obviously," Jade said, then bit the inside of her upper lip, wondering what was wrong with her. She never spoke to a client without measuring her words.

He studied her narrowly for a moment, then apparently chose to ignore her careless remarks. "I'd like you to pick out a bracelet for her at Blumenthal's and charge it to me. I'll call and tell them—"

His office door burst open before he could finish his instructions and a young woman in jeans and a colorful fleece jacket flew into the room.

Jack barely had time to stand before she leapt into his arms and hugged him fiercely.

"Thank you, thank you, *thank* you!" she cried.

Jade presumed this was not the dour girlfriend.

"You're welcome, Di, but—"

"I have never, *never* been so thrilled!" She held him at arm's length and grinned broadly up at him. "It was so exciting to me to know that *someone* saw me as young and sexy enough to wear a black lace teddy. And you know what?"

So that's where the black teddy had landed— on one of his sisters.

Jack looked confused. "What?" he asked.

"I got the boys to bed early and was wearing it when Todd came home." She giggled. "We had the hottest night we've had since the twins were born. I had to push him out the door to work this morning. So thank you, thank you! Gotta go. The boys are outside with Elizabeth."

Jack's sister turned to leave, spotted Jade in the chair and put a hand to her mouth. "Oh, Jack! I didn't know you had a client."

"This is Jade Barclay from The Gift Hunter," Jack said. "Miss Barclay, this is my sister, Diane Draper."

Jade stood to shake her hand.

Diane gasped and caught Jade's arms. "Was giving me the teddy *your* idea?" she asked.

"It was...sort of a collaborative effort." Jade cast Jack a glance that shared the joke.

To her surprise, he gave her a small smile.

"Come on." Jack put an arm around his sister's shoulders. "I'll walk you out so I can say hi to my nephews."

"Nice to meet you!" Diane called over her shoulder.

Jade maintained an innocent expression when Jack returned.

He resumed his chair and shook his head, apparently still recovering from Diane's visit. "So we were somehow twenty-five percent successful," he said. "I was going to send Diane and Todd to the resort because I knew things were a little strained between them, but I thought—"

This time he was interrupted by the phone. And apparently it was his private line because his secretary didn't announce the call.

"Donna," he said. "Hi, babe. Where are you? I've tried to—" He stopped, turned to Jade and said, clearly for her benefit, "Seafoam Lodge?"

Jade put a hand over her eyes. That was the trip he'd intended for Diane.

"Well...good," he went on after a moment. "I'm glad you're having such a good time." He listened a few more moments, his expression changing from perplexity to concern and back again. "Donna, I'm sure a gallery owner seems like a gift from heaven, but you've only—"

Jack closed his eyes, smiling fondly. "He seems like a gift from me, does he? Well, you're welcome. Have a great time but, you know, be careful."

He replaced the receiver, looking stunned. "All right. Fifty percent successful. But who in the hell did Ross Mitchell meet for dinner last night?"

That question was answered not two seconds later when a beautiful middle-aged woman erupted into the office on the arm of a handsome fair-haired man about Jack's age.

Uh-oh. Jade saw it coming. The reservations for dinner at Brighton's. The date Jack had set up for his sister.

Jack stood slowly. "Mom," he said in a choked voice. "Ross?"

Chapter Four

JACK'S MOTHER WORE a chic spruce green pantsuit and a sunny smile. Arms extended, she walked into her son's embrace.

"Mom, I didn't..." Jack began to explain about the mix-up, but his mother drew back and slapped his chest with a grin.

"Darling," she said softly. "I had no idea you had such insightful, creative tendencies."

Jack raised an eyebrow.

His mother reached a hand out to the young man standing a small distance away in a gray pin-striped suit. He took it and moved closer. He met Jack's eyes with a mystified but satisfied expression.

"What ever made you know that Ross and I would enjoy each other's company so much?" Jack's mother asked. "He volunteers at the Portland Art Museum, too. Did you know, that?"

"I..."

She waved away his attempt to answer. "The point is, we had a wonderful dinner. Then he took me dancing, then to listen to reggae music at the Islander, then he hired a boat and we watched the sun rise from offshore." She heaved a girlish sigh and leaned into Ross's shoulder. "I just hate to think of all the other mothers out there with so much life left in them getting fuzzy robes or slippers from their children for Valentine's Day."

Jade looked up at Jack as he glanced her way, seemingly speechless with astonishment.

His mother followed his glance and noticed Jade. She covered the few steps between them and offered her hand. "I'm sorry," she said. Jade noticed that her smile was backlit by a genuine inner warmth. Her escort was fifteen or twenty years younger, but seemed very comfortable with her. "I'm always barging into Jack's office with a question or the latest gossip. I tend to forget that I'm not everyone's top priority. I'm Selina O'Brian. And this is Ross Mitchell."

"Jade Barclay." Jade stood to greet them. "I'm not a client, Ms. O'Brian. I run a shopping service."

Selina's expressive eyebrows dipped in a frown. "Who would hire someone to take over such a charming chore?"

"Me," Jack replied. "Mom...?"

But she'd tuned him out and was concentrating on Jade. "Really? Well, maybe you could shop for a woman who could put a little romance into Jack's life. Is that possible?"

Before Jade could answer, Jack did. "Mom, you've met Natalie."

She blew air between her lips in a scornful gesture completely at odds with her elegant appearance. Jade fell in love with her.

"Natalie is about sex, darling," she said. "I'm talking about romance."

Jack ran a hand down his face. Ross seemed to be concentrating on the light above Jack's desk.

Selina narrowed her focus on Jade. "What are *you* doing on Valentine's Day?"

"Ah...working. I've been getting ready for it day and night for the past two weeks."

Selina signed regretfully. "Don't you young people think of anything but work?" Then she excused herself to freshen up.

The moment the office door closed behind her, Jack turned on Ross. "You were supposed to take my *sister* to dinner!"

Ross shrugged a shoulder, denying responsibility for the turn of events. "You told me you'd made the reservation at Brighton's in my name and that I was to wait for her to meet me there. Your mother showed up, not your sister. If you're going to play Cupid, be careful where you aim your arrow."

Jack looked with disbelief into his friend's pleased grin. "But she's—"

"The most delightful woman I've ever met. Relax, big guy. You know I'm not after notches on my bedpost or you wouldn't have asked me to meet Diane."

"Donna."

"Whatever. You messed up, but the hand of Providence must have been in it because I haven't enjoyed myself so much in years. And Selina says she hasn't, either."

Jack folded his arms, apparently deciding to be merciless. "She'll be fifty-seven next birthday."

Ross's smile didn't slip. "And I'll be forty-one. Doesn't matter. She'll have the heart of a girl until she's ninety. And I've always been the protective type. Lighten up. We like each other. You screwed up, but you did good."

Selina was back in a moment, then she and Ross left, making plans to go skiing at Mount Hood.

Jack fell into his chair, his stunned expression gradually fading to acceptance. Jade sat again and waited, doing her best not to look smug. The Gift Hunter had made a mistake, after all—four of them, in fact. But it would have been a bigger mistake to point out to him that her errors had been more deeply appreciated than his gift selections would have been.

He turned to her finally, his dark eyes revealing self-deprecation. "So you're up to seventy-five percent."

She sat up primly. "It's the other twenty-five I'm concerned about."

His eyes pinned her. "Is it?"

"Of course." She stood and shouldered her purse, the focus of his dark eyes making a licorice whip of her spine. She squared her shoulders. "A woman without a sense of humor should never be given a chenille robe. But it wouldn't have been the right thing for your mother, either." That truth shared, she got back to business. "Am I shopping for gold for Natalie? Diamonds? Something with a heart-shaped charm?"

He stood puzzling over the answer. "What would *you* like if someone was shopping for you?" he asked finally.

She smiled thinly. "The chenille robe. I'll—"

His office door burst open again, this time admitting two towheaded young children, a boy and a girl. They wore blue blazers—apparently school uniforms—and carried books.

They stopped abruptly in front of Jade. "Hi," the little girl said. Jade guessed her to be seven or eight. She was bright-eyed and apple-cheeked.

The boy, taller but with the same eyes and coloring, simply stared at her.

Jack appeared suddenly beside Jade. "Miss Barclay," he said. "I'd like you to meet my children, Andy and Ashley."

Jade put a hand to each child's cheek. Their

beauty was breathtaking, and their bright eyes filled with wit and confidence. She guessed they were very loved and indulged.

"Miss Barclay's going shopping for Natalie," Jack told the children.

"You know her, too?" Andy asked.

"No," Jack corrected. "She has a shopping service and buys things for people who are too busy to do it for themselves."

"Wow!" Ashley's eyes grew enormous. "Buying presents is your *job?*"

Jade laughed. "Cool, huh?" She turned to Jack. "The store will know the price range?"

He shook his head. "There isn't one. Go for it. She was very angry."

As Jade left, Jack pointed to the long table in the corner of his office where the children often did their homework while waiting for him. "Settle in, guys, because it'll be about an hour and a half before we can get you something to eat. And I have work to do that I'll have to concentrate on, so keep it down, okay?"

Andy went to the table, but Ashley followed him to his desk and as though he hadn't even spoken, climbed into his lap. She leaned back against him and crossed her oxfords on his knee. "I didn't know you could get money for shopping."

"Amazing, huh?" He resisted the urge to

reach for the brief he was working on. Ashley seemed to have something on her mind.

"Jane's pretty."

"It's Ja*d*e." He enunciated the d.

"That's a funny name."

"Actually, its the name of a pretty green stone."

"A rock, you mean?"

"No, a stone. Like in jewelry."

"Oh." Ashley put a small hand to her cheek. "She touches like a mom."

"Really?" He guessed where she was going with this and tried to divert her. "Well, I don't think she has any kids. And I'll probably never see her again."

Ashley sat up, her elbow in his throat. He bit her arm playfully, making wolf noises. She laughed hysterically, but she wouldn't be sidetracked.

"How come you're not going to see her again?"

He explained that when she went to buy things for him, she bought things he didn't like, or got the order messed up.

"But you always give me and Andy more chances," she said.

He nodded. "She's had two already. She's just going shopping now to try to make up for the mistake. So I'm not going to see her again—unless, of course, she messes up this time, too. Then

I'll have to see her again just so I can yell at her."

"You're very good at that." From the table Andy flashed him a grin.

Jack sent him a warning glance that he laughed off, then set Ashley on her feet. "Now I have to get some work done, or I won't have time to take you guys to dinner before I pick up Natalie."

Ashley, eye to eye with him as he sat, proposed conversationally, "You could get all your work done, then take us to dinner and forget about Natalie."

"I like Natalie," he insisted.

Ashley looked into his eyes with one of those riveting, adult expressions that always filled him with trepidation. Then she said, "Okay," turned away and skipped across the room to the table.

He congratulated himself on averting a trauma.

But he was a little too premature.

Chapter Five

NATALIE DETECTED the gift box in the breast pocket of his suit coat when they stepped into the elevator to ride up to the Siren Song.

She leaned against him, apologizing with heavy-lidded eyes for her flare of temper the night before. She ran her hands under the lapels of his jacket and across his chest and her right hand collided with the small square.

She smiled seductively. "What's that?"

"Dessert," he replied.

She looked into his eyes and leaned suggestively against him. "But I had *other* plans for dessert."

She claimed repentance all through dinner and forgave him generously with languid looks and tender strokes.

Then the waiter cleared away their dinner dishes and Natalie waited. "Time for dessert," she prodded.

He observed to himself that the dessert he had planned apparently held more interest for her than the dessert *she* claimed to have planned. But he'd resolved to stop analyzing everything and simply get on with his life.

He handed her the box.

Jade had delivered it to his office with a note for him that said, "It's a tennis bracelet that should buy you her forgiveness for twenty years into the future. Good luck. The Gift Hunter."

He'd tucked the note into his desk blotter, the box into his pocket and taken the clamoring children immediately out for pizza.

Now he found himself almost as anxious as Natalie to see what was inside the box.

Natalie pulled off the gold net ribbon that had been tied in a simple bow, and lifted the lid. And stared.

She looked up at him, her eyes saucer-size, and he smiled indulgently, prepared to accept her praise, her kisses and, eventually, her version of dessert.

Then the box came at him like a vicious missile. It struck the bridge of his nose and fell to the table as Natalie stood, her cheeks crimson with fury.

She snatched something off the table and dangled it in front of his eyes. It was a bracelet all right, but it wasn't gold and it held no diamonds.

It was obviously painted steel, or whatever costume jewelry was made from, and several charms hung from it. They were too close to his eyes for him to focus on what they were.

"First you think of me as an old crone and give me a chenille robe!" Natalie shouted at him.

Even the waiters stopped to look. "And now you give me a two-dollar child's bracelet? What's the message here, Jack?"

Before he could try to explain, she dropped the bracelet in his wineglass. "Never mind! I don't want to know! Find a woman who'll be amused by your pranks. I'm not. Goodbye, Jack."

And she stormed away.

To quote the famous Yogi Berra, he thought, *"It was* déjà vu *all over again."*

Jack drove to Jade's, as furious with her as Natalie had been with him. He hammered on the door of her apartment until she opened it.

She wore the same caftan, but he was ready for it this time. He kept his eyes on her face.

"If I have anything to say about it," he threatened darkly, stepping over the threshold as she took a step backward, "you will never shop for me, for my family, for anyone I know or for anyone I communicate with in this country or across the globe!"

Halfway to the sofa, she stopped backing away from him and stood her ground.

"If she didn't like that bracelet," Jade said firmly, "you have to face the fact that there's something wrong with *her* and not with my service."

He held up his index finger, the child's bracelet dangling from it. "I asked you to pick out what you'd like. And this is it?"

Her mouth fell open and she snatched the bracelet from his finger. "No! No!" she said, holding it in the palm of her hand. "This can't have happened. I handled every step myself. I selected a beautiful tennis bracelet, stood over Mr. Blumenthal while he wrapped it and delivered it to Elizabeth myself!"

"Then how do you explain this?" he demanded. "You ruined another evening for me, Miss Barclay."

Her expression changed from horror to confusion. "I don't know. It can't be. Have you talked to Elizabeth? Maybe she can expl—"

"Elizabeth's been with me since I opened the practice eight years ago. She's as honest and loyal to me as my mother."

"I didn't mean she took it. I meant she might be able to expl—"

He caught her right arm and pushed back the sleeve of her caftan. Her wrist was bare. When he reached for the other arm, she kicked him in the shin.

He bit back an oath, deciding in some calm corner of his brain that she was probably within her rights.

"You think I *stole* it?" she asked, her voice shrill. "I'm bonded! And I'm honest! You may check my condo, but don't you *dare* touch me."

"I'll leave that to the police," he said.

"Fine." She walked around him to the still-open door. He turned to follow her and could see a woman and a teenage girl in pajamas and robes standing in the hallway, watching. He recognized the blue hair of the young girl who'd made the delivery to his office the day before.

"And on your way to the police station, you might stop off and have your head examined," Jade went on. "Because any man who'd love a woman whose forgiveness has to be *bought* for something that wasn't even his fault, should have his brain checked for mildew!"

He should have just let it go at that. He wanted to, but he couldn't. He'd planned the night for romance. And strangely, while he'd been with Natalie, he'd felt surprisingly little passion.

But right now, he sizzled with it.

"You owe me, Gift Hunter," he said. "You completely botched my order, and so far you've repaired only seventy-five percent of your mistake. And that was through no skill on your part."

Her eyes bored into his. "You want a sample of my skill, Mr. O'Brian?" she asked, her voice deceptively quiet. "All right. Here it is."

She took hold of his tie and pulled. He could have resisted, but the situation was just too promising. He let her draw his head down, and she wrapped her arms around his neck.

Her lips met his angrily at first, then softened and began to move artfully on him. He responded without taking control and the tension seemed to slip out of the arms around him.

He put his hands at her waist, and she moved closer. He opened his mouth and felt her hesitation. He moved his hand to the middle of her back and splayed his fingers to hold her to him and lift her off the carpet.

She sighed against his mouth and offered no resistance. She parted her lips to explore him and he opened eagerly for her, returning the study, losing all sense of time and place as she kissed him senseless.

He let her slip down his body until her feet touched the floor, finding the experience an exquisite composite of heaven and hell.

She took a step back from him, apparently as astonished by the kiss as he was.

"And let that be a lesson to you," she said in a raspy voice.

"Oh, it *has* been." He tried to appear unaffected by a raging libido. He inclined his head politely to the ladies in the hall and left while he still could.

He was almost home and fortunately on a deserted side street when he braked the Audi to a sudden, screeching stop. He'd been trying to recreate the events of that afternoon in his mind and a seemingly innocent string of facts was coming together into an incriminating noose.

First: The box had been on his desk when he

got back to his office after a discussion in the meeting room with a junior partner. He'd been away fifteen or twenty minutes. And the bow on the box had been so perfect, he hadn't wanted to risk disturbing it to look inside.

Second: Andy and Ashley had been alone in his office.

Third: Earlier that afternoon, Ashley had been very interested in Jade and he'd explained that he wouldn't be seeing Jade again unless she made a mistake on his order, in which case he'd have to yell at her. Something Andy had claimed he was good at.

And fourth: Jack had seen the charms on the bracelet when he handed it to Jade, and though it hadn't registered at the time, he realized now that they were characters from *Pocahontas*. The Indian maiden, Captain John Smith, the raccoon and the hummingbird. Ashley loved the story and had been deluged with licensed products on her birthday.

Suddenly everything made horrifying sense.

He put the car in gear and headed home.

The housekeeper met him with a polite smile and took his jacket. "The children went to bed an hour ago," she said, "but they're still awake. I imagine they want to know how your evening went."

He studied her suspiciously. "Do you know all about it?"

She blinked. "All about what? I never ask questions of your children. It's safer that way."

He patted her shoulder. Of course she didn't know anything. His children never needed adult support for their plans. They were perfectly capable of terrorism on their own.

He walked upstairs.

Andy's and Ashley's bedrooms were empty but that didn't surprise him. They always waited for party reports in his room.

He found them sitting cross-legged in the middle of his bed, playing Crazy Eights. They turned to him with eager smiles. Anyone unfamiliar with their criminal profile might have been deluded by their apparent innocence.

He sat in the chair beside the bed, propping his crossed feet on the edge of the blue-and-beige coverlet.

"Which one of you switched Natalie's bracelet?" he asked. He'd found that direct confrontation brought quick results.

Their smiles faded and they looked at each other, then at him.

"I did," Andy said, dropping his cards.

Ashley added hers to the pile. "But we switched it with *my* bracelet."

Jack's only comfort in all this was that his children did generally tell the truth, and though they often made sport of getting each other into trouble, when it came to the crunch, one never hung the other out to dry.

He noticed that on his daughter's tiny wrist was a several-thousand-dollar bracelet containing a long string of small, round diamonds, each in a simple heart-shaped loop of fourteen-karat gold.

"Why?" he asked.

Andy looked him in the eye. "Because we don't like Natalie."

"Well," Jack said, keeping his voice down, "you weren't dating her, were you?"

"You didn't like her, either." Andy made that declaration bravely, but when Jack raised an eyebrow, quickly busied himself stacking the cards and replacing them in their box.

"I seem to remember telling you that I did."

"But you really didn't." Ashley moved to sit right against his feet. She wore footed Pocahontas pajamas.

"Why do you say that?" he asked, struggling with strained patience.

"Because you never brought her home." Andy tossed the box of cards onto the nightstand and scooted across the mattress until he sat on the other side of Jack's feet. "We all went out together sometimes, but she never came home with us. I don't think she really wanted to. And you knew she'd never be a mom."

"And you said," Ashley reminded him, "that

you were never going to see Jade again, only if she messed up your order. And we think she'd make a neat mom, so we wanted you to see her again."

Their insights often amazed him, but tonight they annoyed him because he found it alarming to know that they understood him sometimes better than he understood himself.

He pulled his feet down and leaned forward to look at one child, then the other.

"Well, I'm glad you had this so well thought out, but I wonder if Jade appreciates what you've done for her?"

"What do you mean?" Andy asked.

Jack pointed to the bracelet on Ashley's wrist. "I sent her to buy that for Natalie, and when Natalie opened the box and there was just a little girl's bracelet in it, I thought Jade had messed up just like you knew I would. But what you didn't realize is that the diamond bracelet cost a whole lot of money and I thought someone had stolen it and put the Pocahontas one in its place. And nobody had touched the box but Jade."

Ashley put a hand over her mouth.

Andy looked pained. "You thought *Jade* stole it?"

"Yes, I did," he replied. He hadn't really, but he was going for effect.

When he'd grabbed her wrist, it had been more because he'd wanted to touch her than because he'd thought her guilty of theft. And she'd gotten her revenge on his shin—and his lips.

"I called the police."

Ashley began to cry. Andy stood up.

"So what do we do now?" Jack asked them.

"You have to tell her you're sorry!" Ashley said anxiously.

"But I didn't do anything."

"Well..." She backpedaled. "You have to tell her *we're* sorry!"

"Close," he said sternly. "*You'll* have to tell her you're sorry."

"Did she cry?" Andy asked in a whisper.

"She was very upset," Jack replied. Actually, she'd spit fire at him, then kissed him. All in all, a rather delicious few minutes. But, again, he was after effect.

Andy took the cordless phone off Jack's beside table and handed it to him. "Can we call her now?"

Jack glanced at his bedside clock. It was almost eleven-thirty, but she'd been angry enough when he left her that she was probably still awake.

"This is an apology we have to make in person," Jack said. "But we'll call her and make an appointment to see her in the morning."

The children huddled together on the edge of the bed while he dialed.

"Hello?" Jade answered. Her voice sounded weary and anxious.

"Miss Barclay, this is Jack O'Brian," he said.

"Did you find it?" she demanded before he could add any more.

"Yes," he replied.

"Thank *God!*"

"Hold on, please. My children would like to speak to you." He handed the phone to his son.

Andy stammered an apology, then said, "We're supposed to make an appointment for tomorrow morning to apologize in person." Andy listened, then looked up at Jack. "She wants to know what time we have to be at school."

"Tell her I can get you there at eight o'clock, if it isn't too early."

Andy relayed the information, then looked up again. "She wants to know if the food court in the mall is okay 'cause she has to start shopping early."

Jack nodded.

"Dad says that's fine. I—"

Ashley grabbed the phone from Andy. "Jade? Um...this is Ashley. I'm sorry, too. But we didn't like Natalie. We like you. We think you—"

Jack read her mind and shook his head at her urgently. "Tell her we'll talk to her in the morning," he prompted.

Ashley looked distressed but did as he asked.

"Dad says I have to go now. We'll see you in the morning. Okay, bye."

Ashley climbed into Jack's lap and opened his hand. She held her wrist down and the bracelet fell off into his palm. "She's mad at us," she said worriedly.

"What did she say?"

"Not much," Ashley answered. "But she was real quiet. Like you get when you're *too* mad to yell."

"Well, I'm sure when you explain, she'll understand." He wanted them to realize the potential harm in what they'd done, but decided it was finally time to cut them some slack.

And they had accomplished something interesting in the process of their lawless activities.

He was going to see Jade Barclay again.

His fingertips went to his lips at the thought.

Chapter Six

JADE WASN'T IN the food court. Jack wondered in concern if her agreement to meet them there had simply been payback for his behavior the night before. Had she lured him there and failed to show just to prove that she could be as mean as he'd been?

Then Andy shouted, "There she is!" and pointed to a tall, slender column of red standing in front of the pet shop window several shops off the court. All the stores were still closed, but morning walkers and others simply planning their purchases wandered up and down the wide mall.

The children ran to her. Jack followed slowly, giving them time to make their apologies and allowing her a little space in which to scold.

But that didn't seem to be what she was doing. She leaned down to them and listened patiently while both spoke at once, then she hugged them to her.

Andy and Ashley were wreathed in smiles as she turned them toward the pet shop window and pointed to something inside.

As Jack came up behind them, he saw that the subject under discussion was a pair of gray Persian kittens. They had flat little faces with brick red noses, and bright green eyes. He noted that the color of their coats was the same shade as the caftan Jade lounged in in the evenings.

His heart thumped at the memory.

Ashley caught his hand and pulled him so close to the window, his nose was in danger of reconstruction.

"Jade's gonna buy those kitties for her client!" She was beside herself with excitement.

"They're for an old lady," Andy said, his hands pressed against the window. "She's all alone in a little house and her daughter wants her to have company."

Ashley sighed. "I wish someone wanted us to have company."

Jack patted her shoulder. "Think how happy they'll make the lady."

He turned to Jade and found her watching him, her expression unreadable until she caught his eye. Then it grew cool and condemning, and he knew he wouldn't be forgiven as easily as the children. Her lustrous hair was caught back in a simple knot this morning, but it gave her an air of hauteur.

"Can we buy you a croissant and a cappuccino?" he asked.

She cast him a glance that was distinctly royal. "If the offer extends to a mocha," she bargained coolly, "you may."

He swept a hand toward the food court.

She caught each child by a hand and led the way.

Ashley glanced at him over her shoulder as he followed. He read the message in her smile. Jade held her hand like a mom.

And like a mom, she gave her full attention to the children. For most of an hour they told her their deepest secrets and their wildest dreams.

"I want to find new civilizations," Andy said grandly, his upper lip lined with hot chocolate. "I want to go everywhere and see everything."

Jade leaned across the table to dab at his lip with a napkin. "Thank you," he said with a love-struck smile.

Jack bit back a grin. Had *he* done that, Andy would have been indignant and embarrassed.

"I'd like to travel." Jade took her last bite of croissant and shared it with Ashley. "But I'm not sure there are new civilizations left to discover."

"There are in space!" Andy insisted eagerly. "I'm gonna have my own ship and crew."

Ashley put a hand on Jade's arm and tugged until she was forced to turn to her. "I'm gonna be a ballerina!"

"That's nice. You like to dance?" Jade asked.

Ashley answered honestly. "I don't know. But I like the shoes and the frilly dresses."

Jade laughed. "Well, that's a good reason. I used to take ballet lessons."

Ashley looked reverent. "You did?"

"Uh-huh. For a couple of years. Until I got a job in high school and there wasn't enough time for everything." Then she glanced at her watch and looked at each child regretfully. "And speaking of time, I have to get busy." She pointed down the mall where shops were opening and moving displays out in front to attract attention. She pushed her chair back. "So, thank you both for your apologies. I understand that you meant well." She turned her smile on Jack but it lost a little of its wattage. "Thank you for breakfast."

She put a hand to the table to push herself to her feet, but Jack placed a hand over it. The gesture stopped her as effectively as if he'd placed an anvil in her lap.

He felt the sudden tension in her.

"Andy—" he turned to his son "—would you take Ashley to look in the pet shop window for a few minutes so I can talk to Jade?"

A wide grin split the boy's face. "Sure. Take all the time you want. I don't want to go to school, anyway."

"Stay right in front of the shop where I can see you."

"Okay." The children ran off and Jack turned to Jade. She was wearing her imperial face, but he stared it down.

"I'm sorry about last night. I knew you hadn't taken the bracelet, but I was angry and frustrated and...I couldn't imagine what else had happened. And you'd made mistakes twice before."

Her expression had softened to mildly conciliatory, until he'd added the last part. Then she angled her chin and asked frostily, "Twice? We did confuse the gifts for your family, but where does the second one come in?"

He knew he was in trouble. "It doesn't matter. I—"

"Where?" Her tone rose a decibel.

He resigned himself to worsening her opinion of him. "The clothes you bought me for that working weekend," he said, leaning back in his flimsy chair.

She looked puzzled. "They didn't fit?"

"They fit perfectly," he admitted. "They just made me look like a Calvin Klein ad."

Her eyes went carefully over him, then met his gaze. "An Armani ad on weekdays, and a Calvin Klein ad on weekends. What's wrong with that?"

He was trying to make contact with her on a personal level, and she kept giving him her Snow Queen responses. He deliberately tried to force a livelier reaction out of her. The way she'd kissed him the night before, he knew there was fire inside.

"Actually," he said, "your fashion sense is what attracted Natalie to me. She was at her father's that weekend and came on to me big-time."

That did it.

Jade got to her feet and looped the strap of her purse over her shoulder. "I apologize if you were unhappy. My instincts are usually pretty good for clothes, but in your case all I had to go on was a voice. And judging by it, I imagined you to be..." She paused, looked into his eyes as he stood beside her. Then she looked away as though embarrassed.

He found that interesting and waited for her to go on.

She drew a breath, seeming to need fresh oxygen for fortification. "I thought you were single," she said, rushing the words, "and therefore childless, and that you were a sort of...a playboy."

He raised an eyebrow. "You got all that from an order over the phone?"

She hunched a shoulder. "Your voice was..."

Again he waited. And noticed that her knuckles were white on the strap of her purse.

She turned and started toward the pet shop. "Well, I can't see that it matters now what I thought about your voice."

He caught her arm and pulled her to a stop, glancing over her head to see that Andy and Ashley were still fully occupied with watching the kittens. He returned his attention to Jade, determined to let her know that this was not ending here.

"It matters," he said, retaining his hold on her arm. "The kiss last night mattered. You don't think I'm going to just let you walk away from me now."

She pulled against him. But he thought he detected a halfhearted effort.

"I think you have no choice in the matter," she said. "Only twelve hours ago you thought I was a thief!"

"I was stupid. Now I know I would be again if I let you go. Have dinner with me tonight."

She looked at him a moment in complete surprise, then her lips parted, as though she might agree. But she shook her head instead. "Tomorrow is Valentine's Day and I have a million things to do."

This time he let her go, but instead of running away from him as he'd expected, she simply stayed a pace ahead of him, headed for the pet store.

"You haven't answered my question," he said.

She kept walking, her low heels clicking on the tiled mall floor. "I told you I was too busy."

"The other question," he said, lengthening one stride to come abreast of her. "About what you heard in my voice."

She stopped abruptly and turned to face him. Her cheeks were pink, her eyes bright, her cool demeanor clearly rattled. "I thought you sounded sexy," she said briskly. "All right? You can add that to my growing list of mistakes."

She strode off and he stopped her again. "Come to dinner with me and let me prove that you weren't mistaken."

"I'm busy."

"You can't shop after five-thirty, no matter how many orders you have to fill."

"Evening is when I wrap everything. I'm busy."

All right. A change of approach was called for. "Okay," he said. "But I think we're missing something pretty big here, because you're not what I thought you sounded like, either."

He turned toward the pet shop where one of the kittens now stood on its hind legs, having a conversation with Ashley through the window. But before he could move in that direction, Jade caught *his* arm.

"What did you think I sounded like?" she asked casually, apparently trying to create the impression that she didn't care.

"If you're determined not to see me again," he said guilelessly, "what does it matter?"

Her eyes registered knowledge of his little game with a delicate roll to the ceiling. "You insisted that I tell you," she pointed out.

He pretended to consider before relenting. "Okay. I thought you sounded like a silly little blonde with a ponytail over your ear who'd found a way to make money out of your favorite pastime."

She frowned. "I'm not silly."

"If you won't go to dinner with me so that you can prove me wrong about you, and I can prove you right about me," he corrected, "you *are* silly."

He headed for the children and she kept up with him. He thought she might be vacillating.

"I really don't have time for dinner," she said, her tone satisfyingly unconvincing.

"I'll bring the kids," he offered deliberately when he was within earshot of them. They were on him like a hat.

"Bring us where? Where you going?" Andy came and insinuated himself between Jack and Jade.

"I'm trying to talk Jade into coming to dinner with us," Jack announced in all apparent innocence.

Ashley, his nuclear arsenal, caught Jade's hands and jumped up and down, pleading, until Jade had no recourse but to agree.

But she gave him a condemning look over the children's heads.

"That was..." She searched for the right word, apparently unwilling to be too denigrating in front of his children. She finally settled on "Ruthless."

He refused to apologize. "Stakes were high.

Ruthless and sexy, that's me. Deal?" He offered his hand.

She studied it a moment, then reached out to shake it. As the cuff on the sleeve of her coat drew back, he noticed that she was wearing the Pocahontas bracelet.

Chapter Seven

"WHAT DO YOU MEAN, sick?" Jack asked the housekeeper as she took his briefcase from him. "Both of them? They were fine this morning."

Isabel nodded, her manner indulgent and amused. "I believe their illness is of a romantic nature." When he looked confused, she added quickly, "*Your* romance."

He closed his eyes, shook his head and started up the stairs. "They're trying to help you, Mr. O'Brian," she said from the other side of the railing. "I'll be happy to watch them tonight. I have nothing planned."

He waved to let her know he appreciated the offer as he loped up the stairs.

Ashley, lying listlessly on her back, a favorite teddy bear clutched in her arm, looked like a victim of something fatal. Her face was chalky white.

Jack sat on the edge of her bed and thought he detected a powdery white residue on her cheeks, and the strong scent of baby powder in the air.

"Hi, Daddy," she said weakly.

He took her hand. It was warm and dry and also smelled of baby powder. "Hi, pumpkin," he said, pretending concern. "Isabel tells me you have the flu."

"Yeah." Her voice was a dramatic squeak. "Everybody at school has it. I don't think I can go with you tonight."

Aha. A plot.

"Are you sure?" he asked. "I was going to take Jade to Michelle's where they have those chocolate sundaes you like so much."

There was a moment's hesitation while she apparently weighed the loss of her favorite treat against the scheme she and her brother had concocted. But she decided on self-sacrifice. "Maybe you could take me next time."

He did his best to maintain a straight face and leaned down to kiss her cheek. "I think I'd better call Jade and tell her you're sick and that I can't—"

"No!" she said urgently. Then she added more quietly, "No. That would be rude. You should go and have a good time."

"Well, if you're sure..."

"I'm sure."

Andy was sprawled on his stomach in the middle of his bed, an arm hanging lifelessly over the side.

Jack sat beside him and rubbed gently between his shoulder blades. "How're you doing, son?" he asked.

Andy had a different approach. His cheeks had

been reddened by something with a cosmetic fragrance, and his fingertips had obviously been colored with something purple.

"I think...I have...a fever," the boy said, pausing now and then to gasp for air. He held up purple fingertips. "And I seem to have...poor circulation. But...I'll be fine. You go ahead...without me."

"Andy, I think you need a doctor," Jack said gravely.

"Ah...Isabel said the phones are dead."

"Really."

"Yeah. Um, she tried to call you to tell you we were sick, but...she couldn't get through. Sun spots, I think. They give NASA fits, you know."

Jack put a hand to his mouth to hide the smile. If his law firm ever failed, he intended to head for Hollywood with his own personal version of the Barrymores.

"But Jade was counting on seeing you and Ashley. Ashley has the flu, you know."

"Yeah...I heard." Andy launched into a coughing spasm. "Maybe you could...bring Jade here after dinner to...see us."

"I'm not sure I should go."

Andy rolled over laboriously and put a grasping hand to Jack's arm. "I want you to go, Dad. You need a little romance in your life. Please. It would make me happy. I won't die before you get home, I promise."

"Well—" he patted Andy's hand "—if you promise."

JADE OPENED HER DOOR and had to tell herself not to stare. Jack wore the black shirt, slacks and jacket she'd bought him for that working weekend, and though he'd insisted that they weren't his style, she congratulated herself on her intuitive choice. Every item was perfect for him.

And whatever he wore, his handsome dark features made him look like an ad for it anyway, so she didn't see the problem.

Despite her objections that morning, she'd anticipated dinner with him all day long. In fact, her preoccupation with it had made Lindy seem like the competent one in the office.

He reached out to the touch the kittens she held in each hand. "You did buy them," he observed.

"They're just what my customer ordered." She nuzzled each one, then put them in a lined basket she'd placed near a heating vent. They meowed in high, tiny voices and looked at her condemningly over the rim of the basket. "The question is whether or not I'll be able to part with them tomorrow. You boys be good."

She turned back to Jack and noticed that something was missing. "Are the children in the car?" she asked.

He shook his head, leaning a shoulder in her

doorway as she reached to the sofa for her coat and purse. "I'm afraid Ashley's come down with a sudden and violent case of the flu, and Andy's suffering from fever and poor circulation."

She frowned at him as he took her coat from her and helped her into it. "They were in cahoots with my housekeeper, who lent Andy rouge for his fever, eyeshadow for his purple fingertips and who dusted Ashley with enough baby powder to clog my plumbing."

She laughed as they stepped out in the hall and he pulled her door closed. "But I thought they'd want to come."

He walked beside her to the elevator. "You mean you don't see the motive behind it?"

Jade reached out to push the down button, then turned to him in perplexity.

"They've selected you," he explained, looking up at the lights above the car that indicated the elevator's direction. The down light lit, the bell rang and the doors parted. "Resistance would be futile."

He took her arm and drew her with him into the car. She couldn't feel his fingers through the sleeve of her coat, but his presence seemed to envelop her. He stood close beside her, his hand still on her arm as the elevator started down with the smallest jolt. Her shoulder bumped his chest and awareness of him made her feel suddenly as though she'd stuck her finger in an electrical socket.

She struggled to think straight, to remain in charge of her behavior. "Selected me...for what?"

"To be their mother." He replied with an easy calm she found surprising under the circumstances. She waited for him to laugh, to do something to make it clear that he was joking.

But his demeanor never changed from the sexy charm and confidence he'd exuded when she'd opened the door.

The elevator doors parted in the lobby of her building. He put an arm around her, resting his hand lightly on her shoulder, and led her out to his car.

"I trust you explained to them that you think of me as a thief and a screw-up?" she asked as he opened her door.

She found herself blocked into a very narrow space as Jack placed one hand on the top of the door and the other on the roof of the car. Her breath caught in her throat.

"But I don't," he corrected, a warm intimacy in his voice and in his eyes. "Lindy called my office and explained about getting the tags and packages mixed up when the skateboarder hit her. I think you were noble and a first-class employer to have taken the rap for your company."

Jade had that warm honey feeling again. "She means well."

"So do I," he said. "And I usually do my best to see that my children get what they want when I think it would be good for them."

She was speechless for a moment. He couldn't possibly mean what that seemed to suggest. Then she asked, her voice breathy, "I...thought that was...Natalie?"

His smile was self-deprecating. "No," he said. "Natalie was pretty potent stuff, but as you pointed out, she has little sense of humor. And when you're raising children, there are times when that's all that keeps you afloat."

She swallowed, feeling as though her heart were thumping its way out of her chest. "Have you missed the fact that if you let them choose their mother, you have to be a husband to their choice?"

"I'm a good lawyer," he said. "No fact ever escapes me. If you'll get in, we can be on our way."

"How do you know I have the requisite sense of humor?"

He grinned. "You bought the red chenille robe, didn't you?"

HE DROVE DOWN the coast several miles to a supper club called The Cove high on a bluff overlooking the ocean. Jade had often made reservations there for her clients, but she'd never been there herself.

It was decorated in a sort of 1930s, Art Deco style with many small tables with tulip lamps that provided enough light to read a menu while still protecting the table's shadowy intimacy.

It was a place for couples, not families, and a band across the room played moody, romantic music. In the darkness beyond the windows, one tiny, single glow from a lighthouse on Wrecker Rock blinked on and off at intervals.

Jade felt the spell of the place entwine itself with her determination to maintain control and do its best to strangle it.

Her dinner of sautéed shrimp, rice and sweet potato sticks was a culinary masterpiece, but she had difficulty concentrating on it.

Jack was charming, witty, and wielded the double-edged threat to her sanity of being both interesting and interested. Often a man who enjoyed entertaining a woman did so for the center-stage attention it gave him. But while Jack shared funny courtroom stories with her, he also asked about her work and gave her the impression that he'd be happy to listen to her talk indefinitely.

Then he reached across the table and caught her hand. His was warm and strong as he studied the Pocahontas bracelet on her wrist. His eyes looked up into hers, filled with amusement. "You're still wearing that."

"It was a gift," she said. "I tried to give it back to Ashley this morning, but she told me to keep it."

He tightened his grip on her fingers. The band began a bluesy arrangement of "Isn't It Romantic?" Without a word, Jack stood and drew her with him to the dance floor.

She was prepared to be taken into his arms. She alerted every nerve ending in her body to be calm, to avoid registering the impact it was sure to bring about.

What she wasn't prepared for was the sudden ignition in his eyes when he turned to her, the underlying darkness in their depths that suggested he'd been truly affected by something. By...her?

That sense of being plugged in ran under her skin again like vibrating voltage.

And when he lowered his head to claim her mouth, she lifted hers to him, power seeking its source.

Unlike when she'd kissed him, he took charge of this exchange, his hand cupping the back of her head, tipping it as he leaned over her. His mouth was tender but passionate and seeking, wanting to know every little detail of her emotions at that moment, claiming a response.

She gave over every secret—yes, I'm a little bit in love, too; yes, I want to know more; yes,

I'm afraid, but I'm even more curious than fearful.

Then she also gave him the response he wanted. She wrapped her arms around his neck and returned the kiss with all the hot emotion he'd brought to it.

And at that moment she felt the loneliness that had shaded her life ripped off it like an umbrella in the wind.

Jack enjoyed her response with all the awe he'd have felt if an arm had reached out of heaven and handed him a gift.

He didn't bother to wonder how it had happened. He knew that life could take things away as effortlessly as it bestowed them, so he'd decided some time ago never to waste time asking why. Fate expected that you accept or enjoy, whatever the situation called for.

It wasn't until Jade's head fell against his shoulder with a sigh and he was forced to raise his own that he remembered where they were. Not that anyone had noticed them. Other couples on the dance floor were gazing into each other's eyes, exchanging wordless messages of love and promise.

"We have to remember that it's only been two days." Jade whispered, looking up into his face. "And during one of those, you thought I was a criminal."

"I did not," Jack denied, forcing himself to

concentrate on moving to the music. "I was angry because I knew the whole thing with Natalie was a fiasco and that your mistake saved me from making a much bigger one. And I hated to admit that. So I yelled at you."

She laughed softly. "You don't think the fact that something worth two thousand dollars had been misplaced had something to do with it?"

He kissed her cheek to assure himself that she was real. "Maybe a little."

"Well, don't worry. My service promises the immediate return of any purchase that isn't satisfactory, so I'll take the bracelet back for you tomorrow and see that they credit your account."

"No need," he said, marveling at how perfectly she fit against him, her breasts embossed into his chest, her small waist nestled in his arm, the softness of the rest of her pressed near and around his frustration. He had to think to form words. "I have to...visit a client tomorrow, so I'll take care of it while I'm out. Should I exchange it for something you'd like?"

Her forehead rested against his chin, and without raising it she moved her left hand until there was a jingling in his ear. "Thanks, but I already have a bracelet."

Chapter Eight

"I DON'T UNDERSTAND," Jade whispered as she and Jack sneaked hand in hand around the house to the back door. "If they were clever enough to try to trick you into seeing me alone, won't they now be pretending to be in bed asleep?"

Jack shook his head over her innocence as he slowly turned the knob on the back door. "Once they get what they want, all pretense stops. Besides, all the *Star Wars* movies were being shown back to back tonight. Andy has his own boxed set of videos, but he still never misses it. And there's no school tomorrow."

"Ah."

Jack had been right. Both children, bright-eyed and exuding good health, sat on opposite sides of the housekeeper. Each held a bowl of popcorn and a can of pop.

Jade followed Jack into the living room. The moment the housekeeper noticed them, she clicked off the set.

Ashley ran to Jade, unabashed at being caught with no apparent sign of illness.

"Did you have fun?" the child demanded.

Jade perched on the edge of the sofa. "Well,

it was hard to have fun when we were both very worried about you and Andy. Did you get over the flu?"

"Ah...yeah." She spread both arms expansively as an expression of her complete cure.

Jade turned to Jack, seated beside her as he inspected Andy's hands.

"And your circulation's fine again?" she asked, noting no purple on his fingers. She put a hand to his cool cheek. "Your fever seems to be gone."

Andy looked from Jade to his father. "I guess when your body cools down, your blood flows better." He waited for their reactions, apparently finding his own story a little thin.

Jack nodded. "Fevers usually run their course over a few days. How do you explain your sudden recovery?"

Andy looked worried for a moment, then suggested hopefully, "It's a miracle?"

Jade's eyes met the amusement in Jack's. "Well, that explains it," she said.

She helped him tuck the children in. While Jack went back downstairs to retrieve the bear Ashley had left on the sofa, the child sat up in bed, her eyes wide in the light of a bedside lamp with a clown base. "Did you fall in love?" she demanded in a loud whisper.

The aggressive question almost shocked Jade into admitting that she had. But she caught herself in time. "You don't usually fall in love in one evening," she said, urging Ashley back to her pillows and drawing her blankets up. "It takes time to get to know someone."

"My dad and my mom fell in love at first sight," she argued. "That means right away. The first time you see somebody."

Jade could imagine a woman falling instantly in love with Jack O'Brian. "And they must have been very happy to have made two such beautiful children. But I do things more slowly."

"Why?"

"Because I like to think about what I'm doing."

Ashley considered that. "Daddy says you should always think before you act."

"That's very good advice." Jade reached behind Ashley's head to straighten her pillowcase, and the child reached up to flick a finger at one of the charms on her bracelet.

"You're wearing it!"

"Of course. A very special little girl gave it to me."

Ashley seemed pleased. "So you love me, even if you're too careful to love him yet."

Jack walked into the room with the bear, tucked it into Ashley's arm and leaned over to kiss her good-night.

Jade was sure Jack had heard his daughter's

remark, but he said nothing as they crossed the hall to Andy's room.

The walls were covered in posters of spaceships of every description, real and science-fiction. And over his bed was a poster of Harrison Ford as Han Solo, captain of the *Millenium Falcon* in the *Star Wars* series.

Jade pointed to it and laughed. "I had that same poster as a teenager."

Andy propped up on an elbow. "You like the *Falcon*?" he asked in amazement.

She leaned down to kiss his cheek, casting Jack a laughing glance. "No. I liked Harrison Ford. But this is a great way to prepare for what you want in life. Surround yourself with pictures of it and someday you'll have it."

"You think someday I'll explore the galaxy?"

"Absolutely. And I'll expect you to bring me orders for earth goods they can't get out there, then freight them back for me."

"You'll be my first contract," he said excitedly. He held his hand out to her and she shook it.

"I'll draw it up," Jack said.

Andy high-fived him. "It'll be a total family operation." He apparently missed the detail that Jade wasn't family. "We'll have to find something for Ashley to do."

"Can't she be in your crew?" Jade suggested.

He made a face. "No. I can't stand her. She'll

have to work on your end of things. Or with Dad."

"She wants to dance," Jack suggested. "We can book her a tour on your route, Andy, and you can keep an eye out for her."

"Well, where are you gonna be?"

"Here. With Jade."

He seemed to like that idea, but not when it left him with Ashley. "Maybe by the time we get this company off the ground, we'll find her a husband."

Jack kissed him good-night and led Jade back downstairs.

"Coffee?" Jack asked.

Jade wanted to stay, but the pull of his home and children was too strong for safety, and as she'd explained to Ashley, she was cautious by nature.

"Thanks," she replied, "but I should get home. Tomorrow is *the* day and I still have a dozen things to wrap. And I'm sure I'll be dealing with many last-minute calls in the morning."

She expected an argument and wasn't sure whether to be pleased or disappointed when he offered none. He drove her home and went up with her in the elevator to her door.

When she inserted her key in the lock, he prevented her from turning it by placing his hand over hers.

She looked up at him in surprise and found

him leaning over her. She parted her lips in surprise and he kissed her slowly, lengthily. Then he raised his head and smiled.

"You lied to my daughter," he accused gently.

She gasped in protest. "When?"

"When you told her you don't love me."

She slapped his chest for alarming her. "I'm not sure what I feel. And you can't possibly be sure, either."

He denied that with a self-assured nod. "Oh, yes I can."

"No, you can't," she insisted, her back pressed against her door by his nearness. On the other side of it, she heard the kittens meowing. "I know you fell in love with your wife at first sight...." When he looked surprised, she explained briefly, "Ashley told me." Then she went on. "But I'm not her. I'm careful and deliberate about everything."

"Well, I'm not," he said, his eyes going over her face, feature by feature, with disturbing intensity. "Being a litigator forces you to think quickly, to be decisive. I fell in love with you at first sight, too. It's the way I operate."

She made a face at him. "Then why did you send me shopping for another woman?"

"Because what you made me feel was bigger than I wanted to deal with," he admitted frankly. His eyes were now focused on her mouth. "And

I thought I could ignore it until I was ready." He laughed lightly, apparently at himself. "But love is power in motion with a life of its own. I saw your face when I closed my eyes. And when I didn't."

He claimed her mouth again and she opened for him, surrendering to the arms that pulled her so close that she felt two heartbeats.

It wasn't until needlelike little claws pierced her stockinged ankles that she came back to reality with a yelp.

Her condo door had pushed open and the kittens had raced out to explore. Jack gave chase, then swept one up in each hand.

She took them gratefully.

"Make no mistake, Jade," he said. "I love you."

JADE SPENT MOST of the night wrapping gifts because she couldn't sleep anyway. And the phone started ringing at seven with last-minute pleas for help, mostly from husbands and boyfriends who'd somehow missed the blanket advertising that filled the airwaves and every store window for weeks.

But she handled every order, delighted to be busy. She didn't want to think about Jack and the children. She didn't want to remember his touch and his lips, the gentle, indulgent way he dealt with Andy and Ashley, and the way they responded to him, confident in his love.

She didn't want to remember Ashley telling her that she knew she loved her, or Andy considering her part of the family.

They were precisely what she'd always wanted, what she'd dreamed every lonely night of having. But now faced with the possibility, she was confused to find herself terrified. How did she know she could give back all they offered?

Jack called at noon. That voice that had started it all made her think of him standing in her doorway in the black slacks and jacket she'd bought him. Every resolution she'd made throughout the busy day to put some distance between herself and him turned to dust.

"What time are you finished today?" he asked.

Lindy and several friends she'd recruited to help her were wrapping the last of the orders and preparing to deliver them. Lindy had been the epitome of efficiency today. Jade guessed that calling Jack and taking responsibility for the mistaken deliveries had given Lindy a new pride in herself.

"Pretty soon," Jade told Jack. "Another hour or so."

"Great," he said. "Can I ask a big favor?"

"What?" she asked warily.

"Isabel's son is down the coast on business

and wants her to join him for the rest of the weekend. The kids are at a neighbor's this morning, but only until two. I can take care of tomorrow, but right now I'm tied up at the office for another couple of hours, and I can't reach my mother. If I messenger you my house key, can you go to my place so somebody's there when the kids come home?"

"Ah..." She tried to resurrect her resolution to keep her distance.

"I'll pay you," he offered.

She made an impatient sound. "Jack, if you were here, I'd slap you for suggesting that."

"Oooh," he said. "Want me to come over?"

"Just send your key."

"Thanks. I love you."

"No, you don't."

"Yes, I do."

"We'll argue about it later."

"Count on it."

THE CHILDREN WERE delighted to see her when they got home.

"How come you're here?" Ashley asked, taking her hand and toying with the charms on the bracelet.

Andy's eyes widened. "And you gonna stay overnight?"

"No," Jade assured him. She explained about their father's call. "I'm just here because Isabel had to leave and your dad had to stay at the office for a while longer."

"That's great!" Andy stopped in the act of removing his jacket. "Can you take us downtown so we can buy Dad a birthday present?"

"Of course." Jade went to the guest closet where she'd hung her coat. "When's his birthday?"

"Today!"

Jade stared at him. "Today? He didn't say anything about it."

Andy caught her hand and pulled her toward the door. "He doesn't like anybody to make a big deal about it. Grandma wanted to have everybody over and bake a cake and all that stuff, but he told her he was too busy and it was too much work for her."

"Maybe *we* could have a little party," Ashley suggested.

Jade's mind began racing with possibilities. Shopping for birthdays, after all, was a major part of her business.

She opened the door and shooed the children out to her car.

Ashley bought her father chocolates because, as she confided to Jade without embarrassment, he was certain to share them with her.

Andy found a pair of boxer shorts decorated with hearts and arrows that glowed in the dark. He insisted they all crowd into a supply closet while the clerk turned off the light and held up the shorts so that Andy could measure the effectiveness of his purchase. He laughed uproariously when the outline of the hearts and the arrows that pierced them shone bright yellow.

Jade bought a cake at the bakery. The children chose one decorated with a hunter with ducks flying overhead and a Labrador at his feet. Green trees made of pipe cleaners trying to resemble a forest decorated one edge.

Jade stopped at her condo to pick up a set of birthday paper plates and napkins and gift bags with tissue so that the children could wrap their purchases.

Ashley found a kitten toy on the floor. "Did you take the kitties to the lady?" she asked. "Did she like them?"

"Her daughter picked them up on her lunch hour," Jade replied, ushering the children toward the door, "and she was going to take them to her mom tonight."

"I hope her mom likes them."

"Yes. So do I."

By the time they arrived back at Jack's house, there were three cars in the driveway. None of them was his.

"That's Grandma!" Ashley shouted, pointing to a small crowd of people standing on the porch. "And Aunt Donna and Aunt Di!"

The children were out of the car before Jade

turned the motor off. She peered into the twilight to see Selina and Ross and Diane, whom she'd met the other day, and another woman and two men she didn't recognize. Almost everyone held a casserole dish. Two toddlers were running in and out of the crowd.

"Jade! Hi!" Selina called to her and met her halfway up the stairs. "Oh, I'm so glad you're here, too. It's Jack's birthday today!"

"So the children told me. Jack asked me to watch them for a couple of hours because Isabel went to visit her son."

"Well, this couldn't be more perfect. I have Jack's key at home, but I didn't think to bring it because I thought she'd be here. Can you let us in?"

"Yes," Jade answered, then realized how that sounded. "Well, he messengered it to me so I could be here when the children got home."

Selina looked surprised that she insisted on explaining. "Yes, dear. Well. We've brought dinner and you seem to have a cake there." She patted the top of the wide, pink bakery box Jade carried, then laughed wickedly. "If Jack thought his birthday was going to pass uncelebrated, he really doesn't know his mother after all these years."

Chapter Nine

JACK PATTED THE BOTTLE of Moët & Chandon on the seat beside him as he rounded the corner half a block from his home. He had Jade right where he wanted her. She was in his home, which was where he intended to keep her for a lifetime. By now, after several hours, his children had either charmed her into submission or worn her to a nervous nub. Either way, she would be his to charm and seduce.

He was sure if he could only make her feel what he felt, she would be his. That wary look would vanish from her eyes when he held her and she would turn her back on the fear love always brought, and surrender to the joy.

Then he spotted the cars lined up in his driveway and felt a primal scream rising in his throat.

"No. Oh, no," he said aloud as he pulled into a spot on the street behind Jade's car. "Not tonight."

He adored his family, but they had an uncanny knack for bursting into his life like a class-five hurricane precisely when he needed quiet.

He sat alone in the car for a moment, trying to brace himself. The house would sound like

Patio Pizza on tournament night, and he wouldn't get a moment alone with Jade, much less an opportunity to seduce her.

Before he could even begin to enjoy his self-pity, the front door of his home opened, lighting the night, and Donna ran down the porch steps in something white and silky. She was followed by a tall man he didn't recognize, who was throwing his suit coat over her shoulders.

Donna intercepted Jack halfway across the front lawn and wrapped her arms around him. "Jack! Happy Birthday! This is Henry Powell. Henry, my brother Jack. He's the reason we found each other!"

In the darkness only partially illuminated by the coach light on his lawn, Jack took the hand Henry offered and recognized a kindred spirit. The handshake was firm, the smile wry. Henry would rather have Donna to himself tonight, Jack concluded, than be at a family party.

"Glad to meet you," Jack said. "But I'm sorry you were dragged here. I imagine you had other plans for tonight."

Henry's grin suggested he was right, but he denied it graciously. "Donna assures me I'm in for an exciting evening. I give you fair warning that your mother's brought Trivial Pursuit."

"Oh, God." Jack noticed the crowned head of a Macanudo cigar protruding from the pocket of his shirt. "Let's stay out on the porch. You can smoke and I'll inhale the aroma."

Henry's grin widened as he patted the breast pocket of the jacket over Donna's shoulders. "I have a couple. Meet you out here later."

Donna got between them, took each man by an arm and led them toward the house. "He didn't come to smoke with you," she said to Jack. "He came to fawn over me."

Henry patted her hand. "I can do both."

From the moment he entered the house, Jack caught only occasional glimpses of Jade in the crowd. He was toasted with the champagne he'd bought for quite another purpose, he was forced to sit at the head of his table while an endless parade of wonderful dishes came past—some old family favorites and a hot Thai concoction his mother and Ross had put together, then he had to hold court near the fireplace while everyone tried to find answers to questions so obscure, God Himself probably didn't know them.

Then he was sung to and made to open presents.

"And not one of us hired a shopping service," Diane said nobly, winking at Jade who stood beside her on the fringe of the group collected on the carpet. "We all did it ourselves."

"*We* hired Jade," Andy admitted, then added by way of explanation, "well, we really didn't *hire* her, 'cause we didn't pay her. But she helped us buy Dad's presents."

"Yeah," Ashley added. "And she bought 'em, too, 'cause we didn't have enough money."

"Get out while you still can." Diane's husband, Todd, with a squirming toddler in each arm, shouted advice from the other end of the group. He wore jeans and a sweater and a cynical smile. "Or before you know it, you'll be shopping for free for all of them. There are birthdays in every month, they celebrate *everything*, even Groundhog Day."

"That's because it sometimes falls on *my* birthday," Diane said, giving him a playful glower. "And there are only eight of us—actually, our twins make nine, but that's only eight birthdays—so there can't be a birthday every month. There are no birthdays in January, April, September and October."

Ross, sitting in a corner of the sofa, with Selina in the curve of his arm, raised his hand. "Sorry, but I'm an April birthday. And I do like presents. I can provide you with sizes and color preferences."

Everyone groaned. They'd made it clear that they liked him.

"I hate to add to your woes," Henry said. He and Donna sat on the floor back to back. "But I'm January twenty-third."

The groan grew louder.

Diane turned to Jade. "And I suppose you were born in September?"

Jade shook her head. "No."

There was a communal sigh of relief.

"October seventh," she said, laughing.

As everyone groaned again and teased her, Jack wondered if anyone else noticed the wide-eyed edginess under her laughter.

He passed around the chocolates from Ashley, and everyone thought it hysterically funny when the box was returned to him empty.

Andy flipped off the overhead light so everyone could enjoy the unique mastery of the glow-in-the-dark boxers.

Jack caught Jade's eye and noticed that her expression had changed subtly to one of softly smiling sadness.

Trying not to panic, he continued to open gifts and unfolded a dark blue sweater from his mother and Ross, a boxed set of John Grisham films from Diane and Todd and the boys, and a box of the coveted Macanudo cigars from Donna and Henry.

His mother carried in an enormous cake, and despite his pleas and protests, his family sang to him.

"Who picked out the cake?" Diane wanted to know.

"We did," Andy and Ashley said in unison.

Diane smiled and indicated the hunting design on it. "But your dad doesn't hunt."

Andy shrugged, as though that had no bearing on it. "I know, but we liked the dog. Can I have a corner piece?"

JACK'S FAMILY LEFT just before eleven, everyone crowding around the cars, exchanging hugs and kisses and last-minute gossip. They hugged again before getting in the cars and driving away.

Jade helped Jack put the exhausted children to bed, then went to the guest closet.

"Whoa," he said, reaching beyond her to push the closet door closed before she could retrieve her coat. He pinned her between himself and the door, a hand to it on either side of her head. "Where do you think you're going? We haven't had a chance to say a word to each other all evening."

There was panic and sadness in her eyes. He forced himself to remain calm about that, but reacted to it in what he knew to be a purely male fashion.

He drew her into his arms with one hand to the back of her head and the other to the small of her back, and held her tightly against him to obliterate the distance between them the evening had brought about. He kissed her with all the longing built up in him since the night before.

He was relieved when she responded. She

wrapped her arms around his waist, leaned into him trustingly and kissed him back. Her hands moved across his shoulders over his cotton shirt, down the middle of his back to his waist and lingered there.

He ran a hand over her hip, holding her tightly to him with it, wanting her hand to wander over him.

But she heaved a ragged sigh and drew a step away from him. And he noted worriedly that while her body had responded to him, her eyes remained troubled.

He entwined his fingers behind her waist, unwilling to let her go.

"I know my family's scary," he admitted, hoping to make her smile. She did, but thinly. "But they're not really dangerous. They just think they have a right to know everything, and then tell you how to handle everything. But it comes from a genuine interest in your welfare."

"I thought they were wonderful," she said, her voice strained and quiet. "I even really liked our mistakes—Ross and Henry."

"They were *your* mistakes, Jade."

"All right. I accept the blame."

"No." He shook her lightly. "I want you to accept the credit. My mother's always happy, but now she's downright ecstatic. And Donna's been lonely for a long time. Henry seems so right for her."

Jade's thin smile became rueful. "And you'll be able to bum his cigars."

"Compatibility is essential in-laws." All right, he accepted. The kiss hadn't restored her to him because, he guessed, whatever the problem was wasn't physical. He had to look deeper. "I'm sure you didn't fail to notice how much they all like you."

"I didn't," she said quietly.

"Then, what's wrong?"

"I don't think you'll understand."

"Then you underestimate me." He kissed the top of her head, then drew her into his shoulder and led her to the fireplace. He pointed her to a comfortable, upholstered chair, added a log to the fire, then turned to see that she'd ignored the chair and folded gracefully to a sitting position on the carpet. Her legs were tucked under her and she leaned sideways, braced on a hand as she smiled up at him.

He stretched out beside her, propped up on an elbow and waited for her to explain.

"I had wonderful parents," she said abruptly. The firelight flickered in her hair and across her pale cheeks. He noticed that with a pang of foreboding but forced himself to concentrate on her words. "I missed them so much after the accident and quickly decided that the only way to deal with the loneliness was to find a wonderful man as soon as possible and fill a house with children.

Loneliness isn't just being alone, you know?" She turned to him, the lingering pain clear on her face. "It's the emptiness you feel when there's no place to put your love. But, then, I guess you know that. I'm complaining, but you lost your soul mate."

"I did." He and Rita had met in college and they'd been friends from the beginning. When she'd died, he'd felt as though everything of consequence inside him had been ripped away.

"But I had my children and my family," he said sympathetically. "You were alone."

"Oh, I adjusted. I got a good job, then I started the business." She gave him a teasingly aggressive glance. "At which I usually do very well. You are one of very few dissatisfied customers."

"I'm not dissatisfied at all," he corrected. "Except that we're talking instead of making love."

He'd thought that remark might make her smile, but it had the opposite effect.

"Yeah, well, see...I'm thinking that maybe the whole thing isn't quite as easy as I thought."

When he said nothing, panicked by her words but afraid to press her, she turned to him. "You know what I mean?"

"No," he said frankly.

She shifted to sit cross-legged, arranging the full skirt of her dress over her knees so that she looked a little like a flower-faced ornament on a red wool base.

He pushed himself to a cross-legged position and sat facing her.

She spread her hands helplessly. "It's just so much harder than I thought," she admitted, her voice taking on a higher note, the words coming out with a kind of desperate speed. "I mean, I've always been loving and caring, but with friends and their children and with customers, not necessarily with...men. And now that I've met the right one, I realize how...how..."

Jack experienced instant relief. She'd admitted he was "the right one." He'd find a way to deal with everything else.

"How silly you are to be questioning it?" he suggested helpfully.

She made a face at him. "No."

"How ungrateful you must seem to the Fates who brought us together?"

She tried to silence him with a look. "I'm trying to tell you what I feel. Do you want to listen or not?"

"It depends," he replied. "Are you going to keep talking nonsense?"

She sat up stiffly, hands on her knees like some very elegant swami. "You consider my feelings nonsense?"

"I consider you questioning your ability to love me nonsense. You do. Just admit it."

"I'm not questioning that I love you," she explained in exasperation. "I'm questioning my ability to return the love you and the children are offering me."

"That's ridiculous." He wasn't about to give her an inch on this. "You're doing it."

"But your family are like gold medalists in loving!"

"You said your parents were, too."

"But when I returned their love, I did it as a child. Now I'm an adult. It's a completely different thing. I have to be everything you need. I have to anticipate the children's needs. I have to—"

He silenced her with a kiss. She pushed against him for an instant then succumbed, all her inherent instincts leaning into him as he'd known she would.

"Every time I touch you," he said, "you open up and invite me closer. Every time the children reach for you, you envelop them. That's all love is."

"I have to go." She pulled out of his grasp and scrambled to her feet. She caught her coat and purse and hurried out the door to her car.

He followed, knowing he couldn't make her stay. Well, he could, but he shouldn't.

"You're acting like a crazy woman," he accused without anger as she climbed in behind the wheel.

She rolled down her window. "I'm trying to protect you."

"I don't want protection," he said, deciding on the spur of the moment that if they were going to battle this out, they may as well go for it. "I want you to marry me."

She stared at him. "You're insane!" she said finally.

"Then we're made for each other. What do you say?"

She backed out of his driveway with a squeal of tires.

Chapter Ten

JADE WAS HALFWAY HOME before she realized she still had Jack's house key. He probably had another, but what if he didn't?

Cursing herself for having forgotten that detail, she turned around in the nearest driveway and reversed direction.

But she wasn't going into his house. She wasn't even going up to the door. She would leave the key in his mailbox and call him to tell him where it was.

Being near him was just too hard. Wonderful, but hard. She'd been shopping for a man like him her whole life, and here he was. The deal of the century with two children added in the bargain.

Only, she was finding she couldn't make the deal. They were all perfect specimens now. What if she married Jack to make herself happy—as she wanted so much to do—then discovered that she'd ruined life for him and the children?

She was a great shopper, but she never kept anything. She delivered it to the person who'd ordered it, or to the one they'd ordered it for. She didn't care for things, they simply passed through her hands.

But Jack didn't understand that. Love was easy for him. He'd been born into it, nurtured by it, shared it with a special woman and their children.

Jade had been born into it, but lost it too soon and had never seen it again until now, when she no longer knew what to do with it.

Her plan might have worked if Jack hadn't been standing on the porch, lighting a cigar.

But he saw her turn into the driveway. She tried to stop the car and run out to the mailbox and back in the time it took him to put out the cigar. But before she'd even opened the box, he was kissing her, his hands moving over her, lifting her off her feet.

She tried to tell him about the key but he was reshaping her lips with his own, preventing her from forming words.

He probably thought she'd come back because she'd changed her mind and couldn't bear being away from him. An uncluttered little corner of her mind accepted that she had.

He carried her into the house and up the stairs into his cool, dark room. He set her on her feet and unzipped her dress.

"Jack!" she whispered urgently.

He framed her face in his hands and kissed her gently, reverently. "What?" he asked.

She wanted to tell him that she'd come to return his key, that she was still afraid to be a wife and mother, that under the circumstances, making love might not be the wisest course of action.

But he was kissing her again and holding her with such unutterable tenderness that the only words she could speak were, "I love you. I love you."

When Jack heard her say the words, his emotions went nuclear. They were more than he could express, more than he could contain.

And they were in his fingertips as he drew slip, bra and panties from her and caressed the glistening moonbeam beauty of her breasts and hips as he tossed the blankets back and put her in the middle of his bed.

He tried to straighten to remove his own shirt and pants, but she had a hold of him and wouldn't let go.

He was surprised but delighted by her boldness when she pulled him down beside her, knelt astride him and kissed him senseless. When he could draw breath again, he found that she'd unbuttoned his shirt. He sat up to help her pull it and his T-shirt off.

Then she strung a line of kisses from his left shoulder to his right, and when he thought he might lose control over the tenderness of the gesture, he felt her hand at the zipper of his pants and knew that his sanity was in danger, as well.

He kicked his slacks and briefs off, pulled her down beside him and leaned over her to plant a kiss on her navel. She gasped with pleasure and he spent long moments bringing the sound out in her again. He stroked every line of her, explored every curve and hollow.

He'd intended to move over every inch of her with his lips, as well, but she stole his plan and started with the underside of his chin and down the length of his throat.

He kissed her forehead, intending to simply follow her, trailing his lips over her ear to her shoulder as she placed kisses down the center of his body.

He remained coherent until she approached his waist, then, knowing she wouldn't stop, he battled her gently for control.

She fought back mercilessly with tender kisses and a wandering hand.

He caught her fingers and held them away from him, placing his own over her femininity.

She made that gasping sound of pleasure again, complaining raspily, "That isn't fair!"

"It is. If you'd have touched me first, I'd have lost all reason."

"I didn't think lovemaking was about reason."

"It's also not about conversation." He covered her lips with his, felt her arch against his hand, and when he was about to congratulate himself on taking control, her hand closed over him and his mind went blank in an instant. As he went over the edge into madness, he wondered if she would ever know what was good for her.

Jade had been unaware that her body held such secrets. Pleasure came from so deep inside her, flowed over and over her until she wondered if she could bear any more; then it placed her in a kind of silken shadow where she was herself again, but the rest of the world didn't seem to exist.

The moment was all about her. Every sense was sharp, every muscle poised, every thought hopeful. She couldn't remember a more wonderful point of time in her entire life.

Then the world came into focus again and she realized that she was sprawled in Jack's arms as he pulled the covers over them.

The thought intruded that this had been too easy, that emotional love would be a lot harder than this, but the world was simply too perfect at that moment to allow her to analyze that thought and decide what it meant to her future.

JACK KNEW the instant she fell asleep. The tension in her ebbed and the breath that had been all gasps and cries only moments before was now even and steady. She had an arm wrapped around him, and a leg hitched over him, and he accepted unconditionally that he was her prisoner for the rest of his life.

He closed his eyes, thinking that he couldn't imagine a more worthy fate.

But his last thought as he drifted off was that he'd have a lot to answer for in the morning. When she'd pulled into the driveway tonight and he'd run to her, he'd seen the key ring looped on her finger. He'd known that she'd come back to return it.

He'd also known that there'd been another, deeper reason behind the key, and she'd proven him right.

He just didn't think *she* understood that.

JADE OPENED HER EYES to see rays of sunlight on the opposite wall of the bedroom.

She knew instantly that it was not her bedroom. In fact, as the memories of last night danced through her mind, she had every suspicion that this was not even her life. It couldn't be. She was lonely Jade Barclay. She didn't know how to be this happy.

Jack's side of the bed was empty.

She noted that in relief and scrambled into her clothes, looking at the sunshine again and wondering what on earth had happened. The sun never shone in February on the Oregon coast.

Last night had even changed the weather.

She was zipping her dress and stepping into her shoes, escape uppermost in her mind, when the bedroom door opened and Jack stood there looking fresh and wonderful in slim-legged jeans and the sweater his mother had given him for his birthday. The blue seemed to burnish his skin and dramatize his dark features.

"Hi," he said, his eyes growing instantly wary as he watched her dress. "Ashley's making breakfast," he said absently. "Cocoa Puffs or toast with peanut butter?"

She pulled a comb out of her purse and turned to the mirror to avoid his eyes.

"I've got to go, Jack," she said.

He came to stand behind her and caught her gaze in the mirror. She kept her eyes on her hair.

"It's Sunday," he said. "The Valentine's Day rush is over."

She straightened the part in her hair and drew the comb through the tousled mess. "But my place is a wreck and I have paperwork to—"

Jack turned her around, took the comb from her and tossed it at the bed near her purse. His eyes were turbulent.

"I thought we settled that 'you-don't-know-if-you-can-love-me' thing last night," he said.

She wasn't going to be bullied into dismissing her fears. "My concern wasn't for loving you physically," she told him, folding her arms.

He tipped his head back impatiently and rested his hands on his hips. "Jade, last night was every kind of love there is. Physical, emotional, even spiritual. We were heart to heart, not just body to body."

"That was one night, Jack. Now we're faced with the rest of our lives."

"Yes, we are. But I'm the one who's done this before, remember. I know every moment isn't going to be like last night. But it has the potential to be wonderful in big and little, and loud and quiet ways, because we're wonderful together. Don't you see that?"

"I think we should just wait," she suggested, thinking that she sounded eminently reasonable, "and see how things go. And in a couple of months—"

"You," he interrupted, "are a lily-livered coward."

She gasped again, only this time it wasn't with pleasure. "Jack, I'm just trying—"

"Don't give me that, Jade," he interrupted again. "Don't tell me you're protecting me, when you're really protecting *you*. And if you think I'm going to date you a couple of times a week for months while you take something big and wonderful and try to cut it down to size so you can deal with it, you're mistaken. And, incidentally, who told me in the throes of passion last night that lovemaking wasn't supposed to be about maintaining control?"

"Making love and making *life* are not the same thing!"

"I beg to differ. They are. You go into both wholeheartedly, you give them everything you've got, you maintain a willingness to be generous and a sense of humor and you have one hell of a great time."

She didn't get it. She looked at him as though he were some picture the Hubble Telescope had sent back from space.

He wanted to shake her, or make love to her again until she saw reason. But knowing neither alternative would work, he did the only other thing he could think of.

He handed her her purse.

She ran.

Chapter Eleven

JACK'S CHILDREN WEREN'T speaking to him.

When he'd told Ashley that he didn't know if Jade was coming back, she'd burst into tears, stomped up to her room and slammed the door.

Andy asked questions. "What did you do to her?"

"Nothing," Jack replied. "But we disagree on a few important things."

"You always say people have to compromise."

Right. Remember the lessons I try to teach only when they can be used against me.

"There are a few things you can't compromise on. Especially if you expect to live the rest of your lives together."

"Like what?"

"Like how to love each other."

Andy frowned. "But you love us all the time."

Jack felt pathetically grateful for that one positive stroke for his side. "Yes, but she's the one who doesn't think she'd be good at it because she's never had a husband and kids before."

Andy looked stricken. "You mean she'd love you if you didn't have us?"

"No," Jack reassured him quickly. "I think she loves *you* and she'd do something about it if you didn't have me."

Andy grinned. "Then we'll send you to Grandma."

Jack folded the Sunday sports section and bopped him on the head with it.

Ashley came downstairs wearing tights and a tutu. She'd gotten the outfit secondhand from a friend, and the left thigh had a three-inch run in the pink mesh. She was also wearing her paper crown from Burger King.

She came to lean her elbow on the kitchen table next to where Jack and Andy sat.

"I'm mad at you," she told Jack.

"No kidding," he said. "I didn't know that."

She studied him suspiciously. She was very bright, but subtlety was often lost on her. "You're being funny, aren't you?"

He rubbed an ache between his eyebrows. "Actually, I don't feel very funny at all. Do you want some lunch?"

"No. I want Jade."

"So do I," he said. "But I'm afraid that's beyond my control."

"I know why she's mad at us." Ashley climbed onto his knee.

"She's not mad at you and Andy," he corrected. "She's mad at me." Then, desperate to find a way through to Jade, he asked, "Why do you think she's mad?"

"'Cause we didn't give her anything for Valentine's Day."

Andy sat up. "Yeah!" he said eagerly. "What could we get her that would prove that we really love her, and that we like the way she loves us?"

Jack stared at his children as an idea began to take shape in his head and quickly developed into a plot. His children, he thought with great pride, were brilliant.

His family insisted they got that from their mother, but right now it didn't matter where the inspiration came from, only that he had it.

JADE WAS DUSTING the lids on the rack of spice jars. The chore was desperate and ridiculous for a Sunday afternoon but she'd reorganized the office that morning, having filled out the form to reorder tissue and ribbon, cut out more tags and caught up on her paperwork. And when she stopped moving and doing, she saw Jack and his children in her mind.

When she'd left Jack's house that morning, she'd kissed each child quickly, and without stopping had explained that she had work to do at home, then had escaped to her car.

And ever since then her brain replayed images of their surprised and disappointed faces, and the insightful expressions in their eyes that told her they knew something was wrong, that the happy world they'd imagined with their father and her wasn't going to happen after all.

She told herself repeatedly that she was trying to protect them, but that brought Jack's image to mind, jaw firmed implacably, eyes angry and unforgiving when he'd told her he didn't want protection.

She was about to remove the lamp shades and dust the tops of lightbulbs when the doorbell rang. A small gray-haired woman dressed in a black coat, a crushed velvet hat with a brim and a pair of black Nike sneakers stood in the hallway with the two gray kittens in the basket.

Standing beside her was the woman's daughter who'd hired Jade to make the purchase.

The older woman thrust the basket at Jade. The kittens meowed. Jade held the basket in one arm and reached in to pet one tiny head, then the other. They accepted the attention eagerly.

"Kittens were a ridiculous idea!" the woman said. "As if at my age I'd want to have to feed them and chase them around. I was hoping for a new purse, or a gift certificate to Denny's." She gave her daughter a look of disgust. "But I get kittens." She turned to Jade, her thin-lipped little mouth set in a firm line. "Well, they'll have to go back. I don't have the time or the patience for them. I'd like a purse instead."

She held up the one she carried. It was a simple, three-compartment square of black leather open at the top. One of two handles was pulling away from the body of the bag.

"Like this," she said. "Maybe a little bigger. When I have lunch out, I like to have room in it to bring half home for dinner. Thank you. Come on, Susan."

The woman headed for the elevator with a stride that belied the claim that she couldn't chase kittens.

Susan smiled at Jade apologetically and rolled her eyes. "I'm about to give up. She lives alone in a pretty little cottage near the water but there is absolutely nothing in her life to give her pleasure. She won't let me put in flowers around her place because then she'd have to water them or hire someone to do it. And she won't have a dog because they bark. I thought kittens would be good because they fend for themselves so well."

She heaved a sigh and glanced over her shoulder. Her mother had reached the elevator and was pressing the button.

"I should have known better," she said, turning back to Jade and reaching a hand into the basket to pet the kittens. "Emotional investments have always been too much trouble for her."

Jade sympathized with Susan, who'd been so excited about her inspiration to give her mother kittens. "I'm sorry. I'll find a great purse for her." Then she smiled. "Do you want the change, or shall I put a gift certificate to Denny's in the purse?"

Susan laughed. "Yes, please."

"Susan!" the older woman called. "Elevator's here. Let's go!"

Susan drew a breath and squared her shoulders. "But you know what?"

"What?"

"I'm not giving up. Easter and Mother's Day are coming. Help me think of *some*thing that'll reach her."

Jade couldn't help but wonder if that was possible. But her job was to find the right thing for her clients. "I'll work on it," she said.

"Good. Thanks." With a parting pat for the kittens, Susan was gone.

Jade sat in the middle of her office floor with the kittens and a spool of ribbon and felt the first little spark of cheer in her life since she'd left Jack and the children.

She watched the lively little kittens race around, chasing each other and the ribbon, jumping in and out of their basket and hiding from each other behind it, and failed to see how anyone could resist falling in love with them.

"How could anyone be unwilling to love something so—" The thought stopped abruptly as her brain processed it as illogical in view of what she'd done that morning.

She'd been unwilling to love. She'd looked

ahead into a future that would undoubtedly demand all her physical and emotional resources and decided she was unprepared to meet it. She'd been afraid that having been alone so long, she would offer a love that was imperfect or incomplete—and so she'd chosen to offer nothing.

She got to her feet as the cold realization broke over her that in a couple of years she could find herself alone in a pretty cottage with no flowers and no kittens. And she wouldn't even have a daughter determined to reach her.

She could have sworn she heard the crash of thunder over her head as her spirit absorbed that new wisdom.

Then it crashed again as she remembered how Jack had looked when she'd walked out on him—hurt, angry, disappointed in her.

She knew a paralyzing sense of hopelessness. She might have experienced an epiphany, but it could very well be too late to save her relationship with Jack and his children.

She dialed Jack's number. The phone rang eight times before she finally hung up. So he and the children had gone out and forgotten to turn on the answering machine. Or chosen not to, so he didn't have to deal with a message from her.

She tried several more times, and the longer the phone rang without being picked up, the more desperate she became to hear Jack's voice, to see him. She felt more stranded and alone than she'd ever felt before she'd met him. And she became more and more convinced that he was staying deliberately out of touch.

Well, she thought fatalistically. That answered that question.

At least with the kittens around, she wouldn't have to resort to dusting lightbulbs.

THE DOORBELL RANG at four-thirty in the afternoon. The kittens scampered along as she ran to the door and unlocked it. Then she picked up a kitten in each hand and shouted, "The door's open! Jack?"

"No, ma'am. Ralphie." A tall young man in the blue-and-red uniform of a delivery service held a small padded envelope out to her. Then, seeing her handfuls of kittens, tucked his clipboard under his arm and took them from her. "Will you sign the sheet, please?" he asked, turning to the side so she could take the clipboard.

Surprised and confused—and disappointed that he wasn't Jack—Jade dropped the package on a nearby chair and signed the sheet. They juggled the exchange of kittens and clipboard, then he pulled the door closed after him with a polite thank-you.

Jade put the kittens down. They scampered off to attack the spool of ribbon as she sat in a corner of the sofa with the package.

Was it from another unhappy client who'd wasted no time returning an unfortunate choice of gift? she wondered.

The envelope had been stapled closed and she ripped it open, pulling a flat square box out of it. The white box with the *B* in gold script for Blumenthal's was instantly familiar.

Her heartbeat began to accelerate. She pulled the lid slowly off the box and screamed. The kittens stopped midfrolic to stare at her like two little statues, green eyes wide, backs arched.

On a bed of glittered cotton lay a simple gold key ring. On it was a key Jade recognized as Jack's. And the bauble on the key ring was a simple gold band with a heart-shaped diamond on it the size of a garbanzo.

Hands shaking, Jade looked inside the envelope again and found a note card embossed with the scripted *B*. With shaking hands she opened it. "Dear Jade. This is the key to our home, our hearts, our lives. Please let yourself in. Love, Jack, Andy and Ashley."

Jade screamed again. The kittens ran into the kitchen.

NIGHT HAD FALLEN and Jack still hadn't heard from Jade. He paced nervously the length of the living room, a child on either side of him, trying to keep up.

"What do we do if she doesn't come?" Ashley asked at a full trot.

"Simple," Andy replied for him. "We go get her. Right, Dad?"

Jack was beginning to believe that was the only way this was going to turn out in his favor. He wasn't usually one to resort to Neanderthal tactics, but he was rapidly losing patience—and hope.

"Right, Andy." He turned resolutely toward the guest closet. "Get your jackets. We're—" He stopped abruptly at the sound of a car in the driveway.

Andy ran to the window, Ashley pushing herself between her brother and the chair to peer through the drapes.

"It's her!" Andy shouted. "Dad, she came!"

Ashley ran to the door, but Jack stopped her from opening it with a shout.

"But, Daddy—"

"We're not sure why she came yet," he said reasonably. "She might just want to give me back the ring. We have to wait and let her do what she's come to do."

"She's coming up the walk," Andy reported from the window. "And she's got something in her arms."

"What?"

"Looks like a basket."

Great, Jack thought. He was waiting for a declaration of love and she was bringing cookies.

Ashley pushed between Andy and the window. "She's ready to knock, Daddy!"

There was a small commotion on the other side of the door, but no knock.

"What's happening?" Jack demanded of Andy.

"We can't see!" Andy said. "The post is in the way!"

Jack suppressed an impulse to run to the door and yank it open. He folded his arms to stop himself from fidgeting and stood his ground, several yards from the door.

Then, like a miracle, he heard the sound he'd longed to hear since the moment he met her. It was the sound of a key in the lock. His key. Her key.

It turned and she stumbled into the front hall, clutching a basket in her arms. It seemed to have a life of its own, spinning out of her grip, climbing her, then tumbling out of her arms, spilling two balls of gray fur.

"The kittens!" Ashley screamed in delight and ran off in pursuit as they dashed for the sofa.

Jade looked as though she'd been to war. Her coat was off one shoulder, her hair was atumble and her purse had fallen to the floor with the basket, the contents scattered across the hallway tile.

But Jack's heart lurched against his ribs as he noted that her smile was bright and filled with love—and focused right on him.

"Hi, honey," she said with a little laugh. "I'm home."

REMINGTON AND JULIET

Rebecca York

Dear Reader,

We've always considered Valentine's Day our own special holiday—a time to celebrate love and romance, no apologies needed. So we were delighted when Debra Matteucci, our editor, offered us the chance to write a Valentine's story.

A note from Eileen Buckholtz:

I love everything about Valentine's Day, most of all my annual Cupid's Brunch with family and friends. For weeks I search the local craft stores for decorations and gag gifts, then on party day we enjoy a bountiful spread of delicious food and have fun designing personal greetings for each other.

A note from Ruth Glick:

When I was fifteen, my father had just died and I realized how sad my mother was going to be on Valentine's Day now that the man she loved was no longer with her and there would be no one to give her a special card that year. No one except me. I don't recall the exact card I gave her, but I remember how my mother's face lit up when she opened it. Ever since then I've thought of Valentine's Day as a time to say things to the people I love that I might not tell them in the midst of our hectic lives. Each year I write personal messages to my husband, son and daughter. I know from the ones I get back that I've cemented a family tradition of making Valentine's Day a time to express the love we feel for each other.

Rebecca York

Chapter One

STATIC INTERRUPTED Juliet Hartfield's favorite old Rod Stewart song. The sun disappeared behind a wall of dark clouds, and a sudden gust of wind whipped a tree branch across the top of her car as she turned in at the gateposts of the Remington estate.

"Bad omens," she muttered, then tried to laugh off the silly flight of superstition. Since when did stable, sensible Juliet Hartfield go around looking for omens?

Since she'd been stupid enough to agree to this foray into enemy territory. Remington territory.

The driveway wound through stands of tall oaks with brown leaves still clinging to the spreading branches. They rustled in the February wind as Juliet rounded a curve and encountered another warning, this time in the form of a sign that said Trespassers Will Be Shot.

She gave a little snort. That sounded like Grant Remington's work. At least the way her cousin Larry Lancaster had described the man, although she had trouble believing *anybody* could be that rotten and not have already gotten himself arrested. Among other things, Larry had told her

Remington's construction company had used substandard building materials on a number of housing projects and that he'd ruined a competitor by consistently underbidding on jobs. He'd driven away his wife by making their marriage a living hell. And most shocking of all, Larry had insinuated that Remington had hired a hit man to knock off his own mother so he could inherit the family fortune.

Juliet gave a little shudder. Then she reminded herself that Larry had a tendency to spin tall tales about the Remingtons—since he seemed to have inherited the family mantle of "Keeper of the Feud." Her ancestors, the Lancasters, and the Remingtons had been at odds with each other since Zebulon Remington had jilted Anabel Lancaster almost a hundred years ago.

Now her family had a chance to score some points on the opposition. Grant Remington was planning to sell some family antiques, many of which had been bought at rock-bottom prices from the Lancasters. And he'd hired her to appraise and catalog them—without knowing that she was a Lancaster descendant. Larry wanted her to undervalue the pieces. Juliet had agreed only to appraise them conservatively. Her other mission was to get some proof of Grant's illegal activities.

As the oaks gave way to evergreens, she slowed the car, thinking it wasn't too late to turn around. Being thrust into the role of spy made her queasy, yet she'd promised Larry she would do her best to uphold the Lancaster honor.

Lost in these conflicted feelings, she didn't see the mansion until she was almost on top of it. It commanded a little rise in the center of a landscaped lot that had once been well tended. Now it was ragged around the edges—like the sprawling house with its flaking wood trim and shingles faded to a dirty gray.

It appeared Grant Remington had decided to do something about the disrepair. A utility van with lumber stacked on top was parked in front of the house, and a workman had turned the wraparound front porch into a carpentry shop. Clad in a pair of dusty jeans and a plaid shirt, he was leaning over a table saw, cutting through a new board. He didn't look up as Juliet pulled into a parking spot across the driveway and climbed out of the car. Afraid to distract him and cause an accident, she waited for the saw to stop buzzing, her interest quickening as she took in the details of the man.

He had thick dark hair that curled over his collar, broad muscular shoulders and one of the nicest pair of buns she'd seen on a guy. Apparently he wasn't bothered by the frigid temperature, because he took his time with the board, his bare hands white against the unfinished wood. His legs were long, and as he straightened, she saw that he was close to six feet tall.

Taking several steps closer, she cleared her throat. "Do you know where I can find Mr. Remington? I'm supposed to meet him here."

"No problem."

He turned, and she found herself staring into a pair of compelling eyes, eyes as dark as midnight.

Grant Remington's eyes, she realized, sucking in a startled breath as she remembered the candid shots Larry had given her. She'd thought Remington was handsome, with a very fortunate combination of high cheekbones, firm jaw and aquiline nose. The photos hadn't done him justice.

She'd also thought she was prepared for Grant Remington. But she wasn't prepared for those eyes. They were sexy and perceptive, and despite the chipper greeting, they were a little wary. Most of all, they made her stomach tighten with nerves and awareness.

His guarded look vanished so quickly that she wasn't sure if she'd really seen it. It was replaced by one of masculine confidence. He might be dressed like a workman, but he stood above her on the porch with the assurance of a tribal chieftain or the president of a Fortune 500 company.

She'd seen that arrogant look before—on men who had been stabbed in the heart and weren't taking any chances on it happening again. She couldn't believe that was the reason Grant Remington was making it clear he held the power in the relationship, because she knew he didn't have a heart to stab. He proved the point by giving her a thorough inspection, starting with the ankles and calves showing beneath her skirt and traveling upward past her hips, waist and breasts. It wasn't a subtle appraisal. But she hadn't expected the man to be subtle. She clenched her hands at her sides, stifling the impulse to pull her coat closed or pat her blond hair into place.

"Miss Hartfield?" he asked.

"Are you Mr. Remington—playing carpenter?" she countered, trying to shift the balance of power. Although she'd prepared carefully for this meeting, it wasn't starting off the way she'd imagined.

He wiped his hands on the sides of his jeans, scattering sawdust. "I'm not playing at anything. I'm repairing woodwork."

She forced a little smile, sorry she'd let her reaction show. "I didn't expect you'd be doing the work yourself. Don't you, uh, have a company to run or something?"

"I've scaled back."

"Oh" was all she could say. Another surprise.

When he didn't offer further explanation, she marched up the steps. "I'd like to get started on the job. I have a commitment this evening, and I want to get back before it's too late." The last part wasn't exactly a lie. She had a firm date to settle down in front of the TV and watch a movie that evening.

"I'm sorry," he said, throwing her off balance again. "I should have been ready for our appointment, but I was trying to get one more piece of board cut before you came." Holding the screen door open, he ushered her into a front hall as large as most people's living rooms. It was also as cold as a deep freeze, making her suspect he'd left the front door open most of the day. She could see where his work boots had left clumps of mud on the marble floor.

"I'll be back in ten minutes," he said. "Why don't you have a look around the first floor. I'm selling most of the pieces you'll see—before I unload the house."

"I didn't know you were getting rid of it."

"Keep that confidential. The last thing I need is a bunch of real-estate agents camping on the porch."

He turned and started up the stairs, making her wince at the trail of dirty footprints on the cream-colored runner. She also noticed he was favoring his right leg. As she wondered how he'd injured himself, he stopped and faced her again.

"Don't go into the back of the house," he called from the landing.

"Why?"

He shifted his weight from one foot to the

other. "I've been tearing up the floor, and I don't want to get sued if you hurt yourself."

"I'm not planning to sue you."

"Good." The word was left hanging in the air as he turned and marched up the rest of the steps before disappearing around a bend in the hall.

IMMEDIATELY ON TURNING the corner, Grant slowed his pace and ordered his pulse and respiration to return to normal. He must have sounded like a jerk, with those remarks about real-estate agents and lawsuits. The comments had sprung from his jangled nerves.

Probably he'd be better off directing his pique at his friend Cameron Randolph. He'd called Cam last week for advice on appraising the Remington relics so he could sell off the collection and get on with his life. Cam had recommended an "established firm" called Antique Authentics. Somehow during their conversation, Grant had gotten the impression that Juliet Hartfield was an older woman, not a stunning little blonde with shoulder-length hair, big blue eyes and just the kind of figure he liked—gentle curves in all the right places.

He closed his eyes but couldn't banish her image. Cam knew his taste in women, all right, and had set him up with the perfect candidate to tempt him out of his self-imposed exile from female companionship. Except that no woman was perfect. He'd learned that lesson the hard way with Cynthia.

He'd parted with a sizable chunk of the Remington fortune to get out of that bad marriage. Although the maneuver had horrified his lawyers, he considered the money well spent. And it would be a cold day in hell before he let himself get twisted around again by an appealing female.

Scowling, he unzipped his dirty jeans, skimmed them down his hips and kicked them savagely into a far corner of the large bathroom, making his bad leg throb.

"Damn." He was supposed to be careful, but he rarely remembered until it was too late. At least there was nothing wrong with his arms, he thought, as he wadded up his shirt and pitched it after the pants.

Of course, the way his life was going, he had to take his little victories where he could get them. He'd weathered enough nasty surprises over the past year to last him for the next hundred. He was still doggedly trying to get his life back together, and he didn't need any distractions. Right now he was hoping that Juliet Hartfield didn't know a Revere porringer from a Wedgwood thimble. Then he could pay her for the afternoon and send her on her way. But first he was going to cool down in a cold shower.

JULIET STOOD on the cold marble floor staring after Remington's departing figure. When she realized her mouth was hanging open, she snapped it closed.

Sue him! The nerve. She'd never sued anyone in her life. She wasn't that kind of scheming person.

The hot denial was followed by an uncomfortable constriction in her chest as she remembered that she hadn't exactly come here with honorable intentions. Probably the best thing she could do was write Grant Remington a note saying that she'd changed her mind about taking the job, although that wouldn't be very good for her business reputation. And then there was Larry. She'd given him her word. She had to stick this out, at least until she could make some kind of report.

With a sigh, she laid her winter coat over the banister and set her briefcase and purse on the floor. At least she ought to take advantage of the opportunity Grant Remington had given her, the opportunity to prowl around unimpeded.

As she started down the hall, she slipped her hand into the pocket of her blazer and wrapped her fingers around the brass skeleton key Larry had given her. Two inches long with a heart-shaped ring at one end, it had been passed down to his parents from Grandma Lancaster and was supposed to unlock a chest or a box that had belonged to her family. Inside were valuables or papers or something else important that Larry was sure the Remingtons had acquired through unethical or illegal means. Juliet had trouble believing that the box could still be locked, but she'd promised to investigate.

A short walk brought her to the living room, a huge space decorated with stunning Adams-style relief work around the fireplace and along the ceiling line. The formal couches and chairs, however, looked stiff and uncomfortable. A caustic smile formed on her lips as she imagined Grant Remington sitting awkwardly in one of the chairs, his bad leg at an uneasy angle. Shocked at herself, she canceled the image. She wasn't supposed to be thinking about him or wondering how he'd hurt himself. She was supposed to be using this opportunity to reconnoiter.

Stalking down a side hall, she pulled open the first door she encountered and found herself in a more comfortable room. It had dark paneled walls, a well-used leather couch and a boldly patterned Turkish rug. This was more like it. She could picture Remington sprawled on the sofa, a drink in his hand and his feet up on the scuffed coffee table as he watched a football game on TV. What did he drink? she wondered. Stepping across the threshold, she peered at the magazines haphazardly stacked on the end table.

She gave herself a little shake. She was doing it again—focusing on the man. His tastes in beverages and reading matter weren't her concern. But if he kept any papers in the desk...

As soon as the idea surfaced, she grimaced. Ancient history was one thing, but in all her years of going into people's homes, she'd never deliberately pried into anyone's private correspondence. Maybe she'd have to tell Larry that pillaging was beyond her capacity.

Making a quick exit, she found the dining room. Back to formality, with an enormous table that looked like it would seat the Baltimore Symphony Orchestra. Behind it was a mammoth china cabinet crammed with serving dishes, figurines and several sets of china—one in the Blue Willow pattern.

The latter was on the list Larry had carefully compiled from a number of sources, the list of Lancaster property sold to the Remingtons when times were tough. Next to the china service was a pretty little burled walnut chest with brass bands, a piece she wouldn't have expected to find in the dining room. The lock looked too small for the key, but she might as well give it a try.

She was reaching toward the chest, when a sound from the hall made her freeze. Palming the key, she turned to find Grant Remington striding into the room. He'd swapped his work clothing for a blue button-down shirt tucked into a pair of gray wool slacks, and traded his work boots for black loafers. His dark hair was damp, and she realized he must have taken a quick shower before dressing. In his dusty jeans he had looked good, but cleaned up, he was absolutely devastating. She forced herself to show no reaction; instead she stared at a Blue Willow teapot.

"Are you including the contents of this china cabinet in your inventory?" she asked, casually slipping the hand with the key back into her pocket.

"That's my intention," he said acerbically.

At the sharp tone of voice Juliet stiffened. Why was he suddenly angry? Unless he'd caught a glimpse of the key...

GRANT HAD BEEN HOPING that when he came back downstairs, he'd realize he'd exaggerated Ms. Juliet Hartfield's appeal. No such luck. She was just as captivating as he remembered. He'd obviously startled her, and she stood with her face slightly flushed and her eyes bright. He wanted to reach across the distance between them and run his fingers through the golden strands of her hair.

Instead, he shoved his hands into his pockets and came out with one of the dumbest observations he'd ever heard himself make. "My friend who recommended Antique Authentics said your company had been in the business for more than twenty-five years. Did you start as a baby?"

She laughed. "Close. My mom started working in an antique shop in Ellicott City six months after I was born, and she dragged me down there in an infant seat. When I was eight, she bought her own shop."

"She still works with you?"

"She passed away two years ago."

"Oh. I'm sorry."

She nodded. "I have an arrangement to sell some pieces from the lobby shop at 43 Light Street," she continued. "But my main focus is appraising."

"Why?"

"I'm good at it."

"So what can you tell me about this thing? Is it worth much?" He casually picked up one of his mother's prized pieces, a hideous Italian teapot, and bobbled it in his hand.

Her eyes dilated, practically overwhelming the blue. Fascinated by the reaction, he almost didn't hear her next words.

"Be careful with that. It looks like a piece from the factory of Charles of Bourbon. That means it was produced between 1743 and 1759."

He snapped his attention back to business. He was supposed to be finding out what she knew, not watching the color of her eyes change. "How do you know?"

She lifted the pot from his hands. Holding the lid securely in place, she turned the piece over and showed him the fleur-de-lis incised on the bottom. "It was made in Naples, before Charles came back to Spain and succeeded to the throne."

He watched her put the piece back on the shelf. Before his mother's untimely death, she'd been fond of spouting that same information to guests.

Turning on his heel, he led Ms. Hartfield around the first floor, quizzing her on various pieces—a seventeenth century toasting fork, a Charles Boulle cabinet, a pair of Huguenot candlesticks. She was familiar with them all. Still, she answered his queries in a voice that became increasingly sharp, and he knew he was making her nervous.

JULIET REPLACED a nineteenth-century figurine on the shelf, wincing as it came down harder than she intended. She recognized intimidation when she encountered it. Grant Remington was deliberately trying to make her nervous.

Not because he knew why she was here, she told herself quickly. He couldn't possibly know. "If you think I'm not up to the job, Mr. Remington, say so," she demanded in a voice that was as steady as she could make it. If he declined her services, she'd be off the hook.

Remington didn't answer immediately, and she felt her heart start to thump inside her chest.

An unreadable expression crossed his features. "I want to give you the assignment."

"Then why the twenty questions?" she shot back, her gaze focused over his left shoulder and toward the French doors at the other end of the room.

He shrugged. "I think I'm entitled to judge your expertise."

"Then—" The sentence died in her throat as her brain suddenly registered what her ears had been hearing and her eyes had been seeing through the panes of glass thirty feet away. "Oh, no."

"What?" Following the direction of her gaze, he whirled to face the double doors where elongated droplets of frozen rain slanted down from the darkened sky, pinging against the windows and splatting to the ground. "It wasn't supposed to sleet," he muttered. "I'd better cover the stuff on the porch."

She scowled, thinking about the worn tires she'd been planning to replace on her car—as soon as she could spare the time. "I have to get back to town while I can still drive," she blurted. "I'll be in touch with you to set up a schedule when I can work." Without waiting for an answer, she walked rapidly down the hall and pulled on her coat.

"Wait!"

"I'll call you tomorrow," she announced over her shoulder as she picked up her purse and briefcase and opened the front door. A gust of wind almost blew it out of her hand.

Although it was only three in the afternoon, the winter sky had turned the color of ashes, and the temperature felt twenty degrees lower than when she'd arrived. Shivering, she turned up the collar of her coat and started across the porch.

The wind blew a stinging spray of icy droplets across her face, but it was a relief to put some distance between herself and Grant Remington. He disturbed her—because of the things Larry had said, she told herself. But she knew it was more than that. She didn't like lying to him—or reacting to him, either.

Shading her eyes, she looked around in dismay at the transformed landscape. A coat of ice shimmered on the grass, encased the tree branches and glazed the driveway.

Remington had followed her outside and was tossing heavy sheets of plastic onto his materials and equipment. As he stepped in her direction, she moved quickly onto the stairs. Almost immediately, her foot skidded, and she grabbed the icy railing to keep from falling.

"Watch out!" he called behind her.

"I'm fine," she shouted into the wind, even as she realized that it was even worse out here than it looked. With careful, tiny steps she made her way more cautiously onto the driveway. But after getting only two or three feet, she slid on a patch of ice. Windmilling her arms, she managed to tumble forward, ending up on her hands and knees.

Remington must have been watching her, because she heard him pounding down the steps, heard him slip and almost fall on the ice as he gained the driveway. But he kept his footing and made it to her side in a couple of seconds.

"Are you okay?"

She drew in a shaky breath and let it out. "Mostly."

"Anything hurt?"

"Only my dignity."

He nodded. "If you can joke, it can't be too bad." After handing her the purse and briefcase, he helped her up and began to move her in the direction of the house.

"No." She tried to pull away. "I have to go home."

Somehow Remington kept them both on their feet. "Not with this ice."

On a little sigh, she acknowledged defeat. Trying not to wince, she let Remington help her back up the steps, into the house and down the hall to the cozy room where she'd assumed he hung out. "Sit down." He gestured toward the sofa.

It hurt to stand, so she sat.

"Let's see your knees and your palms."

"Why?"

"I want to see if you're injured."

Feeling strangely light-headed, she turned her hands over and looked at the raw, red scrapes where her flesh had slid along the driveway. When she pulled up the edge of her skirt, she saw her knees were similarly abraded—under torn panty hose. Looking up, she saw he was taking in the view.

"I'll...uh...get some soap and water, and some antiseptic," he said, making a quick exit.

Juliet tugged at her panty hose, wincing as the fine mesh came away from her wounded flesh. She was in such a state that she found she was dragging down her panties along with the stockings. When she heard her host's footsteps coming back down the hall, she pulled frantically at her underwear, yanking it almost back into place before Remington strode through the door. He was balancing a basin of water on top of a metal box but came to an abrupt halt when he saw her tugging at the skirt hiked around her thighs.

Imagining the picture she must make, she felt her face go red.

"Let me help you," he said in a thick voice, kneeling in front of her. She braced for the touch of his hand against her thigh, then realized she'd misread his intentions as he grasped one ankle and began to slip off her shoe. From anyone else, it would have been an impersonal gesture—dozens of shoe salesmen had been this intimate with her, she reminded herself—yet the brush of this man's warm, strong fingers sent little shock waves along her nerve endings. From the way he went momentarily still, she sensed that he felt it, too.

He switched on a table lamp, isolating the two of them in a little pool of light in the rapidly darkening room.

She wanted to run. She was supposed to be afraid of him. And she was. Yet it wasn't the kind of fear Larry had schooled her to expect. Her throat felt tight, and she was seized with an overwhelming urge to hide somewhere in the dark. There was nowhere to go, though. The best she could do was lean back against the sofa cushions and shut her eyes.

She tried to sit very still as he untangled the nylon from her feet, but the hand lingering for a moment on her instep made her quiver.

"Are you okay?" he asked.

"Yes," she managed to say. Then felt the warm, wet cloth as he gently but efficiently cleaned the wounds on her knees. When a piece of grit made her wince, he apologized softly.

"It's okay," she murmured, wondering if he heard the catch in her voice.

When she caught a strong medicinal scent, she tensed, bracing against the anticipated sting.

"It won't hurt."

He wasn't lying. There was no burning, only

a sensation of cold. Then he took one of her hands, and she caught her breath.

"Relax."

She couldn't manage relaxation, although she willed herself to sit still while he cleaned and medicated first one palm and then the other. But she was melting into the sensation of his fingers pressed firmly to her wrist while he stroked a gauze pad over her abraded flesh. His hands stopped moving. As the seconds stretched, her eyes opened and focused on his face. His unguarded expression almost took her breath away.

Their eyes locked, and she was helpless to prevent her own vulnerability from showing.

"Thank you," she whispered.

He only nodded, and she wondered how his voice would sound at this moment. Would it be thicker? Deeper?

He didn't give her a chance to find out. Making a speedy exit, he carried the first-aid kit from the room.

When she realized she was staring at the doorway through which he'd disappeared, she turned toward the window. While Remington had been tending her injuries, night had crept up on them. Outside it was dark, except for several spots of light from fixtures under the eaves of the house. In their illumination she could see a cascade of white falling from the sky. The sleet had changed to a swirling blizzard.

A gust of wind tore out of the northwest, driving the snow into a blinding curtain against the window. As the old mansion shuddered in protest, an image of the house and landscape buried under a blanket of white flashed into Juliet's mind. And here she was, sitting and waiting for it to happen.

No thank you! She wasn't getting snowed in with Grant Remington.

Her heart pounding, she pushed her feet into her shoes, grabbed her coat and bolted off the couch, gritting her teeth as a stab of pain shot up her leg. She hardly slackened her pace, though, in her dash for the door.

Halfway across the room, she came to an abrupt halt as both the inside and outside lights flickered and died. Darkness enveloped her, a thick, smothering blanket that pressed against her lungs, making it impossible to draw a full breath.

As a little girl she'd been afraid of the dark, but she'd thought she'd mastered that fear long ago. Suddenly, in this creaky old mansion with her nerves already tight enough to snap, the fear came slamming back. She couldn't think. She could only act on instinct—instinct that wiped out any impulse toward rationality.

Hardly knowing where she was going, she started to run and careened into the edge of a small table by the door. The table overturned and crashed to the floor.

She knew she should stand still before she did some more damage in the darkness. Yet she couldn't. The walls seemed to be closing in around her, and all she wanted was to feel the cold outside air against her heated skin. She clenched her fists and bolted through the door, grazing her shoulder on the way out of the room.

"Juliet? Are you all right?" Remington's voice came from what she judged was the top of the stairs.

She answered with a low sound as she stumbled down the hall, her hand on the wall to keep her bearing. In her panic, she'd lost her sense of direction. But it didn't matter where she was going, she told herself. Eventually she would find a door and blessed freedom.

"Stop. Not that way," a sharp voice called after her.

Too focused on escape to pay much attention, she quickened her pace. As she rounded a sharp corner, chilled air and the smell of subterranean dampness wafted toward her. She stopped abruptly, but it was already too late. Her hip collided with a wooden barrier. She screamed as she found herself losing her balance and pitching forward, hanging in midair over an abyss that she couldn't see.

Chapter Two

THERE WAS a scrambling noise behind her, and Juliet felt strong hands catch her, pull her back even as she felt herself starting to plummet into the well of darkness below.

She felt her body sag as Remington tightened his hold, dragging her farther back, around the corner where the air was warmer and drier. Closing her eyes, she made no protest, letting him take her where he would. He didn't stop until they had traveled several yards, leaving the unseen pit behind them.

With a deep, shuddering sigh, he leaned back against the wall, bringing her with him.

For heartbeats, neither of them spoke. As her mind came to grips with what had almost happened, she felt little tremors race across her skin. She was sure he felt the reaction, because he pulled her more tightly against the hard length of his supple frame. His arms felt like a safe harbor. Squeezing her eyes closed, she pressed her face against his shoulder. She'd only stay in his arms until she was breathing normally, she told herself. Yet the moment stretched. Instead of pushing away from him, she found that she was burrowing closer, unable to deny herself the comfort of his warmth and the protection of his embrace.

Perhaps the dark around them made a difference, she thought as she breathed in the masculine scent of soap and spicy aftershave. She couldn't see his face, couldn't guess what expression she might encounter. All she had to go on was his body language. It was welcoming, comforting, and it imparted a subtler message—that he needed the contact as much as she.

When his hands moved, it was to find her shoulders, where he kneaded her taut muscles before starting to stroke the tight cords of her neck.

"It's all right," he soothed. "You're all right."

"Yes," she answered in a voice so soft, she could barely make out the sound. But she knew from the way he drew in his breath that he had heard.

She moved her face against his shoulder, giving herself over to the sensations of being cared for—by Grant Remington. It should feel wrong. It felt strangely right.

They held each other in the darkness for long moments, neither of them speaking. Yet it couldn't last forever. She sensed a change in him as his fingers stilled, and she wondered if he had just realized how intimately they were standing. Quickly he pulled his hand away from her neck.

She raised her head, wishing she could see what was written on his face.

"I told you not to go back there," he growled. "What were you doing?"

She swallowed hard. "I—I'm afraid of the dark. I got scared when the lights went out, and I got turned around." That was part of the truth. She wasn't planning to add that she'd been equally afraid of getting stranded here with him. She didn't want to speculate on what had happened between them during the past few minutes, so she shifted the conversation to a more neutral topic.

"Why is there a big hole in the middle of the floor?" she asked.

"A pipe was leaking in one of the upstairs bathrooms. It ruined the wood. Come on. Let's go back to the den."

When he laced his fingers with hers, she let him guide her back to his enclave. They moved through the pitch darkness of the hallway, yet his footsteps were sure and brisk, despite his limp.

"I guess you know your way around the house."

"I hope so. Billy and Pat and I used to play hide-and-seek back here."

She wrinkled her brow, wondering if the information Larry had given her had been misleading. "Billy and Pat? Did you have brothers?"

He laughed. "Billy was the chauffeur and Pat was the gardener."

She tried to absorb the information. "Your parents let you play hide-and-seek with the staff?"

"Well, my parents were away a lot. When Mom was home, she was busy. Sometimes she didn't pay much attention to what I was doing."

His voice was carefully neutral, yet she could hear wistfulness below the surface. It seemed his parents hadn't lavished a great deal of time and effort on their son and heir.

His strides lengthened as if he was signaling that the conversation had been terminated. Stepping through the doorway of the den, he grunted as he bumped his shin on an unexpected obstruction.

"My fault." She was glad he couldn't see the chagrin plastered across her face. "I guess I knocked over a table in the dark."

He stooped, found the table and set it on its legs with what sounded like a louder-than-necessary thump. Then he led her across the room to the sofa. "Will you be okay if I leave you alone for a little while? I'm going to get a light."

Huddling into the sofa cushions, she wrapped her arms around her shoulders and tried to buffer herself against the cold blackness. Although the house had never been warm and cozy, it suddenly felt frigid. Trying to keep her teeth from chattering, she rubbed her arms and wondered what was taking Remington so long.

THE WIDE BEAM of the flashlight cast eerie shadows around the workroom as Grant searched for the old lantern that Pat liked to use when the power went out. They would need two lights, he told himself. Still, he was honest about his immediate motives as he searched through cans of dried-up paint and glass jars of assorted, nails, screws and bolts. He was stalling while he tried to get some perspective on the interaction that had just transpired between himself and Juliet Hartfield. Unfortunately he didn't come up with any deep insights. The best he could do was admit that holding her in the dark had made him feel as punchy as if he'd been knocked upside the head. He couldn't even remember much about the stupid conversation afterward, except that he'd blurted out some stuff about his childhood he never told to anyone.

When he realized he was standing in the middle of the little room holding the lantern, he set it down on the worktable with a thunk and opened a drawer, looking for matches.

Juliet Hartfield was a complication he didn't need in his screwed-up life, he told himself. He didn't need to be susceptible to feelings and impulses. For a panicked moment he pictured himself packing her into his van and roaring away, taking chances on the slippery roads if only to get her home and out of his life. But he knew that was impossible. He had to stay with her here. Take care of her. Keep her warm. Get her something to eat. Fix a bed for her near the fire. As he cataloged the emergency measures, he silently admitted that he wanted to do all those things—and more.

Picking up the lantern with a jerk, he headed back to the den. When he saw her huddled on the couch with her coat pulled firmly around her body, he felt his chest tighten. Then he came up with another of his piercingly insightful observations: "Let's get you warmed up."

"Can I help you?" she asked through chattering teeth.

"Just stay put."

After pulling on the leather jacket he'd tossed over a chair in the corner, he turned to the pile of logs and kindling stacked on the hearth and began to build a fire—working until he'd coaxed a roaring blaze from the wood.

When he turned, Juliet was leaning forward, sitting with her hands extended toward the blaze. The pose was casual, yet he detected an undertone of tension.

"So why were you running down the hall?" he asked.

She hesitated a moment before answering. "I

wanted to leave—to get some distance between us."

"Is the idea of spending the night here with me so upsetting?" he asked, then cursed himself for the choice of words.

"You've made me nervous ever since I got here," she said in a small voice.

He thought about the way he'd tried to intimidate her. He wasn't going to explain his motives. Still, an apology wouldn't be out of order. "I'm sorry. I've been edgy lately."

She kept her face toward the fire. "It's not all your fault. It's partly my reaction to you. I mean..." Her voice trailed off into silence.

"What?" he demanded, wishing he hadn't been such a bully.

Her hands fluttered. "I guess I'm attracted to you. That's not appropriate under the circumstances. I'm here to catalog antiques."

He had been prepared to defend his disagreeable behavior. Instead he stared at her, feeling every nerve ending in his body quivering. "Anything's appropriate if two people want it to be," he heard himself saying. "I mean—" He didn't know what he meant, so he closed his mouth. He couldn't imagine that he'd deliberately gotten himself into this conversation or that she'd confided such personal feelings. He could have confessed the same thing, of course, if he'd wanted to lay his cards on the table—which he didn't.

Was she telling the truth? If not, what was her motivation? Unfortunately he could supply an answer easily enough, based on his relationship with his wife. Women said things for the effects they created, not necessarily because they were true.

"I guess I shouldn't have confided that," she said with a catch in her voice. "But I've never been comfortable with...dishonesty."

"Good," he replied, hoping it was true. If there was anything Cynthia had taught him, it was that dishonesty was the most dangerous trait in a woman.

"I'm counting on you to be a gentleman."

"I'm always a gentleman," he retorted, thinking about the way he'd kept his mouth shut during the divorce, when Cynthia had made him sound like a first cousin to the devil. He'd told himself he didn't care what anybody thought about him.

He was starting to care now.

But Juliet probably hadn't seen the slanted stories in the *Baltimore Sun,* he decided in the next breath. She wouldn't have taken the job if she'd known his reputation. And she wouldn't be saying the things she had just now, either.

She busied herself pulling out a pair of gloves.

"We'll both feel warmer after a hot meal," he said.

"Don't I wish."

"I'm not kidding. I've been camping out here for a couple of weeks, and I've had the power off while the electrician has worked on the wiring. I've got a propane stove and a sleeping bag."

She nodded gravely, and he wondered why he kept bringing up the subject of sleeping. To test her reaction? He already knew she was nervous.

He was glad the darkness hid his expression. He was nervous, too. Yet he was starting to enjoy himself.

"Come have a look at my canned food collection."

"Is that like being invited to look at your etchings?" she replied with a teasing lilt to her voice.

"More satisfying, I hope."

She stood gingerly, and he handed her the flashlight. He took the lantern and led her down the hall to a vast kitchen with gourmet appliances. Unfortunately, none of them was working at the moment.

The supply of food was on one end of the counter. He'd shamelessly indulged himself in some of his childhood favorites. When her flashlight beam illuminated a can of beefy ravioli, he wondered what she thought of his taste.

She didn't comment; instead she picked up a can of chunky beef soup. "I've had this before. It's pretty good."

"I'll heat it up," he said with relief. "And

there's some seven-grain bread from a new bakery in the shopping center down the road." At least the bakery had a gourmet reputation.

He gave her the can opener while he lit the portable stove. Then he borrowed the flashlight and rummaged in the cupboards for a saucepan.

He was glad for the activity. The way she bustled around, he figured the feeling was mutual. While the soup heated, he sliced some bread and searched in the pantry for a few other supplies—like a bottle of vintage Bordeaux. But by the time the soup was hot, the kitchen was beginning to feel like an arctic wasteland. When Juliet poured the soup into mugs, her hands were shaking, and he could feel his own fingers starting to stiffen.

"Can we eat in front of the fire?" she asked, her teeth chattering as she spoke.

"My thought exactly."

He put the food on a tray and they headed back to the relative warmth of the den.

"Pull over the coffee table and I'll set this near the hearth," he instructed. "That is, if you don't mind sitting on the floor."

"That's fine."

"We'd better save the batteries on the flashlight, in case we need it later," he said as he set down the tray.

She appeared to consider the wisdom of the suggestion, then turned off the light.

The room was illuminated only by the soft glow of the kerosene lantern and the fireplace flames. The effect was intimate.

"It's like pioneer times," she whispered. "When a sea of darkness covered the land, and people huddled in tiny puddles of light."

He'd never have put it that way, but the darkness did have its advantages. He watched the soft light of the flames flicker in Juliet's hair and on her face. It was easy to picture himself moving up behind her, taking her in his arms and warming her with his body the way he had when he'd snatched her back from the edge of disaster. Without warning, he felt a twinge of the fear that had seized him when he realized she was in danger. He hadn't been able to see her in the darkness. But somehow he'd known which way she was headed. Toward the gaping pit he'd left in the floor of the hallway. A shudder went through him as he thought about what might have happened.

He said nothing, fighting the raw need to reach for her, to experience again the sweetness of holding her, of feeling her cleave to him. She'd claimed she was attracted to him. He'd been afraid to put any faith in the words. But the way she'd melted against him had imparted its own silent message.

He didn't realize he'd made a low sound in his throat until she looked questioningly toward him.

"I—I'm starving" was all he could manage.

"Me, too."

He reached for a slice of bread and began to eat, knowing full well it would do nothing to sate the hunger he was feeling.

JULIET TOOK A SLICE and struggled to spread it with stone-cold butter. Giving up the effort, she nibbled on the crust as she tried to relax. Although she had never been much for idle conversation, she cast around for some comment to fill the void.

"This room is different from the rest of the house," she said.

"You mean it's comfortable?" As he spoke, he worked at opening the bottle of wine.

"Informal. Did you furnish it?"

"My father used to hide out in here. I guess my mother didn't have the heart to change it after he died."

He poured them both a glass of wine, then raised his in salute.

She clinked her glass against his. "You said you're selling the house," she murmured after taking a small sip.

"I haven't lived here for over ten years. I don't want to live here now. I'm just getting my mother's affairs in order."

"She's gone."

He nodded. "She was killed in a hit-and-run accident."

She had read about it in the *Baltimore Sun*. And then there were Larry's disturbing accusations....

Fighting to conceal a shudder, she asked, "How did it happen?"

"She was out jogging," he said in a low voice. "I felt partly responsible."

Juliet felt her heart skip a beat. "Why?"

Several seconds passed before Remington replied. "I knew she was upset about something, but I couldn't get her to tell me what it was. Maybe if she'd let me help, she would have been in a better mental state, she would have been watching where she was going."

The answer was completely unexpected. So was the pain in his voice. "Don't blame yourself," she said, laying a hand gently on his arm.

He went on as if she hadn't spoken, hadn't touched him, and she sensed that he was telling her things that had been bottled up inside him for a long time.

"She didn't have close friends—like other women do. I'm not sure she needed other people. Even my father."

"Everybody needs someone," she whispered.

"Well, she and Dad made a perfect couple. He was a real type A personality—a corporate wheeler and dealer. She loved being his hostess, helping build his career with the right social contacts so she could be Mrs. Business Executive. Unfortunately he worked himself into a heart attack when he was still in his fifties."

"How sad."

"It didn't make much difference in my life. Mom found new activities to occupy her time." He sucked in a breath and let it out. "I always knew I didn't want to be like my parents. Then I woke up one morning and realized I was following the exact same pattern. I married a woman who wanted me to be important so she could shine in the reflected glory. When I realized I was working myself toward an early grave like my father, I opted out of the rat race."

"And you're happier?" she asked.

He gave a harsh laugh. "It depends on how you look at it. My wife didn't like the change in life-style. When she found out she wasn't married to a mover and shaker, she bailed."

"Maybe you're better off being alone." She realized as soon as she'd made the assertion that it had come out wrong.

The words hung between them. After several painful seconds, Juliet leapt back into the conversational breech.

"I mean, sometimes it's for the best. Six months ago I made the decision not to get married." She took a quick swallow of wine. "I mean, I was engaged. And Dick wanted me to sell my business and stay at home. The more he tried to persuade me to his way of thinking, the more I realized I just couldn't do it."

"You didn't want to be a wife and mother?" he asked.

She didn't like the note of disapproval she thought she detected in his voice. "I want that eventually," she said quickly. "But my mother's experience made me realize that it's dangerous for a woman to be too dependent. She gave up a teaching career to marry my dad. He wasn't a high-powered type, he was a manager at the Social Security Administration."

"If he liked working there, that's what counts."

It was her turn to give a bitter little laugh. "I believe he hated it. He went through an early midlife crisis and left her with a six-month-old baby to go to New Mexico and make silver jewelry. For all I know, he's dead."

Remington looked astonished at the revelation. She was astonished herself at having blurted out a story she'd kept hidden from all but her most intimate friends. It seemed that the dark and the cold—and the company—were conducive to confessions.

"I guess his leaving you must have been rough," he said.

"Mom was devastated, because she'd tried to be the kind of wife he said he wanted. While she was out of the job market, they changed the requirements for teachers, and she wasn't certified any longer. She didn't know how she was going to support us. A friend offered her a job working in his antique shop, and that gave her a chance to learn the business. When my aunt died and left us some money, Mom used it to open her own shop. By the time I was ready to graduate from high school, we were finally doing reasonably well."

"Money doesn't buy happiness."

"Of course not, but it's easier to be happy when you don't have to worry about paying the bills."

He shook his head. "I would have traded parents who sent me with my governess to buy designer jeans, for parents who helped me with my homework, took me to the zoo and watched me play soccer."

Taking a small sip of soup, Juliet tried to imagine his childhood, tried to imagine parents who chose not to nurture their son. She couldn't stop herself from seeing the lonely little boy...just as she couldn't stop looking at the handsome man he'd become.

With a mental shrug, she reminded herself why she was here. Not to devise little romantic fantasies about the man, but to compile information about him and his family antique collection. She kept forgetting the mission. In fact she *wanted* to forget it. Larry had as much as told her Grant Remington was evil. But all she could detect was a man who was pretty well adjusted, given what sounded like a deprived childhood.

"I think we've had enough confessions to last us the evening," he suddenly said as if he were able to follow her thoughts.

Her face heated, and she hoped the darkness hid her embarrassment.

"Look on the bright side. Tomorrow you'll be able to start right in on the Remington relics."

"The Remington relics? Is that what you call a house full of valuable antiques?"

"Yeah. Unloading them will be a relief."

So Larry was wrong on another count, she thought.

Before she could investigate the subject further, Remington stood, walked to a grocery bag that sat on the floor beside the sofa and pulled out a package of marshmallows. "Dessert," he said with a flourish.

His enthusiasm was infectious. "You've been holding out on me!" she exclaimed.

"I was just waiting until we finished dinner." As he spoke, he skewered a marshmallow on a long-handled fork and held it over the flames.

"I always used to burn them," she said.

"Are you saying you've got no patience?"

"No ten-year-old has patience," she countered. "Everybody in my Scout troop burned her marshmallows."

"I never did."

"You were a Boy Scout?"

He shook his head. "No. Sometimes in cold weather Pat used to make a fire in an oil drum. When he was in a good mood, he'd let me pretend we were camping in the woods."

"Pat the gardener?"

"Right." As he spoke, he pulled the fork toward him and with a critical eye inspected the marshmallow before returning it to the flames again. "Not quite done."

He was indeed patient. She would have opted for a charred exterior long ago. Finally when he was satisfied, he tipped the perfectly toasted offering toward her.

"It's yours," she demurred.

He shook his head. "You're my guest."

"Okay." She accepted the fork, blowing on the marshmallow before taking a cautious bite. "Delicious," she declared as she swiped her tongue over her lips. When she saw he was watching her every move, she flushed and popped the rest into her mouth.

When she was finished, he loaded her fork again and fixed another for himself. "You can do your own this time."

"Fair enough." She held her marshmallow above the flames, raising it and turning it quickly when it began to singe on one side. There was nothing more pressing to do than concentrate on toasting her dessert, and as she focused on the simple task, she found herself relaxing.

"Too bad you don't have graham crackers and chocolate to go along with the marshmallows," she mused.

"This is decadent enough."

She laughed. "I won't tell, if you don't."

"Deal."

They smiled at each other, a glow of genuine warmth between them. He stretched and began to gather up the remains of the meal. "I'll take the tray back to the kitchen."

"I should help." To her surprise and chagrin, the statement ended with a yawn.

"Guests get to relax."

"You weren't planning on company."

"I like it better than I thought I would," he said in a bemused voice.

She hardly had time to think about the implications before he continued. "With the electricity off, we might as well turn in early. Unless you want to play Abraham Lincoln and read by firelight."

"I don't think my eyes are up to that."

"The powder room is two doors down the hall. You can wash up before it gets any colder."

"All right."

Opening the door of the den was like stepping

into the blizzard. The only thing missing was the snow and wind.

"Get your coat," he suggested.

She didn't protest.

He brought along the flashlight, and showed her where to find the bathroom.

"When you're finished, go back to the den where it's warm," he instructed. "I'll be back soon."

With a quick nod, she stepped into the bathroom and closed the door. As she shined the flashlight around the room, she saw shaving cream, a razor and other toiletries arranged neatly on a shelf above the sink, and a couple of towels on a stool in the corner.

She used the facilities, then quickly washed her face and hands in the sink, clenching her teeth at the cold water. Turning toward the window, she saw a layer of frost on the pane. As she watched, more flakes piled up. With a shiver, she wondered if they'd be under two feet of snow by the time the storm broke.

Reflexive panic tightened her chest as she realized she'd been lulled into relaxing. She was still trapped in Grant Remington's lair, except, things weren't turning out quite the way she'd expected.

Slipping into the hall, she heard the sound of rattling pots coming from the kitchen. Remington might have left them in the sink earlier, but the neatness of the bathroom suggested that he wasn't the type of man who waited until morning to clean up. He was probably washing dishes and she should probably help. But her hands had already stiffened from the brief exposure to the cold water.

With a sigh, she took her host at his word and let the warmth of the fire draw her back to the den, where she moved the coffee table to the side, gathered a handful of pillows and propped them against the bottom of the sofa.

When she switched off the flashlight, the low flames of the fire cast a flickering glow in the room. Picking up the poker, she turned the half-burned logs, then added a couple more. As the fire licked around them, she covered herself with her coat and stretched out on the thick rug, intending to relax for a few minutes. She hadn't realized, though, how exhausted she was. Almost as soon as her eyes closed, she was dozing off.

Sometime later she was aware of blankets being laid over her. When she struggled to sit up, a gentle hand on her shoulder pressed her back.

"You look too comfortable to move. Stay there."

"I should have helped you," she murmured.

He lowered himself beside her. "I'm used to doing for myself."

He sat close to her right shoulder, his back against the bottom of the sofa, his long legs stretched toward the fire, and she lay peacefully beside him. Time passed as she drifted in and out of a light sleep. When his hand stroked gently across the top of her head, she made a small sound.

"Your hair's soft. I thought it would be."

How did his feel? she wondered. Languidly she turned her head toward his touch. His fingers lingered, lightly stroking the tender line where her hair met her cheek. This was a dream, she told herself. If she didn't open her eyes, it was only a dream, and she didn't have to worry about what was happening between them.

His thumb traced the outline of her lips, which opened so that he could skim the tender skin inside.

He was so close, leaning over her, the warmth and scent of his body familiar now.

"You should sleep."

Drowsiness had stripped her of control. "Only if you don't go away," a reedy voice whispered, and she realized she had spoken her thoughts aloud. The little hesitation while she waited for his answer made her heartbeat quicken.

"I'LL BE RIGHT HERE." He heard himself answer. Where? In bed with her? Well, not exactly a bed. A rug in front of the fireplace. With a lot of cozy quilts.

Still, he was in the wrong place. He should stop touching her and get up.

But instead of taking his hand away, he found the gentle curve of her ear. Leaning closer, he breathed in her fresh, flowery scent. She'd used some cologne or perfume that morning. He couldn't tell what it was, but he loved the way it mingled with the warmth of her flesh as she slept.

In the dim light, he admired the sweep of her lashes against her cheek. They were light, like her hair. Yet the tips were dark. Nature? Or artifice? He'd know in the morning when any makeup she'd put on today would be gone.

Not that he objected to makeup. It heightened a woman's beauty. Yet there was something to be said for seeing her as nature had intended.

While he'd been in the kitchen, he'd opened the back door and found a foot of snow on the terrace. It was still coming down, and he was willing to bet they weren't going anywhere in the morning. The knowledge brought a little forbidden thrill of relief. He'd have her to himself again tomorrow, even if he wasn't precisely sure what he should be doing with her.

He ordered himself to take his hand away from her. When he did, he touched his fingers to his mouth, imagining he could detect the taste of her where his thumb had stroked his lips. He was getting turned on. His whole body felt hot and flushed as if he were trapped on a tropical island instead of in a frigid mansion in a snowstorm. For long moments he allowed himself to enjoy the sensation of arousal as his gaze lingered on the tender vee of flesh visible at the top of her blouse. Her breasts would be soft, soft as flower petals. His mind began to spin a fantasy of gathering her to him, of waking her, of feeling her respond.

He'd sensed a change in her as they'd eaten dinner and exchanged confidences about their lives. She was less shy, less skittish. And when she was half-asleep and her guard was down, she was very sweetly seductive.

He wasn't reckless enough, though, to consider her request that he stay as an invitation to make love to her. He knew he was treading on dangerous ground even by sleeping beside her. He didn't know her well enough for this. And he wasn't sure how far he could trust himself. It had been a long time since he'd shared a bed with a woman. He should get up and take a nice cooling walk in the snow.

Instead, he rolled to his back, arranged a couple of pillows behind his head and lay staring into the darkness, listening to the gentle breathing of the very desirable woman next to him.

Chapter Three

ONE MOMENT Juliet was sleeping, warm and cozy and filled with a sense of well-being. In the next, she was disoriented, uncomfortable and alarmed. It took only a few seconds to figure out what had caused the abrupt change of status—a persistent buzzing that seemed to pulsate through her entire body. Well, not a buzzing, exactly, her sleep-fogged brain decided. More like a silent vibration.

Her pager, she realized with a start. She never wore it to bed, but last night she'd forgotten all about it.

When she reached to shut it off, her hand collided with another fumbling hand—a large masculine hand that searched along the front of her body for the source of the disturbance.

Grant Remington's hand.

She remembered drifting off to sleep beside him. Somehow during the night, the two of them had snuggled up against each other so tightly that there was barely space to fit a sheet of paper between them.

She tried to push herself away and realized her fingers were pressing against the fly of his slacks.

Behind the zipper was an unmistakable ridge of distended male flesh. Her face flamed as she tried to wiggle free, only succeeding in making the situation worse.

When he made a strangled noise in his throat, she answered with a little "oh" of abject embarrassment.

In the next second, he rolled away and lay on his back, his breathing rapid.

Freed from the awkward contact, she scrambled off the makeshift bed as if bent on escape from a pool of molten lava. Turning her back, she pressed the button on the pager to shut off the vibration and stood trying to calm the frantic pounding of her heart. When she felt a little more in control, she looked at the number of the screen. It was Larry.

Oh, great. Her cousin was trying to reach her. And if she didn't respond to her page, he was going to try again. Or maybe he'd descend on the estate in a helicopter.

She shuddered, realizing that the reaction was partly from the cold. The fire had gone out, and the temperature in the room had dropped considerably. That was why she and Remington had gravitated toward each other under the pile of blankets, she told herself.

Her eyes shot to her bed partner, who was sitting with his knees drawn up and his face turned toward the window. When she followed the direction of his gaze, she had to shield her eyes against the glare of sunlight hitting blinding whiteness.

Remington half turned and cleared his throat. "Sorry about that. I threw my pager away six months ago, but I guess I still have the reflex reaction of reaching for it."

She winced when she saw the color in his cheeks. He was just as embarrassed as she. But the worst part hadn't been his reaching for the pager; it had been where her hand had landed when she'd tried to push him away. "Not your fault," she whispered.

"It wouldn't have happened if I'd slept somewhere else," he said in a gritty voice.

"And frozen to death?" As she finished the sentence, she shivered again. To give herself something to do, she lurched toward the stack of logs on the hearth and began picking up pieces of wood.

"Let me." Remington was beside her, lifting a split log out of her hands.

"So who needs to get in touch with you at a quarter to eight in the morning?" he asked.

Juliet hesitated for a split second, and in that pause she made a decision. "My cousin. We, uh, have some business to discuss."

"If you need privacy, there's a phone by the back door of the door of the kitchen."

"Thanks."

"When you finish, I'll heat some water for coffee."

If the den was North Dakota, the rest of the house was Siberia. Zipping her coat, she headed for the kitchen. When she got a good look at the landscape outside, she couldn't repress a little exclamation.

With a sigh, she called Larry's number.

He answered on the first ring. "Juliet. Where are you?"

"I'm at Remington's place."

"What the hell are you doing there?"

"We got snowed in."

Larry whistled through his teeth. "Clever girl. What have you found out?"

Hearing a noise in the hall, she looked guiltily toward the kitchen door. But Remington was nowhere in sight. "You don't think I'm going to discuss anything with you now, do you?"

"Yeah. Good thinking."

"Larry, I'm not comfortable with this job."

"Come on. Where's your Lancaster loyalty? You agreed to—"

"Stop," she said in a firm voice. Lord, what if Remington picked up the phone in the den? She didn't think he'd do something devious like that, but it would be a disaster if he did. "Don't say anything else. I'll call you when I get home."

"Juliet! Don't waste the opportunity to—"

"Bye." After slamming the receiver into the

cradle, she closed her eyes and leaned against the wall. Her heart was pounding like a jackhammer inside her chest and her palms felt sweaty. Larry was a jerk. Didn't he realize how incriminating his end of the conversation would sound?

Sucking in a deep breath, she let it out slowly. Had she ever experienced so many emotions in such a short span of time? she wondered. When she'd come here, she'd been primed to mistrust Grant Remington. Then she'd gotten to know him, and she'd had to cope with a disturbing mixture of attraction and guilt. A few minutes ago she'd felt mortified by the intimacy of their awakening. Now she had moved past embarrassment back to remorse at her role as spy.

She craned her neck toward the window, looking at the blanket of snow. If there was any way she could get out of here, she would. Yet she didn't see how it was going to happen.

Grimacing, she returned to the den. Remington had gotten a roaring fire going, then folded up the bedding and stowed it in the corner of the room. But he wasn't anywhere in sight.

When she stepped into the hall again, she felt a cold breeze blowing from the front of the house. The door was ajar. Looking through the gap, she saw Remington inspecting the snow piled around his equipment and their cars. Digging them out would be a major undertaking. But why bother? Without a plow, there was no possibility of maneuvering through the foot-high snow.

The cold stung her face and worked its way through her clothing as she stepped outside.

Remington turned and shrugged apologetically. "I just called the company that used to come up here and plow. They said they'd get to us when they could."

"I wonder how long I'm going to have to wear these clothes." She said the first thing that popped into her head.

"There's no reason you can't change into, uh, something more comfortable."

"Are you offering me a pair of your jeans?" she asked in a slightly querulous voice. Last night they'd gotten comfortable with each other. This morning was another story.

He pulled open the door and ushered her back into the house.

She stood in the hall, rubbing her cold hands, staring at the little drift of snow that had followed them inside and trying to calm her nerves.

"There's got to be a ton of female stuff here," he answered, then sighed. "I haven't been able to make myself sort through it."

"I don't want to wear your mother's clothes."

"You don't have to. Shopping was one of her chief recreations. I guarantee you'll find everything from underwear to designer gowns—still with the price tags on. Why don't we go up?"

She sighed. "Okay." Why give him a big argument? Finding clothing and fixing a meal were as good a way as any to fill the long hours stretching ahead of them.

He led her up the stairs to a dramatically decorated room with dark green walls and a bedroom set that looked like it had come from an English manor house. Beyond it was a huge bathroom, opening into an even bigger dressing area.

"Check some of those drawers," he suggested, waving toward a bank of built-in cabinetry.

Reminding herself that Mrs. Remington wasn't going to object, Juliet took a quick step forward. The first drawer she opened was filled with designer scarves—thousands of dollars' worth of neatly folded silk. The next held an impressive collection of athletic socks. In the third were silk and lace panties. Those on the right had obviously been worn. The ones with the price tags were on the left. Reaching in, she pulled out the stack. Underneath was a small pile of papers that looked like letters.

Well, she wasn't going to stoop to reading personal correspondence stuffed in the bottom of an underwear drawer, Juliet thought. But as she started to turn away, some boldly underlined words leapt out at her, making her draw in a sharp breath.

"WHAT'S WRONG?" Grant had been turned in the opposite direction, staring out the window. He stepped quickly to Juliet's side, wondering if she'd found a spider hiding in the drawer.

She gestured toward a pile of papers that his mother had obviously hidden. What hadn't she wanted anyone to know? he wondered as he reached for the stack of correspondence.

"Dear Edith, You have been marked for death," the top letter began.

Grant echoed Juliet's startled exclamation. Then he quickly shuffled through the notes. There were four of them, each on a square of heavy, creamy stationery. The formal script had obviously been produced from a computer. Each missive was addressed to "Dear Edith." Each contained a short, threatening message. And each was unsigned. The last one, sent about two weeks before her death, advised his mother to get her affairs in order.

Grant felt the blood draining out of his head, the muscles of his face stiffening. Raising his eyes, he looked pleadingly at Juliet. "Why the hell did she keep these secret?" he demanded. "Why didn't she ask for my help?"

"You said she didn't confide in you."

"And I also told myself I had my own problems to deal with," he muttered, barely able to talk around the sudden constriction in his throat. "So I didn't press it. She'd never needed me or anybody else, why should things have gotten any different?"

Juliet reached out her hand and touched his shoulder. When he uttered a low curse, she responded by opening her arms. He resisted as long as he could—perhaps half a dozen heartbeats, then stumbled forward with a shuddering sigh.

They'd gotten off to a pretty bad start this morning. Ever since then, she'd been diffident with him, probably trying to deny the accidental intimacy of their awakening. When he needed her, though, the diffidence vanished, replaced with generosity and caring.

"Grant." She whispered his name, her hands moving soothingly over the knotted muscles of his back and shoulder. He held on to her for dear life, shamelessly drawing on the warmth and goodness he'd sensed in her.

"You didn't know," she said in a voice that rang with conviction. "She didn't tell you because she didn't want you to know."

He wanted to believe her. He couldn't let go of the guilty feeling that he hadn't done enough.

"I should have—"

"You're not a mind reader. You had no reason to know she was being threatened," she said as she threaded her hands into his hair, moving his face so that she could look into his eyes. Hers were large and filled with compassion—more than compassion. What he saw drew him toward her with a need that he was no longer able to deny. He'd wanted to kiss her last night, but he'd convinced himself it was the wrong thing to do. Now he was helpless to keep from gathering her close and slanting his mouth over hers, drawing forth the sweetness she was offering.

When she murmured something incoherent, he deepened the kiss. He wanted to lose himself in the generosity of her embrace. He allowed himself only a few more seconds of pleasure—then managed to stop while he could still string coherent thoughts together. He couldn't, however, resist one last brush of his lips against hers before he raised his head. They stood together without speaking, but now the silence was comforting. What was it about this woman that gave her the power to soothe his turmoil? he wondered.

He sucked in a deep breath and let it out slowly as he realized he was still clutching the letters. "Who the hell sent this?" he asked.

"Maybe it was somebody who wanted to frighten her. Maybe she thought that was all they intended to do," Juliet answered.

He took a step away but kept his free hand on hers, needing the contact of her fingers entwined with his. "She'd had some pretty bad fights with various neighbors. The latest one was about a year ago. The Jordans wanted to build a modern addition to their house. She persuaded the local preservation committee to block it. Tim Jordan acted like he was mad enough for homicide. But the police investigation into her death cleared him."

Juliet squeezed his hand. "Well, now they have some new evidence."

"I'd rather give it to a private detective who's been working for me. Mike Lancer."

She looked surprised. "I know Mike. His office is at 43 Light Street—the building I have some of my antiques for sale in. But why not the police?"

He sighed. "Mom used to pull rank on the police regularly. When people parked along Long View Road, she'd call the governor. I think the cops were glad she was out of their hair."

"Surely they wouldn't deliberately let a murder go unsolved."

He continued over her objection. "They conducted an investigation, but when they didn't turn up anything, they chalked it up to an accident."

"But you believe it wasn't?" Juliet asked.

He nodded. "Call it a feeling." That was only part of the truth. Shortly after his mother's death the back stairs at the site of a house he was building had collapsed when he'd been standing on them. He'd been lucky to escape with only a broken leg and a bruised kidney, but the injuries did nothing to further his belief in coincidences. "I decided to let Mike poke around and see if he could come up with anything," he said finally to

Juliet. In fact, Mike had discovered the stairs had been partly cut through, but he hadn't found out who'd done it.

He turned toward the window, determined not to let Juliet read the grim expression on his face. "I wish I could fax him these letters right now. This might be the proof he needs that the 'accident' was murder."

"He probably can't get down to the office," she murmured.

"Yeah," he conceded, although he was champing at the bit to jump on the first new piece of evidence in months. Yet he understood there was nothing he could do at the moment. More than that, he'd come to realize over the past few years that when you can't take effective action, you might as well relax and wait for the right opportunity.

So he deliberately forced his mind on to other things. Like the very lovely woman who was still holding his hand. The woman who had made it clear she cared about him. The two of them were stuck here for a while, and he could think of several good ways to take his mind off his troubles. Only, he'd gotten the message that she wasn't the kind for casual fooling around.

"You pick out something to wear. I'll put the evidence in a safe place and fix breakfast," he said.

The way she looked at him made him suspect

she'd forgotten why they had come up here in the first place.

"Find a warm sweater and slacks," he advised, "and feel free to use any one of the five bathrooms up here."

BY THE TIME Juliet finished washing, she was shivering again—partly from the cold and partly from emotional overload. Quickly she pulled on the new panties, beige slacks and powder blue sweater she'd selected, and fluffed out her hair with her fingers. She'd even found a pair of light boots that were a size too big but stayed on her feet. As she peered at herself in the mirror, a sudden film of moisture clouded her vision, and she squeezed her eyes shut.

She was in a heck of a fix. Trapped with Grant Remington. Falling for him. Lying to him. The combination was intolerable. She had to tell him why she had come here. Yet he'd said he hated deceit in a woman. What if she destroyed the feelings that had been building between them? Her fists clenched and unclenched. She had another problem she hadn't even considered. She could tell him about herself, but she couldn't talk to him about Larry until she got her cousin's permission. And there was no way she was going to get into an extended discussion with Larry Lancaster until she had some privacy.

Pulling on her coat, she shoved her hands in

the pockets and headed for the stairs. She had been feeling hungry a little while ago. Now the smell of food wafting toward her made her feel slightly sick.

As she stepped through the door, she saw Grant had fried several thin slices of ham and was scrambling eggs in a pan on his portable stove. He was also listening to the news—on what must be a battery-powered radio. The commentary was on the terrible road conditions. Motorists were being advised to stay at home.

When he saw her expression, his face grew grave. "I guess it sounds pretty bad," he said.

"It's not that. I have to tell you something—something that's making me uncomfortable."

"Oh?" His expression was instantly wary.

She gulped, then forced herself to say, "When you called to ask if I'd appraise your family's antiques, I should have told you who I really am."

He eyed her skeptically. "And who is that?"

She took a deep breath. "I'm a descendant of the Lancasters."

His eyes narrowed. "You mean the family that's been feuding with mine for almost a hundred years?"

"Yes. I was going to turn down the job. But some—uh—some of my relatives were curious about some pieces that used to be in our family—pieces we sold to the Remingtons. I should have told you that but—"

"The Lancasters have always been jealous of the Remingtons," he replied in a voice that mirrored the look in his eyes. His surprise of a moment ago had been replaced by outright anger.

"That's not true!" She'd come downstairs, intending to make a confession. Now she found herself defending her family. "The way I heard it, the feud started when Zebulon Remington jilted Anabel Lancaster."

"The way *I* heard it, *she* jilted *him*," Remington shot back.

"I suppose you think your family didn't ruin us by hiring away the workmen who were going to empty our warehouse after the Baltimore fire of 1904?"

"We were simply willing to pay premium prices."

"That's a self-serving way to look at it."

The eggs he'd been cooking suddenly began to smoke. Remington lifted the pan off the burner and with a clank set it onto the granite counter. Unmindful, he continued, "It sounds like we've heard the same stories—with a slightly different perspective."

She nodded tightly.

"Why are you bringing this up now?" he asked, speaking slowly, emphasizing every word.

She hadn't started the conversation to stir up

ancient accusations. This was about the two of them—today, last night. She held out her hand to him, then dropped it at her side. "I came here prepared to dislike you. You were supposed to be one of the enemy. But you're so different from what I expected," she said in a wistful voice. Her palms turned up in a helpless gesture. "I like you a lot. I respect you. I know you've been through some rough times."

He snorted. "You mean you feel sorry for me. That's what this is all about."

"No. It's nothing like that. I was hoping we—" She stopped because everything had suddenly gone wrong. And she knew that if she continued to stand in front of him explaining her feelings, she was going to start crying. With a quick shake of her head, she turned and rushed out of the room.

The tears came as she hurled herself down the hall—away from the room where they'd slept. When she came to the giant hole in the floor, she pulled up short. If she'd tumbled into the basement, she might have been killed. But Grant had saved her—and then hugged her to him as if he cared about her.

She couldn't cope with that memory any better than she could cope with the harsh words they'd just exchanged. She could only skirt the hazard and keep going blindly. Away. As far away as she could get.

Chapter Four

FOOTSTEPS POUNDED after her, fast and hard. Running out of the hallway, she ducked through a door and found herself in a small utility room—with no way out.

When she felt a hand on her shoulder, she drew away. "Leave me alone."

"I'm sorry." Grant's voice was soft. "I've gotten into the bad habit of reacting first and thinking later."

"Please leave," she whispered, swiping a hand across her eyes and trying to get control of herself.

"It took guts to tell me the things you did," he replied, his tone as raw as a new wound.

Several seconds passed before she could answer. "I had to."

"Why?"

If she explained maybe he'd leave her be. "I couldn't stand the idea of getting close to you and having dishonorable motives hanging over me," she said honestly, simply. "It wasn't fair to either one of us."

"Juliet." He said her name in a kind of

stunned wonderment as he turned her toward him and pulled her into his embrace.

She came to him with a little sob that ended as she wrapped her arms around him and clung. When she lifted her head, he lowered his, and their lips met in a kiss that was hard and frantic. She felt a shudder go through his frame as her hands moved under his jacket and flattened against his back.

"Grant. Oh, Grant."

He turned his head, first one way and then the other, his mouth hungry as it ravaged hers. And she was no less hungry. Everything that had happened between them seemed to unleash intense emotions. She felt wild, out of control. And when his stance shifted so that he could cup his hand around her breast, she arched into his touch, her nipple beading tightly as she quickened to him.

Heat built to a flash point between them. Desire for this man pounded through her like a force of nature.

She heard hot, sexy words rumble in his chest. With his free hand, he grasped her hips and pulled them tightly against his, letting her know he felt the same wild arousal as she.

Her breath came in gasps. So did his.

He was reaching around to unhook her bra when his hands suddenly went still. "Hell, what am I doing?" he asked.

"Making love to me," she murmured.

"We can't," he said with a hard finality.

She lifted questioning eyes toward his. "I didn't ask you to stop."

"I don't want to," he said, putting space between them. "But I'm not going to take advantage of you."

"Because of what I told you?" she whispered.

"Yes."

She felt as if he'd slapped her.

He must have caught the utter despair in her expression, because he added quickly, "I don't mean that the way you think."

"How do you mean it?" she asked with a little gulp.

He lightly touched her cheek with his knuckle. "We've been thrown together in a weird situation, and we're going through a lot of emotions in a very short time. Like when you told me you were a Lancaster, I had a knee-jerk reaction." He laughed, a strangled sound. "This one's equally inappropriate."

"I hope not."

"We may feel differently when we get some perspective."

She knew she wouldn't. The things that were happening between her and Grant—good and bad—were like mountains shaking, tidal waves sweeping over the land.

His sigh was long and heartfelt. "You're the first woman I've wanted to get close to since my divorce. Maybe I'm so out of practice that I'm not responding normally."

She tipped her head to one side. "You hardly seem out of practice."

"The moves come back. It's the emotions that worry me."

She didn't know how to answer that objection. She only knew that he was being as honest as he could, the way she'd tried to be honest. He'd been through a devastating divorce; she could understand why he didn't want to get hurt again. And she hadn't given him much reason to trust her.

"Do you want me to find you another appraiser?" She hoped she sounded more composed then she felt.

Seconds ticked by, seconds during which her chest grew steadily tighter.

"No, I'd like you to do it," he finally said.

"Why?"

"You were highly recommended. You know the field. And you wouldn't have told me about your background if you weren't honest."

She nodded tightly. "One more thing." One more item she had to get off her conscience, she realized, pulling the key out of her pocket and holding it in the palm of her hand. "Do you know about this?"

He shook his head.

"It's supposed to fit a box or a chest or something that belonged to my family. Something the Remingtons acquired. I can't believe it's still locked after all these years, but one of my relatives asked me to keep an eye out for it."

His mouth tightened. Gingerly he took the key and turned it in his hand, examining the heart-shaped loop at the top. "I never heard that particular story."

"Either the box was opened long ago, or it's a Lancaster secret. I...thought maybe we could look together, if that's okay with you. And if we don't find it, I'd like your permission to continue the search."

"Thank you for sharing that with me," he said, trying to hand the key back.

"Keep it."

"Were you going to search anyway—without my permission?"

"That was the plan when I got here. But I've found I can't look myself in the mirror in the morning after sneaking around behind your back."

"Glad to hear it." He hesitated for a moment, then pocketed the key before turning and headed back toward the kitchen.

She followed more slowly, feeling a little better and a little worse.

GRANT DUCKED into the bathroom and splashed cold water on his overheated face. If she was trying to get him to back off, she'd picked a pretty good method. Only, he wanted to believe that wasn't her purpose. She'd said she was uncomfortable with dishonesty. He'd like to take that at face value. The trouble was, he'd started to examine in a different light everything they'd said and done. She'd seemed so open, so contrite. Either she was being brutally honest, or her confession was a clever ploy to get him to drop his guard.

It seemed like a roundabout technique. Yet he'd damn well had enough experience with women to know that they didn't have to make sense to you for something to be perfectly logical to them.

Like a few minutes ago, when he'd made himself stop kissing her. He'd started because the wounded look on her face had made him want to comfort her. Once he'd touched her, he'd wanted to do more than comfort. And she'd seemed hurt—disappointed by his withdrawal. But Cynthia had been terrific at making him think she was as hot for him as he was for her. Later he'd realized she was probably more turned on by his earning power than his lovemaking.

He sucked in a strangled breath and let it out slowly as the water turned his hands and face icy. He'd practically given Juliet permission to come back and search the house, if that was what she wanted to do. Was he hoping to catch her in something dishonest—or hoping against hope that he wouldn't? With a grimace, he dried his hands and face and opened the door. All he knew was that he had to get some emotional distance from her now.

When he came back into the kitchen, she'd cleaned out the pan of ruined eggs and started another batch. She'd also cut the now-chilled ham into small pieces, which she stirred into the eggs as they cooked. The other burner held a pot of hot water—for the coffee he'd put in a filter over a glass pot.

He stood watching the water slowly come to a boil. Then he lifted the pot and made the coffee.

Neither of them spoke until she cleared her throat. "I guess we should eat in the den again, where it's warmer."

They sat at opposite ends of the table, neither one eating with much enthusiasm. After a few minutes, he found he couldn't take the silence.

"Thanks for starting a new batch of eggs."

"You're welcome."

The conversation lurched to a halt, and they picked at the food again.

"After we eat, I could do some work," she offered.

"You don't have to."

"I enjoy my work."

"Which part do you like best?" he asked, realizing he really did want to know the answer.

"That's hard to say. I like touching things that people long ago used in their everyday lives. Ordinary things. Like a spoon or a baby's bed. And I like discovering the jewels among the common stuff. Like a piece of carnival glass that's become a collector's item. Or a Williamsburg candlestick at the bottom of a box of stuff someone was going to throw out." As she spoke, her voice lost its flatness, took on some of the color he liked.

"Does that happen often—finding valuables in the trash?"

"Often enough. I was helping a family clean out their mother's house once, and I found some rare glassware in the attic. It ended up paying her medical bills."

"You could have told them it was junk."

"I'd never do that," she said with deliberate seriousness.

He wanted to believe she wouldn't. He wondered why he was so eager to give her the benefit of the doubt. To break the mood, he deliberately jumped in with a question he knew he shouldn't ask. "So were you going to let me make love to you? If I hadn't stopped."

Color flooded her cheeks and she lowered her head. "I was reacting. I wasn't thinking."

"Do you do that often?"

"Make love? Or react?"

"Either."

"I usually think instead of react," she answered in a level voice. Standing, she picked up her plate and left the room.

He found her in the kitchen scraping the better portion of her eggs into the trash. Setting his own plate on the counter, he shoved his hands into his pockets. "I'm sorry. That was out of line."

"Yes it was. I think it would be better if you found another appraiser."

"You're probably right. Why don't you go back to the den? I'm going to do some work on my repairs," he said, wondering how he was going to do that without electricity. She was polite enough not to ask.

She was sitting rigidly on the sofa when he brought in an armload of wood. Neither of them spoke as he added more logs to the fire and waited while they caught.

Then he stamped out of the refuge and down the hall to the utility room where he grabbed a snow shovel and waded onto the porch. His mouth set in a grim line, he started shoveling a path from the porch to the van, knowing it wasn't going to do him much good. But he couldn't simply sit around doing nothing.

He'd been working for forty minutes, his bad leg was aching and he was starting to turn into an icicle when he heard the noise of an engine disturbing the silence of the frigid air. A minute later, a small four-wheel-drive truck came around the bend, clearing the access road with the plow attached to its bumper. Grant turned and waved.

"I thought you couldn't come now," he called out.

The driver rolled down his window and laughed. "I figured you'd pay for the service."

"You figured right. How are the roads?"

"The main ones have been plowed."

Behind him, Juliet appeared on the porch. "Thank God," she whispered, and he felt his stomach clench. She called to the driver of the plow, "Can you help me dig out my car?"

"That'll cost you extra."

"I'll pay it," Grant said in clipped tones, as if he couldn't wait to get rid of her. It wasn't true, he silently admitted, yet he couldn't help reacting to her obvious desire to get as far away from him as she could.

"You don't have to," she said in a small voice, giving him a glimmer of hope. Then he told himself he was being foolish. She was simply being polite.

"My treat," he insisted.

They stood staring at each other, as if there might still be time to change their minds. Then the driver jumped out and grabbed a couple of shovels from the back of the vehicle. When he tossed one to Juliet, she caught it and moved toward her car.

With the three of them working, the vehicle

was freed in half an hour. Grant's fingers were icy through his gloves, and his face burned with the cold. Juliet looked equally cold, yet the fixed expression on her face told him she wasn't going to change her mind about leaving.

While he settled up with the driver, she ducked inside.

He was about to follow her when she reappeared on the porch again with her purse and briefcase.

Absurdly he wanted to ask her to stay. But he knew she wouldn't do it. He settled for "Please be careful."

"I will."

"Call me when you get home."

She stared at him.

"I want to know you made it all right."

She nodded. "If the phone rings twice and stops, it's me."

He started to protest, then checked himself as she turned and marched through the snow toward her car. He held his breath as the engine turned over, and called out as she started to skid. But she got the car under control and forged ahead, and all he could do was stand there watching her drive out of his life.

Chapter Five

WHEN JULIET REMEMBERED the next few days, they always came back to her in a series of vivid phone calls that stood out against a feeling of gray depression.

Larry phoned the next morning, demanding a blow-by-blow description of her twenty-four hours with Remington, and she was instantly plunged into a very unpleasant conversation.

"You had a perfect opportunity, and you screwed up!" his angry voice shrilled in her ear.

"Right. I don't make a very good spy," Juliet retorted. Before she could stop herself, she added, "And I don't share your opinion of Grant Remington. He's a nice man." At least he'd been nice until he made that last crack about making love, she thought, feeling a painful stab in her heart. He'd driven her away. He'd wanted her to leave. But maybe that was because he was afraid to trust her—afraid of getting emotionally involved after all the things that had happened to him.

But Grant Remington wasn't the one on the other end of the line. It was her cousin, and if she had to pick which man had made her the most upset, it was Larry, for putting her in an untenable situation. "I don't want to discuss it anymore," she said and slammed down the receiver.

Five minutes later the phone rang again. Once, twice. On the third ring she snatched it up.

"Juliet, I realize I wasn't fair to you," the voice on the other end said. It was the wrong man—Larry.

"Why are you calling back?" she asked.

"To apologize. I shouldn't have yelled at you. I should have realized your sensibilities would get in the way."

"Thanks a lot."

"I'm not doing this right. I was thinking, maybe we can take another approach."

"No."

"Juliet—"

She hung up again.

The next important call was two days later. When she answered the phone, a deep voice said, "Don't hang up."

"Grant," she breathed, then stopped short.

"Don't hang up," he said again.

"Why not?"

"I want to say I'm sorry."

"Okay."

"I want to see you again."

"I don't think that's such a good idea." She'd

opened up to him and gotten hurt. She wasn't sure she could take that again.

"Come with me to the Valentine's Dance that the Light Street Foundation is holding on Saturday night," he said, his tone full of longing.

At least that's what she told herself she heard, and her heart started to pound. "I don't know." Even as she protested, she wanted him to persuade her.

"Juliet, I haven't been able to get you out of my mind. I keep thinking that maybe if we tried again—under more normal circumstances—we could..."

"Could what?" she pressed, her voice breathy.

"Could make a relationship work," he said.

"What about the Lancaster-Remington feud?" she asked, reminding him that there was a long history of bad feelings between their families.

"I don't see why it has to affect us," he said dismissively.

"How can you be sure? We hardly know each other."

"You don't really think that's true, do you?"

She closed her eyes, willing herself to steadiness. He was taking a chance by calling her. She could take a chance, too. "I'll go with you to the dance," she said in a husky voice.

"Great! I'll pick you up at seven."

Juliet didn't have a dress that was suitable for a Valentine's dance, but she'd find something.

Something beautiful and romantic. Because Grant had reached out to her and she wanted their second chance to work.

Larry called the next day. "I've been thinking," he began. "It could be you're right about Remington. If I sit down and talk with him, there's a good chance we could bury the hatchet. I could tell him which family pieces I want, and maybe he'll sell them to me."

"Oh, Larry, I'm so glad you've changed your mind about him."

"I hear he's taking you to the Light Street Foundation's Valentine's Dance."

"How do you know about that?"

"I have my sources. That might be a good place to meet him—on neutral territory."

She didn't want him horning in on her date. "Maybe we should wait until I see how things work out."

"No. It's a good plan. I'll be at the dance. If it looks like he's approachable, I'll come over and introduce myself. It won't be any big deal. I'll just let him know I'm not an ogre and arrange to meet with him at a convenient time." He cleared his throat. "But don't, you know, mention it in advance. I don't want him getting all worked up about meeting me."

"I don't know," she said. She and Grant would have enough problems without throwing Larry into the mix.

"Trust me, Juliet. This is the way to do it. It won't be any big deal. I'll only take up a few minutes of his time. And I'll be on my best behavior. But give me your word you'll keep it a secret."

She sighed, wishing she hadn't let Larry maneuver her again, and promising herself that it would be the last time. "Okay."

SHE FOUND the perfect dress in a little shop on Charles Street. It was a soft crepe gown in an icy violet that did wonderful things for her pale skin. She spent Saturday in the beauty parlor having her hair swept up into a romantic crown of curls and her nails manicured and polished a delicate pink. Then she splurged on a makeup session at a cosmetics boutique.

She hadn't gone to this much effort for a date since her senior prom. But she was able to justify all the frantic activity. It was better to keep busy than to sit around wondering how the evening would go.

The nervousness came back the closer it got to seven o'clock. By the time she went to answer the door of her Ellicott City town house, her heart was pounding. It had been almost a week since she and Grant had seen each other. And all sorts of fantasies and fears had run through her mind.

When she opened the door and saw him standing on her doorstep, her breath caught. He was devastating in a tuxedo with a burgundy bow tie and matching cummerbund. And his eyes were warm and welcoming.

For several seconds, he didn't move as his gaze swept over her. "You're beautiful."

"So are you," she answered, then flushed. "I mean—you look wonderful." That wasn't much better. Too revealing. Yet seeing him again made it hard to hide her feelings.

As he stepped into the foyer, she saw him swallow hard. "I've been praying I wouldn't make a mess of things this time," he said.

The wistfulness and contrition in his voice was so palpable that she held out her arms to him. He came into them, and she gave a deep, contented sigh, sinking into the warmth of him, the familiar scent, the strength of his embrace. They held each other tightly. Just held. It was enough, a sharing of overwhelming feelings neither of them could quite handle.

"Oh, Grant, I've missed you," she whispered, her cheek pressed tightly to his shoulder.

"It can't be more than I've missed you."

The joy inside her bubbled up into a little laugh of relief.

"What?" he asked.

"I'm happy."

"Same here. And relieved. And we're going to be late if we don't get going."

"Why is the dance being held so far out in the country?" she asked.

"The Light Street Foundation got a great deal on the mansion. Erin Stone decided that would mean more money for charity and less for expenses."

Juliet nodded. Several years ago, Erin's husband, Travis, had set up the foundation, which supported a number of Baltimore charities. Both of them were active in administering the funds.

Grant helped Juliet on with her coat, then escorted her outside into an almost balmy evening. Tonight the temperature was thirty degrees warmer than it had been during the snowstorm, offering the promise of an early spring. Grant's vehicle was another contrast to the previous week—not the utility van he'd used in his carpenter mode, but a stunning gray Mercedes sedan with glove-leather seats and thick carpet.

"I wasn't expecting such luxury transportation," she murmured as she slid onto one of the contoured seats.

He gave her a little grin. "It's one of the remnants of my old life. I haven't had it out of the garage in a couple of months, but I enjoyed driving over here."

"You're lucky it started."

"I thought of that just before I put the key in the ignition. Otherwise, you'd be riding next to a load of lumber."

Juliet shrugged as he pulled out of her driveway. "You may not realize it, sir, but I've ridden with all sorts of unlikely loads. On one antique-buying trip with my mother it was a chest of drawers we'd dragged out of a musty old basement. The thing smelled so bad that we had to keep all the windows open. Then halfway home, a mouse climbed out from one of the drawers and started running around the van. My mother almost drove into a utility pole."

"And what were you doing?" Grant inquired.

"Screaming my head off."

He laughed, and she joined him. She had thought the conversation might be strained after the way they'd parted. But the communication was easy and natural.

She hated turning the ambience more serious, but she wanted to know what had happened with the letters. "Did Mike Lancer find out anything?" she asked.

Grant's hands tightened on the wheel and she instantly wished she'd thought longer before she'd spoken.

"Yes," he answered. "He's got a friend in the FBI who's going to check out the fingerprints on the notes through their database."

"He'll find yours and mine—and your mother's."

"And somebody else's, if we're lucky. Unless the sheets of paper were wiped clean."

"I hope he thought the letters would never surface. And I hope he's in the computer."

"You're assuming it's a man?"

"I guess it could be a woman," she conceded, trying to imagine who would be so foolish as to leave written evidence.

They came around a curve in the road, and Grant pointed toward a brightly lighted mansion commanding the top of the largest hill in the vicinity—a small mountain, really.

It had been an hour's ride to the hilltop estate, but the time had flashed by. They were directed to a parking place in a nearby field where scores of cars were already parked, lined up in neat rows.

An attack of nerves hit Juliet as Grant took her arm and escorted her toward the front door. Many of her friends would be here, and they'd be observing her and Grant with interest. As if sensing her tension, he squeezed her arm.

She glanced up at him and saw a possessive look on his face. All at once she wondered if he'd brought her to such a public venue because he wanted people to know they were an item. If she'd been in a different mood, she might have resented the ploy. Tonight the knowledge that he wanted people to know about them made her giddy.

A smiling Travis and Erin Stone were greeting guests in the foyer, which had been transformed into an indoor garden planted with hundreds of spring flowers. Twinkling among the blossoms were tiny red foil hearts. And large heart-shaped balloons were festooned in an arch above the entryway. Juliet stood for a moment, enjoying the display. It was like stepping from a winter evening into a balmy spring day.

After Grant had checked their coats, they both greeted the Stones.

"I'd better warn you..." Erin started to say to Juliet.

But it was apparently already too late. A dark-haired boy dressed in a super hero suit and wearing a small black mask dashed up to Juliet and pointed a bow and arrow at her. She looked at him quizzically. It was the Stones' son, Kenny.

"He told me he'd play Cupid," his mother explained. "Then he saw the costume he was supposed to wear and balked."

"It looked dumb!" the youngster explained, putting away his weapons and reaching for a jump rope hanging at his waist. He looped the ends around Juliet, holding her prisoner and looking knowingly from her to Grant.

"You're Cupid's captive, until somebody rescues you with a kiss and a check for the Light Street Foundation," Erin explained with a grin.

"Is this your idea of politically correct?" Juliet managed.

"My question exactly." Travis entered the

conversation. "But I was overruled—for this one day of the year."

Not wanting to spoil the fun, Juliet let herself be led through an archway of flowers. On the other side was a large room full of well-dressed partygoers. Many of them were her friends, the men and women she saw daily coming and going in and out of 43 Light Street offices. They were all regarding her and Grant with extreme interest.

"Did you know this was going to happen?" she whispered.

"No," he murmured. "The entertainment was billed as a big surprise."

"I can see why."

"Come on," Cupid ordered.

Juliet let him lead her though the crowd—like a virgin sacrifice, she thought wryly. However, from the looks on the faces of the other women, she surmised most of them had already lived through the ordeal. Too bad she and Grant hadn't arrived a little earlier, when the audience was smaller.

She was led to a place of honor on a slightly raised platform in the corner, under a bower of pink and red roses and hearts. Cupid dropped a garland-twined bar in front of her before stepping away—blocking her escape.

All eyes were on her, and she would have ducked behind the arch of flowers, except that

Grant stepped quickly up onto the platform, screening her from view.

"Sorry," he whispered.

"It's not your fault."

"I invited you. I didn't know we'd be on display like this."

"Are you upset about that?" she heard herself asking.

"Not at all. It's the perfect way to let people know that we're a couple."

"Oh!" She'd suspected his motives, but she hadn't expected such a blatant declaration. Her eyes sought his, and he smiled as he stepped forward and took her into his arms.

Somewhere in the distance she heard people clapping and a band playing, but they all receded into the distance as Grant folded her into his embrace. He could have chosen to give her a restrained kiss on the cheek. But she'd learned that he didn't do things halfway. Either he was committed or he wasn't. In one swift motion, he gathered her to him and brought his mouth down firmly on hers, his lips moving urgently, heatedly. Her eyes closed, and she was lost in the sensation of kissing him again, silently acknowledging how much she had secretly longed for this.

He murmured something she couldn't catch, but the vibration of the words traveled down her nerve endings. Then he pulled her more intimately against his body, and she drifted off on a cloud of longing.

She was brought down to earth by clapping and whistling. Her eyes snapped open as Grant raised his head. He blinked, and she knew in that moment that he'd been as oblivious of their surroundings as she. They were in a room full of people, but they might as well have been alone in a bedroom.

"That's a five hundred dollar kiss if I've ever seen one," an amused male voice called out.

"I think they just melted any remaining snow on the property," someone else observed.

Juliet ducked her head against Grant's shoulder.

He pitched his voice so only she could hear. "I guess I got carried away."

"That makes two of us," she admitted.

He raised the bar, freeing her from the bower, but not from captivity, because he kept his hand firmly locked on hers as they were directed toward a nearby table where Cameron Randolph sat behind a cash box.

Grant pulled a checkbook from his pocket and wrote an amount that made Juliet's eyes bulge. After handing over the check, he steered her toward a quiet corner of the room. Everyone else was turned toward the door, watching the next victims parading toward the bower. It was a married couple. Lucky them, Juliet thought. The scrutiny wouldn't be quite so intense.

"No kiss is worth that much," she whispered to Grant as he shoved his checkbook back into his breast pocket.

"It was to me."

She met his eyes and caught her breath at the heat in their blue depths.

They stood, regarding each other for long moments. Then the band began to play a slow, romantic tune, and he pulled her against himself, swaying to the music, although she suspected that dancing was simply an excuse to hold her again. She knew it was for her.

"Sorry I can't do any fancy steps with this leg," he apologized.

"This is fine. How did you hurt it?"

He hesitated for a moment. "Some stairs collapsed at a house I was building. I was on my way down at the time."

She squeezed her eyes shut as a frightening image of the accident flashed into her mind. "You could have—"

He cut her off before she could finish. "Don't worry about it. I'm fine. My physical therapist says I'll end up with hardly any limp."

"How long ago did it happen?"

"Four and a half months."

After his mother had died, she thought. Another accident.

The knowledge that he could have gotten killed made her cling to him more tightly. She'd tried to tell herself that she didn't know him very well. That might be true if you thought strictly in terms of the hours they'd spent together. But time wasn't the important factor. She was beginning to understand there was a sense of connection between them that few couples could match. Around them, other people danced and talked and laughed, but everything except Grant stayed in the background. This time when she closed her eyes, it was so she could focus on his touch, the way his body moved against hers, the feel of his lips as they skimmed her hair. She felt him guiding her gently from where they were swaying. Trusting him to take her to the right place, she didn't bother to open her eyes—until he stopped moving and she found they were in the corner under the staircase.

"Coming here was a mistake," he said in a low voice.

"You didn't like ransoming me?" she asked, wondering if she'd been conjuring up a fantasy that had no basis in reality.

"I don't like sharing you with a room full of people."

She raised her face, so close to his. "Then let's leave."

She saw the color of his eyes deepen. "Where do you want to go?"

"Anywhere you want." She'd never been so aggressive with a man. Yet this was different. Right.

Again their gazes caught and held. She felt a thrill rush through her as his fingers knit with hers, and he began to lead her back through the crowd toward the door.

Things were moving fast again, and she didn't really want to slow them down. She could see some of the other guests were taking note of them, but she didn't care. Then a sudden thought struck her. Larry had said he would meet Grant tonight. But she hadn't seen him.

When she stopped, Grant gave her a questioning look. "It's okay. We can stay here. I keep forgetting we haven't known each other very long."

"I feel as if I've known you all my life," she countered.

"Yes," he said.

"I was only remembering that I'd told someone I'd look for him here. But I guess he changed his mind." Larry had warned her not to say anything. If he hadn't shown up yet, and if he didn't think the time was right, they could always arrange another meeting. Only, the next time she wouldn't stand for any more of Larry's games. She would insist on telling Grant what to expect.

He left her in the foyer while he went to retrieve her coat.

"You're leaving early," Erin said after she greeted a latecomer.

"It's a wonderful party, but I, uh..."

"You don't have to explain," her friend murmured. "I can see the two of you don't need anything as subtle as Cupid to rope you together."

Juliet had hoped it wasn't so obvious. And she'd thought she was beyond blushing, but she was helpless to stop the reaction. "I'm sorry. I didn't mean to be rude."

"Nonsense." Erin dismissed the apology with a wave of her hand. "What's a Valentine's party for?" Then she gave Juliet a little smile. "I've been worried about Grant. He's been withdrawn since his divorce and his mother's accident. It looks like you've made a difference in his life."

"I hope so," Juliet answered with deep sincerity.

By the time Grant returned, Erin was chatting with another guest.

Hands clasped, Grant and Juliet made their escape into the night. Few guests had left, so they threaded their way back through the ranks of cars to the gray Mercedes.

When they were sitting in the front seat, he turned to her. "There are no strings attached to the rest of the evening. If we end up sitting in a quiet corner of a restaurant and having a cup of coffee, that's fine by me. I just don't want to share you with a crowd."

"Coffee first," she said in a husky voice. "And we'll see what develops from there."

Grant squeezed her hand. "Whatever you say." Then he slid the car out of the parking slot and headed slowly for the steep access road. It wasn't until he pointed the vehicle's nose downhill that the real trouble started.

When he skidded on a patch of ice, she felt him instinctively hit the brakes, but there was no effect. The car didn't slow.

"Grant?"

He pumped the pedal again, then swore when the car picked up speed. As they hit a curve and skidded again on some loose gravel, Grant fought to stay on the pavement. He pulled up on the parking brake, but there was only a slight slowing of their dangerous downward spiral.

He swore again, his hands moving rapidly on the wheel as he tried to control the hurtling automobile.

Chapter Six

ALL JULIET COULD DO was watch in horror as the twisting road rushed toward them at incredible speed. They were on a private driveway, on a surface that would need repair after the hard winter. On the left side there was no guardrail, only a narrow shoulder before a long drop into a stream valley below. On the right, tall cliffs rose, blocking any means of escape.

They skidded around another curve, the wheels on the right kicking up stones as they came perilously close to the edge. Thrown to the side, Juliet clenched her teeth and tried not to scream.

"Hold on," Grant shouted, and she dug her fingers into the edge of the seat.

"I've got to slow us down," he grated. "Scoot over toward me. I'm going to sideswipe the cliff."

She gasped and pressed close to Grant, hooking her arm over the back of his seat as he eased off the road. The wheels on the right side dropped with a clunk as they hit the shoulder. Though she had her head turned, she could still see the gray wall looming closer and closer. Then the car shuddered, the movement accompanied by a terrible grinding noise as the bumper and the chassis scraped along the obstruction. The speed slowed a little.

"Juliet, are you all right?" Grant shouted as metal crunched and tore off.

"Yes," she managed, imagining the side of the car being scraped off in layers. Yet Grant had no other option. And even this maneuver might not be enough to stop their wild ride.

He did it again, battering the car mercilessly as they came around a curve. When they reached the bottom of the long grade, she let out the breath she'd been holding. But they still weren't out of the woods. Grant shot through the stop sign at the end of the road and careened onto the two-lane highway. Thank God there was no traffic coming in either direction.

The grade was level for several hundred feet. But another downward hill loomed ahead.

Juliet squeezed her eyes closed, sure that there was no escape from disaster. Then Grant bumped onto the shoulder, and her eyes snapped open as she saw him steering toward a low field where runoff from the recent snowstorm had turned the ground marshy. The thick mud sucked at the tires, slowing them down. By the time the car came to rest against a fallen log, there was only a slight jolt from the impact.

Grant cut the engine and leaned back with his

eyes closed, his breathing rapid. After the roar of the motor, the silence was deafening.

"Thank God," she gasped, hardly able to believe they were still alive.

"Yeah, I thought we were going over the side," he admitted in a hoarse voice. Swinging toward her, he found her hand and held it tightly. "Are you all right?"

"Yes. Thanks to you."

"Let's get out of here."

She nodded, feeling strangely disconnected from her body. When she forced her hand toward the door handle, she realized the whole side of the car was caved in, the leather padding bulging toward her.

Grant made a quick exit, and she sat staring through the windshield, unable to function.

Turning, he reached inside for her and snapped open the seat belt. She still didn't move, and it took a moment to figure out that she'd have to slide behind the wheel and get out on the driver's side. Her movements were jerky as she exited the car and stood swaying on a patch of grass that stuck up above the general morass. Shivering, she looked back along their route. From this vantage point, the mansion seemed to be perched at the top of a dark mountain that rose at an almost vertical angle, and she marveled that Grant had made it down the steep road without getting them both killed.

She expected him to inspect the damaged side of the car; instead he put his arm around her shoulder and led her toward the road where dark houses loomed.

"Damn. I thought I remembered seeing a place where we could get some help," he muttered.

She stumbled, and he kept her from falling, cursing again. In some corner of her mind, she knew that she was probably in shock, but she couldn't seem to pull herself together.

Grant kept her close to his side as he led her toward town. When they rounded a curve, she saw lights a few hundred yards ahead.

"There it is," he said, urging her toward a rambling white-painted house. When they drew close to the picket fence she spotted a sign that said Sadler's Bed-And-Breakfast.

Grant led her along the fence, through the gate and up the steps.

"What are we doing?" she asked.

"Getting off the road."

She nodded in agreement as he rang the doorbell, hoping that she could sit down before her knees gave way.

A gray-haired woman answered the door and looked inquiringly at the couple in party dress on the front porch.

"We've had an automobile accident," Grant said. "I wonder if we might come in."

"Oh, my. You poor things. Do you need a doctor or the police?"

Grant shook his head. "My brakes went out. The car's in a field just down the road."

The woman stepped aside and led them into a small parlor decorated in a warm country style. Ordinarily Juliet would have been interested in the furnishings. Tonight she barely looked around as she dropped gratefully onto a chintz sofa.

"Do you want to lie down?" the woman asked.

"That's a good idea," Grant answered. "We were in town for the Valentine event. Maybe we could spend the night here and take care of things in the morning."

"I do have several rooms—with private bath," the woman said. "By the way, I'm Mrs. Sadler."

"Grant Remington and...Juliet."

Mrs. Sadler bustled over to a pine desk. "Well, Mr. and Mrs. Remington, if you'll sign a registration card, I'll show you to a room."

Mrs. Remington, Juliet thought, momentarily startled out of her reverie. Grant didn't disagree, and she knew he was protecting her reputation. But her muddled brain was still confused. Why were they sleeping here?

Mrs. Sadler led them to a sweetly furnished room on the second floor, in the back—with the two double beds Grant had requested. Juliet waited patiently as Mrs. Sadler showed them the bathroom and how to operate the heater. As soon as they were alone again, she turned to Grant.

"Why are we staying here?"

"It's safer."

"Safer than what?"

He hesitated, then said, "Safer than going back to the city. There have been too many unexplained accidents in my family recently. If someone is tracking my movements and arranged this little surprise, I don't want them to check and see I got home in one piece."

She stared at him. "You think somebody...did something to the car?"

"It was pretty strange for the brakes to go out at the top of that hill. But I won't know for sure if it was deliberate until a mechanic has a look at it tomorrow." He swallowed. "I've put you in danger, too. I'm sorry."

He was worried about her. But all she could think about was that suspicious accidents had happened to *him* before. Like the stairs collapsing, she realized.

She reached toward him, but he didn't move. So she took several shaky steps closer until she could circle his waist with her arms and press her face against his chest. It was a relief to lean into him, a relief to feel the solid strength of his body against hers.

"Juliet, don't," he said in a strained voice.

"Why not?" she asked, conscious as she spoke that her breath was warming the front of his shirt, warming the flesh beneath.

"I forgot about being on guard this evening. That was a mistake. I think you just had a pretty vivid demonstration that getting messed up with me is bad for your health."

She shook her head in denial. "No. We'll find out who did it."

"You're not safe with me until we do."

"I thought you wanted to be alone with me."

"What I want isn't important."

He raised his hands to her shoulders as if to push her away. The gesture only made her hold on to him more tightly. As she did, she felt his hands change their hold, millisecond by millisecond, cupping her closer instead of shoving her away. Some of the tension seeped out of her as she let her body flow against his.

Then she heard him draw in a ragged breath. "I didn't check us into this room so I could take advantage of the situation."

She raised her face to his, gave him a slow smile that she hoped would hide the quaking sensation in her stomach. "You're not taking advantage. I'm seducing you." Then, gambling her self-respect on one wanton gesture, she moved her hips provocatively against his erection.

He lowered his mouth to hers, in a kiss that said his feelings ran deep and strong. It was a soul-shattering kiss that demanded even as it offered.

His hands were in her hair, his fingers greedy as they stroked through the golden mass, tangling her carefully arranged coiffure into a wanton tumble of curls.

Her own hands were busy, slipping under his jacket and pulling the tails of his shirt from his dress pants so that she could touch the warm skin of his back.

She had always thought of herself as a little shy with men. There was nothing shy about her as his hands went to the zipper of her gown, and she helped him remove the unwanted garment. Underneath was the sheer silk slip she'd bought because it went so well with the lines of the gown.

Heat curled in her stomach as his eyes swept over her curves.

"You're beautiful." He reached out to stroke her breast through the sheer fabric, watching the nipple bead at his touch.

He drank in her little sound of pleasure, then began to work open the front of his dress shirt, scattering gold studs on the floor in his haste.

There was no longer time for slow seduction, only frantic need to rid themselves of unwanted clothing.

Moments later, he pulled her naked into his

arms, and they both gasped at the pleasure of flesh touching flesh.

Luckily the beds were only a few feet away, because she knew she couldn't have remained standing for much longer. He chose one, threw the covers aside and brought her down to the yielding surface, rocking her, kissing her, touching her in ways that sent the blood pumping hot and fast through her veins.

She thought she was ready for him then. She didn't know that he could take her to unimagined heights that would have her writhing on the bed, begging for release.

Finally he shifted his body above hers. There was a breathless moment of anticipation as his dark eyes focused on her face. Then with a growl of satisfaction, he sank his body into hers. She clutched his shoulders, holding him to her as he began to move—hard and fast. And she matched him thrust for thrust, frantic in her desire to reach fulfillment. It was quick and shattering and joyful. And as she lay in his arms afterward, she knew that this night was the beginning of something new and precious in her life.

She longed to tell him how she felt, but she didn't want him to feel obligated to say things that he wasn't ready to say. So she simply snuggled against him, enjoying the stroking of his fingers on her arm and his lips against the side of her face.

"Sleep," he murmured, and she knew that there would be time in the morning for anything she needed to say.

HER EYES SNAPPED OPEN the moment she felt him stir beside her. When he started to swing his legs out of bed, she put a hand on his arm. It was early, a little after sunrise, she judged by the light showing through the crack in the drawn curtains.

"Where are you going?" she asked.

"Back to town."

She sat up in bed, dragging the covers with her. Had she been wrong about the two of them? Had she made up a fantasy that was more wishful thinking than reality?

Her face must have registered her distress, because his expression softened immediately. Slipping back under the covers, he turned to her, gathering her close. "I want you to stay here until I find out what happened last night."

She gestured helplessly with her hand. "You were going to let me wake up and find you'd left?"

"I was going to leave you a note," he answered quickly. "If I know you're safe, I'll have one less thing to worry about."

She sighed, understanding his reasoning. Yet the thought of his walking out the door made her heart start to pound. And she had a sudden sharp sense that if she let him leave, she'd never see him again.

"Where will you be?" she asked in an almost-normal voice.

"At Mike Lancer's office. I'm going to pay Mrs. Sadler a great deal of money to let me borrow a car."

She nodded, yet she couldn't stop her stomach from clenching. Maybe if she could keep him here for a little while, she could convince him to let her come to town with him.

She brushed her lips against his arm. "It's early. You don't have to go yet," she whispered, wanting him, wanting to keep him in her bed as long as she could.

"Are you trying to seduce me again?"

"Am I that transparent?"

"It wouldn't be too difficult to get me to stay. I think we're on the same wavelength. But I'm not going to take another chance with you. Last night I was too charged up to think about protection. This morning, I'm going to act responsibly."

She blinked. She hadn't been thinking about that last night, either. Apparently she still wasn't. Maybe it was because the idea of letting him go was so terrifying.

"Then just hold me for a little while," she whispered, full of foreboding.

He slid down beside her, and as he pulled her

close, she could feel his body responding. He wanted her. Yet he did nothing more than cradle her in his arms and gently kiss her.

All too soon, he was easing away, his expression regretful. "I have to go."

"Take me with you!" she pleaded.

"Stay here. Do that for me. I have to be sure you're safe."

She nodded, not trusting herself to speak.

"Go back to sleep. I'll call you in a few hours," he said gently.

Again she nodded, then silently watched him climb back into his rumpled tuxedo and leave the room. She managed to give him a little smile after he kissed her. But the moment the door closed behind him, the tears she had been holding back began to trickle down her cheeks.

Chapter Seven

PRESSING A FIST against her mouth, she tried to stop the sobs from shaking her body. She was simply on the down side of the roller coaster ride she and Grant had been on since they'd met, she told herself. The emotional highs took her to the clouds, the lows plunged her into a bottomless pit.

Burrowing into the covers, she sought to wrap herself in the warmth they had created. If she could just sleep for a few more hours, the time would pass quickly. But sleep was impossible. Instead, her thoughts began to circle back to recent events and conversations.

And as she lay there in bed, she remembered something she'd forgotten the night before. She'd met Grant because her cousin Larry had sent her to spy on him. Larry hated the Remington family. When she'd confronted him, he'd changed his tune and said he intended to speak to Grant at the party. Yet she hadn't seen him there.

Goose bumps rose on her arms, and she rubbed them with her hands. Sitting up in bed, she reached for the phone and dialed her cousin's number.

He answered on the second ring.

"Juliet?" he asked, sounding puzzled when he recognized her voice.

"You weren't expecting me?" she asked.

"I—" he stopped. "I thought—"

"Thought what?"

He hesitated for a moment. "I thought I heard Grant wrecked his expensive Mercedes last night."

Juliet felt chilled to the bone as she contemplated his choice of words—and how he might have gotten that news, since presumably nobody but Mike Lancer had been informed.

"Where did you get that information?" she asked in a quiet voice.

"Maybe I was mistaken. I'm glad to hear you're all right."

"We're fine," she answered automatically, feeling far from fine. It sounded like Larry had just confirmed her worst fears.

"Where's Remington? Is he with you?"

The question made her heart start to pound. "I've got to go. Talk to you later," she said, carefully replacing the receiver in the cradle. But the damage was done. She'd just told Larry that his plan had failed, and, knowing he had caller ID, she'd just told him where to find her.

She had to warn Grant. Dialing again, she got Mike's number from Information and called his office. The answering machine picked up, and she clenched her fists in frustration. She wanted to talk to Grant in person. Her only option was to leave a message—and hope she wasn't too late.

"Mike, this is Juliet Hartfield," she began in a shaky voice.

"Tell Grant that I think my cousin Larry is the one coming after him. Tell him to be careful."

Then she leapt out of bed. Her ball gown was lying in a heap on the floor, and the idea of putting it on made her feel almost physically sick. Luckily Mrs. Sadler had provided guests with a terry-cloth robe hanging on the back of the door.

The innkeeper was in the kitchen making muffins when Juliet found her. "Did you sleep well, dear?" Juliet nodded.

"My...my husband said he was going to borrow one of your cars."

"That's right. And you'll be spending the day with us."

"I know that was the plan. But I remembered I have an important appointment. Is there some way I can get a ride into Baltimore? And, uh, do you have something I can wear?"

Mrs. Sadler looked doubtful. "You're supposed to stay here."

"I can't," she answered, feeling her desperation rise.

"Your husband told me you'd be needing some clothes. I can lend you some of my daughter-in-law's things."

"That would be wonderful. But I need transportation, too. Please, it's very important."

"This is all so strange. Are the two of you in some kind of trouble?" the woman asked.

Juliet nodded, hoping she could win the woman's cooperation. "Yes. Someone has been stalking my husband. And I remembered some important information I have to give him."

Mrs. Sadler considered the answer. "Well, Jimmy Lewis works downtown. If you hurry, you could catch a ride with him."

"I'd be so grateful," Juliet answered.

An hour and a half later, she was standing in front of 43 Light Street. Under her dress coat, she wore a pair of baggy jeans and a flannel shirt, and her feet were squeezed into tennis shoes a size too small. But she was here.

Mike Lancer shared an office with one of her friends, Jo O'Malley, on the fifth floor. The doors to both offices were closed when Juliet entered the waiting room, but she could see a light shining from underneath Mike's door. After knocking briefly, she turned the knob and stepped into the room. Mike was seated at his desk. Grant, who had changed into wool slacks and a blue shirt, was standing by the window. Both men looked up as she rushed in.

The breath whooshed out of her lungs in relief as she saw that Grant was unharmed. All the way into Baltimore, she'd been afraid that somehow Larry had figured out he was here and had gotten to him before she could.

"I have to talk to Grant," she told Mike.

The two men exchanged glances.

"Would you give us a few minutes alone?" Grant said it almost grudgingly.

Mike nodded and stood up. "I'll be downstairs getting a cup of coffee."

The moment they were alone, Juliet started toward Grant. But before she'd taken two steps, the stark look on his face stopped her dead in her tracks.

"I talked to Larry this morning. I have to tell you—"

"I got your message." He cut her off, his voice frigid. "Mike already told me that your cousin Larry tried to kill me last night. And you helped him. You told him where I'd be."

She heard the words, but they seemed to come from a thousand miles away.

She shook her head, but she wasn't sure what she was denying since she'd just heard her worst fears confirmed.

"He's a real piece of work. His fingerprints were on the notes threatening my mother. And he was seen at the party last night, but he left early—after he drained the brake fluid from my car."

She felt her knees buckle and braced herself against the edge of the desk. She'd had a premonition that something terrible was going to happen this morning. Now she knew what it was.

"Grant, you have to believe me. I didn't know!"

He ignored the exclamation and went on

calmly. "Then why did you phone Larry this morning?"

"I—I started thinking about the way he'd been acting. So I called him to—"

"To get your stories straight?" He cut her off before she could tell him anything about the conversation. "Did he pay you to spy on me, Juliet? Or were you doing it for family honor? The revenge of the Lancasters against the Remingtons?"

"Family honor..." she choked out, feeling the world around her crack and splinter into jagged pieces.

Grant gave her a curt nod.

"But...but he tricked me," she added in a rush of words, trying to make him understand how she'd gotten sucked into Larry's clever trap. "He told me all kinds of lies about you. About your company. About your life. As soon as I realized you weren't anything like the monster he described, I told him the deal was off. Then he said he wanted to talk to you and suggested he'd meet you at the Valentine party."

"But you kept that piece of information to yourself," Grant pointed out.

"He said that if you knew he was coming, you'd back out."

Grant snorted. "Right. I'm so wound up with an ancient family feud that I make it the basis of all my decisions!"

"Of course not. Larry was the one who was

obsessed. I understand that now." She held out her hand toward him. "Please, I didn't know what he was doing. I swear. He would have killed me, too."

"Yeah. The joke's on you." He gave a grating laugh. "I guess he decided you were expendable. But that doesn't really change anything. All the time we were together, you were playing me for a prize fool."

"No." Her throat was almost too dry to speak, but she forced out a few more words. "Last night, I thought we—"

His features hardened. "Did he suggest you seduce me into dropping my guard? Or was that your idea?" he flung at her.

Her shoulders sagged, but she managed to say, "Neither. I fell in love with you."

He answered with another harsh laugh. When he spoke again, she strained to hear him above the roaring in her ears.

"Juliet, it's time to retire the naive little cousin act. If you're trying to stay out of jail, that's out of my hands. It's up to the police."

The harsh words stabbed at her. Did he really think this was about staying out of jail? Yet she understood how difficult it was for him to believe her now. He had given her his trust, and it looked to him as if she'd paid him back with lies and wild plots to kill him.

His eyes were shuttered, his expression almost

blank, and she knew he was fighting to hide the terrible pain he felt at having let her hurt him.

With jerky movements, she stumbled across the distance between them, hoping that if she touched him she could break through the barrier he'd erected. But he stood rigid as she grasped his arm, rigid as she laid her head on his shoulder. God, if he'd only raise his arms, only pull her close and tell her everything was all right. But he stood like a man turned to stone by an evil wizard.

"I know how it seems to you, but the only thing I did wrong was trust my cousin," she whispered, because if she tried to speak louder, her voice would crack.

He said nothing.

"Grant?"

He didn't answer, and the breath locked in her throat, turning solid so that every gasp for air was agony. She'd thought last night was the beginning of something joyful. This morning she understood—finally—that she was touching him for the last time. When she realized her fingers were digging into his arm and her tears were spilling onto his shirt, she turned and ran from the room.

Chapter Eight

DESPITE the promising weather of Valentine's Day, spring was late that year. Juliet hardly noticed. She was too busy trying to get her life into some kind of order.

As she stacked Victorian glassware on the open shelves behind the counter of her new shop, she thought about all the things that had happened in the past three months. In some ways, she was very lucky. The biggest blessing was that she hadn't been charged with any crime, for which, ironically, she had Larry to thank. At the urging of his mother, he'd signed a statement saying that Juliet was innocent of any involvement in his scheme against the Remingtons.

Too bad that declaration had surfaced after the newspaper articles detailing the generations-old feud between the Remingtons and the Lancasters, the murder of Edith Remington and the part Juliet Hartfield had played in the stalking of Grant Remington.

She'd been pictured as malicious and jealous of the Remingtons, and the bad publicity had killed her business. Several clients had called to cancel appointments the day the headlines hit, and no one else had requested her services. She couldn't blame anybody but herself. Going into people's homes and appraising their possessions meant being trusted, and she'd lost that trust in the Baltimore community.

Which was one of the reasons she'd sold her house, moved away and started up with a new antique shop. She'd found one in Fredericksburg, Virginia. The shop had been her salvation, but it didn't solve all her problems, she thought, fighting off the scared, sick sensation she always got when she thought about her dilemma. Feeling light-headed, she sat down on the stool she kept behind the counter and closed her eyes.

Grant's face floated in her mind. She still missed him so much. She'd loved him and lost him in such a short space of time. Yet they would always share something very precious. The night they'd made love, they'd made a baby together. *That* was what she'd sensed when she'd realized something new and wonderful was starting.

From the moment she'd learned she was pregnant, she'd vowed to make a good life for herself and her child. Her mother had done it alone, and she could, too. Yet her determination was dampened by fear. She knew what Grant thought of her, knew that he would hardly consider her a fit mother for his child. Remembering his anger had made her want to run away to a place he'd never find her. Yet she'd promised herself she'd never lie to him again.

Sooner or later she'd have to tell him about

the baby. Then what would he do? Would he try to take the child away from her? Could she possibly win a custody case, given the facts he'd present to a judge? Or would he write the baby off the way he'd done with her? The first alternative made her throat close in despair. The second was so sad that she could hardly think of it without crying.

The bell over the door jingled, and she looked up to see that an older couple had come in. Plastering a smile on her face, Juliet asked if she could help them. They were looking for early-twentieth-century lace to use as a pillow cover, and she had several good examples. After they left, she waited on a young housewife who'd gotten into the habit of dropping by in the afternoons to see if she had any new goodies.

They chatted for a few minutes. Then Juliet went into the back room to sort through some early *Life* magazines.

The bell rang again, and she snatched up the stack of periodicals. "I'll be right out," she called, pleased that business was good for a weekday.

As she stepped through the curtain, her hands went limp and the magazines slipped through her fingers and spilled around her feet. Standing six feet from her was Grant Remington—looming like a giant among the delicate antiques in her little shop.

Her heart started to knock against her ribs, but

she held her ground, thankful that the counter hid the slightly rounded curve of her abdomen.

She reminded herself to breathe, knew that if she didn't, she would pass out. If only she could decipher his expression, but his face was deliberately unreadable as he stood and contemplated her.

"You didn't just wander in here, did you?" she finally asked, hearing the quaver in her voice.

"No. I had Mike find out where you'd gone."

Her chest felt hollow. This was the moment she'd been dreading. Somehow he'd found out about his baby, and he'd come to tell her what he planned to do.

"Don't," she whispered, unconsciously folding her arms protectively across her middle.

"I understand why you might not want to see me," he answered. "I said some pretty awful things to you."

She nodded tightly, unsure where the conversation was leading.

His stoic expression dissolved into one of pain, and when he spoke, his voice was raw. "Juliet, I've been miserable without you."

She gaped at him, unable to believe what she was hearing.

"I don't have anything left to lose," he rasped. "So I'm throwing myself on your mercy." He held out his hand toward her, took a step closer. "Please, I have to know whether I have another chance with you," he begged.

Her head was spinning, and she grasped the edge of the counter that still separated them. In the lonely months without him, she had never dared imagine this scene. "I didn't stop loving you," she finally managed.

His face registered relief, then uncertainty. "Does that mean you'll forgive me?"

Speech had become impossible. She could only nod, only reach toward him.

He looked as if he was going to jump over the counter. Instead, he surged around the end and scooped her into his arms before she could catch her next breath. Then he was hugging her, lowering his lips to skim her forehead, her cheeks, her mouth, like a man with a chest full of riches so tempting that he doesn't know what to reach for first.

It was the same for her. She couldn't stop touching him, stroking him, kissing all the places she could reach.

"Juliet, I can't believe it. You still want me."

She clung to him, trying to keep from dissolving in tears.

"You said the only mistake you made was trusting your cousin," he rasped. "I didn't believe you then. I was afraid to take the chance of trusting you." He stole a quick kiss. "So many people have disappointed me. My parents...my wife...I wanted to wall myself off again, but I couldn't get you out of my mind. So I—I had some sessions with a therapist."

She gave a stunned little nod, marveling that he had asked for help—and that he could tell her about it. "I'm glad you could talk to someone," she whispered.

"Yeah, I've never talked so much in my damn life. And the more I went on about your lying, the more I realized I was only trying to protect myself. You were being honest, but I couldn't accept it."

She raised her head, searched his face. "You believe that now?"

"Yes." He swallowed hard. "And I believe that the time I spent with you was the best time of my life."

"Yes," she echoed.

He raked a hand through his hair. "Everything happened so fast—I mean, falling in love with you. I felt like I was being swept along by a tornado. I wasn't prepared."

She nodded, understanding the feeling perfectly. Then the words sunk in. He'd said he loved her!

"I was afraid to trust my feelings—afraid to love you," he said again. "But I couldn't help myself."

Lightness and warmth began to radiate through her. But she couldn't give in to it while her heart was still pounding inside her chest. "Grant," she whispered. "Grant, there's one more thing you have to know...something I was afraid to tell you."

She felt his whole body stiffen. Then he eased away from her, his face as wary as it had been the last time she'd seen him. "Something I won't want to hear?"

"I don't know." She forced herself to keep her eyes on his face as she spoke past the tightness in her throat. "The night we made love—" She took a strangled breath before beginning again. "The night we made love, we made a baby."

His face was a study in stunned disbelief.

Trembling, she took his hand and carried it to the little swell where his child was nestled within her.

He closed his eyes, moving his hand against her, gently, reverently.

Her own eyes filled with moisture, and she dropped her head to his shoulder.

"I sent you away like this," he whispered. "Alone. Pregnant."

"You didn't know," she answered softly. "At first I didn't know. Then, when I found out, I was afraid to tell you. I was afraid you'd try to take the baby away from me—that you'd tell the court I wasn't a fit mother."

"Oh, God, Juliet. You must have been going through hell." He cradled her against his body, his hands moving over her. "I came here to tell you how much I love you and to ask you to marry me. Will you? Will you let me take care of you and be a father to our child?"

"I don't need anyone to take care of me," she murmured. "But I want to be your wife. I want us to be a family."

"Thank God."

She felt the tension ease out of him as he held her. After a long while he looked toward the door and she noticed something she hadn't seen before. A canvas carrying bag was sitting on the floor. "Stay right there," he said, loosening his hold and crossing the room again. First he picked up the bag, then he turned the sign on the door so that it read Closed from the outside.

Setting the bag on the counter, he pulled out a small box. It was delicately carved and inlaid with swirling ivory designs. Then, from his pocket, he produced the heart-shaped key she had given him.

"I kept looking for the box," he said in a gritty voice. "I guess it was a way of feeling close to you. And I finally found it in the attic, at the bottom of a pile of old books."

"What's inside?" Juliet asked.

He shook his head. "I turned the key and heard the lock snap open, but I couldn't lift the lid. I thought you should do that."

She was overwhelmed as he pressed the key

into her palm. With shaking hands, she inserted it into the lock and turned. When the mechanism clicked, she gave Grant a trembly smile. "You open it."

"Together," he whispered, placing her hand on one side of the top.

Together they opened the box. Inside was a packet of letters tied together with a red ribbon. Slipped on top was a folded note.

Gingerly Juliet lifted out the packet. The envelopes were addressed in a bold masculine hand to Anabel Lancaster. The return address was Zebulon Remington. And the note on top was signed Felicia Lancaster.

"Anabel's sister," Juliet explained. As she quickly scanned the words, her hand began to shake. The note was a confession, written when Felicia was in her sixties. Jealous of her younger sister, Felicia had intercepted the messages Zebulon had written to Anabel. Felicia had prevented the lovers from communicating, and had been the reason Zebulon and Anabel had never gotten together.

"All these years, my family thought he jilted her, but he didn't," Juliet whispered, gently touching the bundle of letters.

"And my family thought she'd broken his heart," Grant added. "But it was her sister who kept them apart." He reached for Juliet's hand, his grip tightening possessively. "Zebulon was a bitter, angry man," he said in a rough voice. "I think his losing the woman he loved affected our whole family. And I could easily have ended up the way he did."

She raised her face, her gaze shining into his. "But you didn't let it happen. You came looking for me, and that took courage. More courage than he had."

"I shouldn't have waited so long."

She shook her head. "No. I think you waited until the right time. For you. For us. Now we both know what we might have missed."

"Oh, yes." He moved swiftly around the counter again, gathering her close, holding on to her with the strength of a man who knows he has taken control of his own destiny.

Juliet nestled deeper into his embrace, unable to stop the surge of pure joy that made her blood sing. She couldn't help a little laugh from surfacing.

"What's funny?" Grant wanted to know, his mouth against her hair.

She eased away from him, not too much, but just enough so that she could look up into his eyes. "I was just thinking what a brilliant appraiser I am. I went to your house hunting for hidden treasure." She stood on tiptoe, reaching her arms up to link them behind his neck. "And I certainly found it. You."

He shook his head. "I'm the lucky one. But I'm not going to get into a debate about it."

His fervent kiss stopped her rejoinder, and in moments she had forgotten what she wanted to say as she lost herself in the bliss of her reunion with the man she loved so much.

DEBBIE MACOMBER

invites you to the

HEART OF TEXAS

Join Debbie Macomber as she brings you the lives and loves of the folks in the ranching community of Promise, Texas.

If you loved Midnight Sons—don't miss Heart of Texas! A brand-new six-book series from Debbie Macomber.

Available in February 1998 at your favorite retail store.

Heart of Texas by Debbie Macomber

Lonesome Cowboy	February '98
Texas Two-Step	March '98
Caroline's Child	April '98
Dr. Texas	May '98
Nell's Cowboy	June '98
Lone Star Baby	July '98

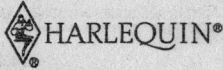

HPHRT1

Take 4 bestselling love stories FREE

Plus get a FREE surprise gift!

Special Limited-time Offer

Mail to Harlequin Reader Service®

3010 Walden Avenue
P.O. Box 1867
Buffalo, N.Y. 14240-1867

YES! Please send me 4 free Harlequin Superromance® novels and my free surprise gift. Then send me 4 brand-new novels every month, which I will receive before they appear in bookstores. Bill me at the low price of $3.57 each plus 25¢ delivery and applicable sales tax, if any.* That's the complete price and a savings of over 10% off the cover prices—quite a bargain! I understand that accepting the books and gift places me under no obligation ever to buy any books. I can always return a shipment and cancel at any time. Even if I never buy another book from Harlequin, the 4 free books and the surprise gift are mine to keep forever.

134 HEN CCMK

Name	(PLEASE PRINT)	
Address	Apt. No.	
City	State	Zip

This offer is limited to one order per household and not valid to present Harlequin Superromance® subscribers. *Terms and prices are subject to change without notice. Sales tax applicable in N.Y.

USUP-696 ©1990 Harlequin Enterprises Limited

Coming in August 1997!

THE BETTY NEELS RUBY COLLECTION

August 1997—Stars Through the Mist
September 1997—The Doubtful Marriage
October 1997—The End of the Rainbow
November 1997—Three for a Wedding
December 1997—Roses for Christmas
January 1998—The Hasty Marriage

This August start assembling the Betty Neels Ruby Collection. Six of the most requested and best-loved titles have been especially chosen for this collection. From August 1997 until January 1998, one title per month will be available to avid fans. Spot the collection by the lush ruby red cover with the gold Collector's Edition banner and your favorite author's name—Betty Neels!

Available in August at your favorite retail outlet.

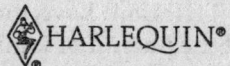

Look us up on-line at: http://www.romance.net

BNRUBY

Look for these titles—
available at your favorite retail outlet!

January 1998
Renegade Son by Lisa Jackson
Danielle Summers had problems: a rebellious child and unscrupulous enemies. In addition, her Montana ranch was slowly being sabotaged. And then there was Chase McEnroe—who admired her land and desired her body. But Danielle feared he would invade more than just her property—he'd trespass on her heart.

February 1998
The Heart's Yearning by Ginna Gray
Fourteen years ago Laura gave her baby up for adoption, and not one day had passed that she didn't think about him and agonize over her choice—so she finally followed her heart to Texas to see her child. But the plan to watch her son from afar doesn't quite happen that way, once the boy's sexy—*single*—father takes a decided interest in *her*.

March 1998
First Things Last by Dixie Browning
One look into Chandler Harrington's dark eyes and Belinda Massey could refuse the Virginia millionaire nothing. So how could the no-nonsense nanny believe the rumors that he had kidnapped his nephew—an adorable, healthy little boy who crawled as easily into her heart as he did into her lap?

BORN IN THE USA: Love, marriage—
and the pursuit of family!

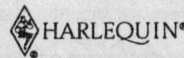 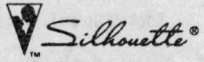

Look us up on-line at: http://www.romance.net

BUSA4

HARLEQUIN ULTIMATE GUIDES™

Every woman's guide to finishing first!

Harlequin Ultimate Guides™ brings you another *how-to* book that will help you take control of your life!

Here in one volume are easy, workable suggestions for getting where you want your future to be:

- from setting goals in love to setting up a nest egg,
- from managing your dream home to managing your health

Visualize the goal, identify the obstacles and go for it! It's time to find out how to

Get What You Want Out of Life—

SECRETS OF FINISHING FIRST

And Keep It

Available in February 1998 at your favorite Harlequin/Silhouette retail outlet.

Look us up on-line at: http://www.romance.net

HNFLIFE

Cupid's going undercover
this Valentine's Day in

The Cupid Connection

Cupid has his work cut out for him this Valentine's Day with these three stories about three couples who are just too *busy* to fall in love...well, not for long!

ONE MORE VALENTINE
by Anne Stuart
BE MINE, VALENTINE
by Vicki Lewis Thompson
BABY ON THE DOORSTEP
by Kathy Gillen Thacker

Make the Cupid Connection this February 1998!

Available wherever Harlequin and Silhouette books are sold.

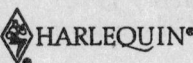 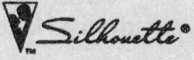

Look us up on-line at: http://www.romance.net

HREQ298

Make a Valentine's date for the premiere of HARLEQUIN® Movies

starting February 14, 1998 with

Debbie Macomber's
This Matter of Marriage

on the movie channel tmc

Just tune in to **The Movie Channel** the **second Saturday night** of every month at 9:00 p.m. EST to join us, and be swept away by the sheer thrill of romance brought to life. Watch for details of upcoming movies—in books, in your television viewing guide and in stores.

If you are not currently a subscriber to The Movie Channel, simply call your local cable or satellite provider for more details. Call today, and don't miss out on the romance!

the movie channel tmc
100% pure movies.
100% pure fun.

HARLEQUIN™
Makes any time special.™

Harlequin is a trademark of Harlequin Enterprises Limited. The Movie Channel is a trademark of Showtime Networks, Inc., a Viacom Company.

An Alliance Production

FREE VALENTINE NECKLACE!

Harlequin's Valentine's Day gift to you.

See order details below.

On the official proof-of-purchase coupon below, fill in your name, address and zip or postal code, and send it to: In the U.S.: 3010 Walden Avenue, P.O. Box 9077, Buffalo, N.Y. 14269-9077; In Canada: P.O. Box 609, Fort Erie, Ontario L2A 5X3. Please allow 4-6 weeks for delivery. Order your free Valentine necklace today—quantities are limited. Offer for the free necklace expires December 31, 1998.

Proof-of-Purchase Coupon:

Key to My Heart
Valentine Necklace Offer

Official Proof of Purchase
Please send me a free Valentine Necklace

Name: _____
Address: _____
City: _____
State/Prov.: _____ Zip/Postal Code: _____
Reader Service Account: _____

097 KGQ CSA3 785-6

PHKGQ349